Orphan Station

Orphan Station

John Kent

2014

First Printing: 2014

ISBN 978-0-9937285-2-5

John Kent
299 Warburton Road
Lansdowne, Ontario, K0E 1L0

www.johngkent.ca

Dedication

To my beautiful wife, Veronica for teaching me how to smell the roses.

Acknowledgements

I would like to thank my editor, Marg Gilks, for turning my clumsy words into art. I have learned so much from your teachings.

I would also like to thank the team that helped bring my cover to life; Ashley Dungan, the Bookish Brunette, Claudia McKinney of Phatpuppy Art, and our photographer Teresa Yeh and her team.

The cover turned out better than I could have hoped for.

Thank you all for your patience and guidance.

Orbiting the seventh planet of Eta Cassiopeia, the yellow star, Orphan Station was small compared to the stations in the Tau Ceti, Sigma Draconis, and Alpha Centauri systems, her traffic limited. Even so, it was perilous at the centre of the station, where officers created a seamless transition for settlers on their way to a new home on the farthest colony from Earth. It was no place to raise a child.

Chapter 1

Selene waited a few seconds to jump from one corrugated grate to the next, listening to the echoes of her footfalls reverberating down the hall. It ran the length of Orphan Station. Lights blinked on as she arrived in a section and dimmed as she left for another. The hall was otherwise silent, the thrumming of the station's machinery muffled from the public section.

Imagining herself bouncing across an asteroid, Selene counted aloud to thirty, then huffed as she leapt and landed on another grate. She was a miner, slicing through the rocky crust to gather altite, the most important mineral ever known to man. It would save Earth from its dismal existence and she, Selene Sotana, was the only person brave enough to step into the void of space to mine it.

She paused again, tucking her hair into her tattered shirt before hiking the man-sized jumpsuit higher on her shoulders, but not before her left foot caught in the voluminous pant leg and tripped her up. She threw her scarred hands out to break her fall as she crashed to the floor. "Son of a—" she hissed at the pain that lanced across her palms, then bit her lip to force herself to silence.

Selene stood, wiped her bloodied hands across her pants, and continued down the wide hallway until she came abreast of a double-wide air lock door crisscrossed with yellow emergency tape. She stepped closer to peer into the darkened bay, then squeezed her misty eyes shut as she caressed the *Savir Sotana* embroidered on the jumpsuit she wore. "Papa," she mouthed, her throat too tight to release sound.

Selene frowned as the small creature following her darted closer, its tiny metal legs clicking on the floor. She sighed as it nuzzled its metallic nose against her leg, and knelt to brush its back. Her breathing slowed and her furrowed brows relaxed as her petting produced coos. "Shush, Spike. Don't let the people hear you," she whispered as she patted his metallic backside. He puffed his chest out before arching his back, as if he were more a cat than a dog.

But Spike wasn't really a dog, either. He walked on six crooked legs that looked more like fingers. He barked like a real dog and followed her without tiring or whining to be picked up, and he was always ready to listen to her stories or complaints. He never made a mess on the carpet of her spacious cabin, as she'd heard real dogs might do. She'd also heard they smelled like her Uncle Callum. She liked Spike more.

Selene's hand froze as her wristwatch rang. She shuddered, her wide-eyed stare lingering for a few seconds on the black screen before she stuck her hand into her pocket to retrieve a green pill the size of her thumbnail. With a sigh, she threw the pill into her mouth and chewed.

Her breathing shallow, she ducked her head and skittered down the hall on her hands and knees, glancing through the open windows into the adjoining halls until the watch's screen faded to a soft grey. Only then did she stop, sit back on her knees, and wipe the tears from her eyes with her grimy hands. She sighed, shook her head, and glanced at the ceiling. *It's easier to be an astronaut mining altite.*

Bunching her legs under her, Selene jumped into the air. End over end she floated, all the while holding her breath. She bent her legs as she touched down and rolled into the wall before bursting into laughter. After a minute her laughter faded and she pushed herself off the floor again.

She froze at the sound of muffled voices. Curious, she crept toward the closest hatch and peered through. Spike wound his way between her legs.

"I'm telling you, I heard it. That laughter. It's the Orphan Station ghost," a man insisted as he shuffled down the hall beyond in a long line of travellers. Selene caught her breath.

"That's just a myth. Keep moving, you donkey," someone beyond her vision called.

"No, I'm telling you, the place is haunted. A pilot radioed back that it was true. They say there's a girl that haunts the starboard halls."

"Shut your gob, Michaels, and get to the ship. Make sure she's ready to fire up."

Selene felt her face warm as she ducked back, chewing the corner of her chapped lips. The line shuffled on, then the hall fell silent. After a few seconds she slipped away from the hatch. Captain Tulk would have her head if he heard any of the travellers talking about the "ghost."

They would soon be gone, she reminded herself, on their way to the colony. *Thank God.* The massive transport ship *Orient* had been docked for two and a half days—long enough to fuel the ship, but not so long that her crew and passengers discovered the effects of drying out from cryosleep. That was a lesson Captain Tulk preferred they learned after leaving the Orphan.

Metal clanged on metal, the sound echoing down the hall and bringing Selene's head up. Heart racing, she sniffed and wiped her bleary eyes. They darted from one side of the hall to the other until she found an access to the utility corridor: the air intake grate. Everything ran through the halls; they couldn't let any travellers see the piping, could they? Some corridors were too cramped to pass through and some where she required a stool to move from one level to the next. It had taken her weeks to explore the ducts honeycombing the station, but over time she'd mapped them all. Three quick steps brought her to the air intake's latch; she released it and slipped inside, Spike close on her heels.

She turned, bending low to peek through the opening. Sweat beaded on her forehead. "Please don't be the captain. Please don't be the captain," she breathed. Then she shivered, and pulled her arms tight to her chest for a second as her breath began to mist. Fumbling around the darkness, her hands finally contacted soft material. She straightened, shrugging the sweater onto her back before reaching out to close the grate. She caught her breath as she recognized the voices of the station's captain and his first officer. *Crap.*

"There's something wrong, Captain," her Uncle Dallas said as he and Captain Tulk approached.

"I'm listening," the captain said, pausing to look down at the rotund man. His brows furrowed and he crossed his arms. His face was shiny and his hair had been cut to exactly the regulation length. Selene knew without looking any closer that, unlike her uncles, his perfectly pleated uniform was devoid of oil stains or bits of food.

In contrast, her Uncle Dallas looked as though he'd just awakened from a drunken stupor. His hair was in disarray and the two-day-old stubble on his face made him look more like a passing traveller than the man responsible for getting them to their destination. Dallas cleared his throat. "The ship is ten hours late."

Even at her distance, Selene could see Captain Tulk's brows draw so close together that they looked like one continuous brow. Finally Captain Tulk bowed his head and said, "That isn't uncommon, Dallas. Why are you panicking?"

Selene eased her white-knuckled grip on the grate handle as blood from the wound on her palm trickled down the metal. *Why does it matter if a ship is late? They come and go all the time.* Mention of time made her look at her watch. A countdown was cycling toward zero. Her eyes grew and she caught her breath. *It must be the last.* They were going into the dark side pass of the planet in less than twenty hours. She slapped her forehead. *Why else would the halls be empty?*

Radiation! Selene grimaced and licked her lips. Still watching the officers, she slipped her hand into her pocket to finger another green pill. She pulled it out and placed it on her tongue before swallowing hard.

Captain Tulk glanced her way. *Can he hear my breathing?* She pulled back as if the door was on fire, careful to be silent, and held her breath. It was all for naught; Spike shifted under her feet, the metallic clicking of his feet on the floor sending shivers down her back. *Did you hear that?* "Damn it," Selene whispered, grimacing. She bent and scooped Spike into her arms before setting off down the narrow corridor.

Thirteen steps and a quick turn to the right brought her to a junction with a ladder leading down. Seventeen steps to the left brought her to the junction leading back up. She stopped to stare at the hatch opening on the hall where she'd heard the travellers talking about the ghost. She shook her head and looked down to Spike. "They've all gone to the ship," she whispered. "There aren't enough people to hide in."

The sound of grinding metal got Selene moving again, and she heard nothing after that beyond the pounding in her ears. Did they think she was a stowaway, creeping through the station unchecked? There had been a couple of those through the years, but Captain Tulk's response had been extreme.

Selene screamed, tension making her overreact as she stumbled against a low bulkhead. Dropping to kneel on the floor, she gulped for air, rubbing her shoulder. She was going to be in so much trouble! She'd never be allowed to leave her quarters again.

Selene sat back, eyes scanning the darkened hall, her gaze drawn to every flash of light. She should admit her guilt and tell the captain she had been listening. *No*, she thought. That would get her into trouble. He would know if she lied. She couldn't lie to him. He could see right through any lie. *He can read minds.*

A tear raced down Selene's face. She knew how hotly Captain Tulk's temper could flare. Though she hadn't experienced it herself, she had seen and learned many things while crawling through the utility corridors. She knew his ire wouldn't just be roused this time. *He's going to kill me.*

Selene wiped her face with the back of her arm and started off again. She had to be where Captain Tulk couldn't find her. He would see her tears and know the truth. *Maybe he'll just ground me.*

She scampered toward the aft section of the station, passing through the environmental purification system and alongside the cables leading from the power generators. She stopped, her breathing laboured, as she was stopped by another wall. Her counting was off. *I have to slow down.*

She bent to release Spike, then rubbed arms reddened by the pressure of his weight as she continued, consciously slowing her steps. As she approached the next exit, the lights flashed on. *That's it*, she thought as she skidded to a halt before the door to the Farm. She could pretend she'd been in the Farm all day; her Uncle Sasha wouldn't know the difference. Selene pushed Spike through the hatch that would seal off the farm from radiation when the station swung toward the dark side of the planet, then followed the robot through.

Pausing to pull the large sweater over her head and wipe her face and hands, Selene glanced around the massive bay behind her. The Farm ran most of the station's length. Here, she stood hip-deep in barley, one of her Uncle Sasha's main crops. *Topea,* she thought as she counted the variations of the plant. Some were for flour, others were for pasta. There was even one variety planted for its medicinal properties. They all helped with the air purification, though that wasn't by Sasha's design. Selene's mother, Robin, had dictated that need when she'd designed the station. *I'll do that someday,* she thought as she stuffed the sweater into the corner.

With a last glance back into the hall, she closed the door. Then she let her shoulders relax and a smile find its way to her face. She'd made it. Captain Tulk wasn't following her. He wouldn't find her in the fields.

She couldn't see her Uncle Sasha, but that didn't mean anything. He was likely hunkered down talking to one of his plum trees or scraping the dirt for a row of soybeans. Regardless, Selene knew she only had to walk through the apple grove to find him—or rather, have him find her.

Selene prowled catlike toward the apple trees, her head shooting up at every movement until she recognized its origin. Then she'd sigh and her shoulders would relax, and she'd set off again.

Though only a little taller than Selene, the apple trees were prolific in the fruit they bore, and they were almost ready to harvest. She couldn't see him, but Selene was sure Sasha hovered nearby, ensuring none of the station's crew ran off with more than their daily allotment. It wouldn't be the first time an officer hoarded something. Some travellers would pay anything for fresh food.

Selene froze as the hatch clanged open. Her breath caught and her nostrils flared as her Uncle Ray ducked his head to enter. She licked her lips. *I have to leave. I can't let him see me.* She found no comfort in Ray's eyes. His gravelly voice made her shiver, reminded her of a feral beast from one of her Uncle Callum's stories. Ray was Captain Tulk's sword; he was here to give her trouble. *Damn.*

A flash of movement in her peripheral vision drew Selene's eye. Her Uncle Sasha approached, dusting his hands against his leather coveralls. He winked as he crossed her path, then leaned down to say, "Alo, Selene. Why don't you tend to my waterrrrr lilies?"

Selene swallowed hard, nodding. Then she darted toward a babbling pond surrounded by hundreds of colourful flowers. Their fragrance reached her even before she was within ten paces. Her smile returned as she knelt to play in the moist dirt. Instantly she was Selene Sotana, the great botanist trying to save Earth.

Behind her, Sasha shuffled off toward Ray. Ray was wise to keep his distance, Selene thought. It wouldn't surprise her to see a vine move of its own will to protect itself from Sasha's hostility. From her vantage, Selene could hear them speak, though they couldn't see her face.

"Hello Sasha," Ray said with a curt nod.

"Good morning, Lieutenant," Sasha replied, returning the nod.

"You are the only one who knows whether it's morning or afternoon, Sasha," Ray said nonchalantly, his gaze locked on Selene.

"'Ere on ma Farm, it *is* always morning. The sun always shines on my family." Sasha bowed low and swept his arms out wide, like wings.

Ray stared at the man for several seconds before shaking his head. "When did she get here, Sasha?" His cheeks twitched as he spoke.

Sasha cleared his throat. "She's been here for at least three hours. You know, you look like you've swallowed a mouthful. What's your problem?"

"Are you sure of that?" Ray asked with a sigh.

"Of course," Sasha lied. He was the only man Selene knew who could lock gazes with either Captain Tulk or Ray and lie so easily. His mouth didn't twitch, nor did his eyes narrow as he returned Ray's measured gaze. It made Selene wonder how much of what Sasha told her was the truth.

Ray inched forward. "Captain Tulk has informed me that someone may have been hiding within the environmental systems."

"*Mon dieu*," Sasha said, covering his face. "What in the world would the child want in therrrrre?"

Ray growled and turned away. For his part, Sasha glanced at the ground for several seconds before lifting his hand. Wagging his finger in the air, he said, "You know, I bet that robot that Lieutenant Benson gave 'er is to blame. It likely reverted to prowling for rats again. I do hope they aren't back."

Selene glanced down at Spike as she reached out to pat the robot's head. Her father had told her about the invasion of rats. The rotten animals had managed to board an ark on Earth. When the ship docked at the Orphan, it took minutes for the rats to race through bio-security, then chew through the steel walls to raid what was in storage. That was one of the reasons Spike had been created. His unique ability to pass through the bio-security system was paramount to tracking down the tiny beasts. The whole incident had given Selene nightmares of red-eyed cyborg rats chewing into her quarters. It had taken her weeks to visit the Farm without crying, but Spike was her constant companion and stood guard at night.

Sasha, however, hated Spike almost as much as the rats the robot was designed to hunt. Sasha had crafted the Farm to be free of technology. It struck Selene as odd that her Uncle Sasha could be so smart and focused on genetics, yet despise any other technology.

She watched through the trees as Ray balled his fists when Sasha refused to bow to his demands. His nostrils flaring bull-like, Ray said, "Perhaps you should lock your entrance to the halls. We will be going through the dark side soon and you don't want Dallas in here, sealing it tight."

"*Sacre.* No, I suppose not," Sasha replied as he turned away, wide-eyed. He walked toward Selene.

This is it, Selene thought, *the last few seconds of freedom.* In a moment Ray would turn and restrict her to her quarters. She was going to spend her birthday tied to a chair. She was never going to see Spike again.

"Sasha," Ray called out. Selene caught her breath and leaned forward to listen.

Sasha turned back. "*Oui*—ahem . . . aye, Lieutenant."

"The ark Lieutenant Dallas has been waiting for has been delayed. He isn't sure if Benson will have enough time to process it. You should prepare a larger supply of food. Perhaps Selene can help you."

Sasha's brows furrowed as he turned away. Selene heard, "*Sacre bleu*," then other words he must have thought she couldn't or shouldn't hear. *I've heard 'em,* she thought. She heard all kinds of words while playing in the utility halls. No one held their tongue when they didn't think she was around.

Selene sighed. *Company?* They had never had company during the dark side. Captain Tulk wouldn't be pleased for sure. That was why Dallas had been worried. *He was hoping to dump them before the dark side.* They would have to deal with crazed officers drying out. Though Selene was curious—she'd never seen the process—she knew it wasn't good.

With that, the towering Ray marched from the bay. Selene watched him leave, her heart pounding. *Am I free?* It almost didn't matter, with the news of visitors. *Visitors. They're going to stay.*

Selene jumped, startled, as a scowling Sasha appeared in front her, his hands balled into fists. "Was that because of what you did?" he asked. "*Non*, I don't want to know. Next time, don't come to *moi* to fight your battles. I have enough of my own."

Sasha marched away, calling for his assistants. Within seconds both were scurrying to his side. Selene stared after him, her hands still wrist-deep in the soil. Her eyes welled, and she felt herself trembling. Sasha had never been short with her. He'd never been cross with anyone except Dallas and Benson, and he hated them. Selene shook her head. *No.* He was her uncle. He loved her. *But, why . . . why would you yell at me like that?*

Selene stood on shaky legs, her upper lip twitching. *Fine*, she thought as she blinked away her tears. "If you're going to be like that, you son-of-a-cow," she muttered, "we're never coming back." She'd never talk to him again, even when she was forced down to the section on the dark side pass. She turned away, calling through clenched teeth, "Come here, Spike. *Now!*"

Fists clenched, she stomped toward the hatch and pushed it open hard, smiling as it clanged against the back wall. On the other side, she jerked her arm back as she moved to close the door. *Stupid Sasha.* She pirouetted and pushed her way through the crowd of officers walking down the hall.

Why shouldn't she be allowed to walk through the station? She knew what she was doing. She knew how to get out of any problems. She'd been on her own for almost a year. She was almost an adult. *Of course, that's it*, she thought as a scowl crept onto her face. *They think I'm just a kid*. She could have been twenty and it wouldn't matter to them.

Selene turned her head to the side and curled her lip before spitting on the wall. "I just wish they would . . ." She clenched her teeth and stomped silently down the hall without noticing whether Spike trailed after her.

Chapter 2

Selene was curled into a ball in the corner of her bed when she woke the next morning. Spike, nestled in the curve of her knee, stirred when her breathing changed. The creature poked his head over her thigh, then crawled up her back.

She dug her palms into her eyes to rub the crust away, then blinked and stretched her arms, opening her mouth to yawn. She paused when she noticed the numbers blinking on the large clock hanging on the wall of the outer room. Her eyes widened. *It's here.*

Selene's toes scraped the floor as she pulled herself over the side. The floor was the exact temperature that she remembered. She wouldn't have even thought about it, except the first thing her father had always said he woke was, "The floor is the same. I guess I'm still an Orphan." An inside joke between the officers he couldn't have understood would become her reality.

Selene shuddered as a dull computerized voice piped through the suite, breaking the silence. "Are you up, Miss Selene?"

"I'm up, Cecile," Selene said to the computer as she rose and, eyelids still heavy, shuffled into the bathroom. She finished her ablutions by brushing her teeth and combing her hair. It took longer than usual because of the dirt and grease she'd acquired while climbing through the utility halls the day before. She had to unwind the hair and brush it clean. *I don't have to wash it*, she decided. She would have lots of time when they were on the dark side. *It's here!*

The scrapes on her hands had scabbed over. She reached for a pill bottle in the cabinet above the sink, pausing to read the large label on the bottle before fishing out a pill and swallowing it. She chewed the corner of her lip for a second, then fished out another pill.

"Good morning, Miss Selene. Do you require any assistance?" The computer's tone rose at the end of the sentence, making it sound human. Selene knew it didn't care whether she needed assistance or not, though; it couldn't do anything for her, even if it wanted to.

"No thank you, Cecile." She sighed as she glanced at the dents in the wall. She had learned the hard way that the computer didn't care how she responded. Swearing and kicking the wall accomplished nothing. *Only a child would do that, not an officer.*

"Would you rather have porridge or—"

"I would like whatever the special is, Cecile," Selene said. She shivered as she left the bathroom. Glancing at the speaker, she said, "I'm not really hungry." *I have places to go.*

"I'm sorry, Selene. I don't understand your request," the computer replied.

Selene frowned as she entered her living room. Spike was still sprawled on the large bed in the starboard room as she moved into the smaller one to port. She pulled clean clothing from the dresser and dressed quickly. "Hmmm . . ." She pulled at the neck of her shirt.

She returned to the larger room where she'd slept. Spike stirred again when she entered, then jumped to the floor as she bent to retrieve a pair of orange coveralls flung against the wall. She bunched the greasy uniform under her nose and sniffed it twice before laying it out far enough that she could pull it on over her other clothes. She rolled up the sleeves, then skipped over to grab her watch from the bed table. Before she could fasten it around her wrist, the computer chimed and the woman's voice said, "Your food has arrived, Selene."

Selene rolled her eyes as she walked to the hatch. *Stupid seaman.* She threw the door open and leaned out to grab the plastic food tray sitting on the floor. Before she retreated, she glanced down the hall, frowning when she saw movement—someone striding around the corner. She sighed and shook her head. "Stupid seaman. I'm not going to give it back to you."

Selene walked over and dropped the tray on the table to look it over. A grilled cheese sandwich nestled within a circle of fruit. It wasn't the special, but then again, Cook knew her tastes: grilled cheese for breakfast, grilled cheese for lunch, and macaroni for dinner. She lifted the edge of the crust and grimaced. *That doesn't look like cheese.* It was more green than yellow, and there were several swirls in the centre. They always managed to find new ways to hide vegetables in the food. When she saw them, she got rid of them in honour of Sasha. She couldn't be party to destroying the vegetables' souls and, in turn, Sasha's family. Today however, a smile played on her lips as she squished tiny peas between her teeth.

There weren't many, however. *Maybe they're mashed into the cheese.* It was possible; it was even possible that they had always been the cheese. *Where else could cheese come from?* Was it possible to stock enough cheese for her daily intake, let alone what the rest of the crew ate? She gave up counting after reaching 30,614 slices, and that didn't include the cheese on the pasta.

"Miss Selene, I have an incoming alert from Lieutenant Benson. Would you like to connect?"

Selene froze for a second, then slapped her forehead. *The ship. It's here. It's really here.* She paced back and forth across the room, rubbing her thighs. Then she stopped in front of the screen. "Yes please, Cecile."

The small screen near the bathroom flickered for several seconds before focusing on a thin man wearing an orange jumpsuit. He had several new cuts on his sweat-drenched face. "Hey there, kiddo," he said, looking at her with dancing eyes through the video screen.

"Hello, Uncle Benson. Can I help you with something?" She wiped her mouth with the back of her hand.

"Listen, kiddo, we had a late docker and we want to get the stick men out before we hit the dark side. I'm not really sure I'll have time to teach you this morning. Can we push your appointment to this afternoon?"

The ticking clock above the viewscreen stole Selene's attention for a second as it rolled over the hour. *They still want to send them away before the dark side.* She glanced away, silently counting the hours. Her Uncle Dallas had said twelve to fifteen hours. That meant they had five or six hours left to eject the ark. She smiled. "Can I help, Uncle Benson? I've seen you use the robots before and I'm really good at the VR interface."

The man's shoulder's fell for a second as he sputtered, "I . . . I'm . . ." He looked away for a second before he looked back and nodded. "Sure, kiddo. You can help. Meet me in the Lab, okay?"

Trembling, Selene stepped away from the screen. As soon as it flickered off, she threw up her hands and jumped squealing into the air. *I did it. I did it. AWESOME!* She'd been permitted to use some of the equipment now and again, but to help was unprecedented. *Here's my chance,* she thought. She'd prove how valuable she was to the crew. She would do her parents proud.

Selene danced around for several minutes, arms raised. She was going to the Lab, a place she'd only been to once before. Deep within the protected section, the Lab was the heart of the station. It housed the computer core. Cecile's true kernel was saved there. Spike had been devised there. Her mother had designed the secondary systems there. Her father had worked there.

Selene stopped, her arms dropping. She stood still, eyes blinking. She'd never thought about it before. Her father had been sick for so long, she didn't remember the whole event. He'd been in bed for most of the last month, but during those last days when he refused to let her see him, Savir had moved down to the Lab. In the end, they'd found him slumped over one of the computer terminals.

Selene shivered and reached into her pocket for a pill. She swallowed it, gulped, and took a deep breath, wiping her eyes. Again composed, she stopped at the door to slip on her shoes and called, "Come on, Spike."

Spike must have powered down, as it took several calls before he bounded off the bed to follow her. She bent and flipped a small switch on his belly, waiting long enough to ensure Spike's measured steps were following her before she rushed from the suite and skipped to the end of the hall, whistling. Up to the right, a massive hatch now closed off the outer ring of the station. She moved out of the way as a pair of officers rushed by, carrying medical kits.

Turning into the hall that would take her toward the Lab, she passed several officers as they worked. Most operations continued during the dark side, though not as much got done. Most would be attempting to find solutions to the whole process. In twenty-plus years, no one on the station had been able to solve the dilemma of the radiation emanating from the planet. Selene shivered, fingers playing with the small pills in her pocket. *Damned radiation.* During the closest pass to the planet, a few minutes of exposure could burn a man's insides to dust.

Marching—one, two, one, two—she reached out and dragged her fingers along the cool metal walls. Unlike the smooth walls of the outer ring of the station, these were bumpy like the goose bumps Selene got when she was cold and the hair stood up on her arms. The hallway lights were dimmed, so she could detect the texture of the dark walls only with her fingers.

She glimpsed movement within one of the non-commissioned officers' sleeping quarters as she passed its open hatch, as officers hunkered down for sleep. *How can they sleep through this?* she wondered, eyeing the full bunks. It was a trick Selene hoped to learn someday. No way could she sleep through the blaring klaxons, especially when they crossed into the dark side. Cocking her head and closing her eyes, she imagined she could hear snoring as she moved beyond the room and its inhabitants. She sighed and her shoulders relaxed. She couldn't remember the last time she'd heard that sound; not since her father had gone away.

Lost in her thoughts, Selene stopped as a firm hand fell on her shoulder. Her nose wrinkled at the foul stench that came with it. *Fuel,* her mind supplied, as tears sprang to her eyes and she swallowed hard to keep her breakfast down. She didn't have to look up to know the hand and odour belonged to her Uncle Callum.

"I haven't seen you in a couple days, my dear," Callum said, his eyes dancing. He tipped his head back and howled like a wolf before leaning forward to sniff loudly.

Selene rolled her eyes as her smile widened. "Oh, Grandmother, why are your eyes so big?"

"The better to see you with, my dear," Callum said with a smile and another sniff. He waited a second before they both broke into laughter.

Selene tapped her thigh as she split her attention between her uncle and the hall that led to the engineering bay. She shifted, her gaze catching on the digital clock hanging above the hall entrance as it counted down from five hours. She forced her eyes away from the red flashing lights of the clock and slid her hand into her pocket to retrieve one of her green radiation pills. She surreptitiously slipped the pill into her mouth, and her shoulders relaxed as the sweet taste spread over her tongue.

"I know yer goin' down to the Lab, hon. I can walk with you." Selene knew that her Uncle Dallas kept many of his supplies— thousands of miles of cabling and wiring—in the Lab.

They entered a main hall filled with dozens of officers hurrying in both directions. Those dressed in environmental suits, like her Uncle Callum, ran full-out, still working to latch their helmets. Others in regular uniforms moved aside at the last second to let them pass. Selene stopped, but before she could comment, Callum reached out to cover her ears long enough to yell, "Goddamn it, people, get your arses in gear!" At the sound of his voice, the officers pulled to attention and quickened their steps. Selene pretended not to have heard.

They were outside the activity room. Nothing stirred within; the training equipment and card tables sat unused. *Maybe later,* she thought. Captain Tulk expected absolute discipline for the transition, and if the ark was docked, no one had the luxury of being off duty if they weren't sleeping. The thrum of machinery kept Selene from continuing down the hall. Back to the activity room entrance, she watched two man-sized robots shuffle down the hall carrying massive crates, their operators close behind.

Oblivious to the chaos, Callum said, "The guys and I wanted to know if you were going to grace us with your presence."

Looking at the floor, Selene said, "Oh, Uncle Callum, I've been *so* busy." She caught her breath. *Is this a test?* He would get sad if he realized she'd just been playing in the empty halls of the public sector. They smelled better, though, and didn't make her gag.

As the robots shuffled closer, Callum reached out to pull Selene behind the painted line that ran the length of the hall. "You know, when I was your age I made sure to get around to my poor uncles before they got old and grey."

The corners of Selene's mouth twitched before curving into a smile. Selene opened her arms wide to embrace him. "Um, maybe tomorrow while we're still stuck inside, we can come down and see you and the gang." Spike jumped from behind her legs long enough to bark his agreement. A second later he stepped behind the painted line to sit on his haunches.

"That would be wonderful, hon. The gang would really appreciate it," Callum said as he pulled away, his fresh environmental suit crinkling under her arms. "Soooo . . . I heard you had a little tussle with Sasha last night. I hope everything is—"

Selene's face contorted. "I hate him." She curled her lip to spit on the wall, but held back and looked up at Callum, who raised an eyebrow in query. "He yelled at me."

Callum sighed. "I'm sure he didn't mean it. He was probably having a bad day."

Crossing her arms, she set off again. "I don't care. He yelled at me. Papa wouldn't have done that. It was mean."

Callum took two quick steps and slid sideways to block Selene's path. Kneeling, he said, "You know that sometimes adu . . . your uncles say things we don't mean. I'm sure he was just having a bad day."

Selene closed her eyes and covered her ears. "I don't care. I don't care."

"Okay, okay." Callum threw his hands in the air. "Just remember that he loves you. We all do."

Selene sighed and looked at the wall. *I don't think so. He's stupid.* But she sighed at Callum's frown and mumbled, "I know."

"Good," Callum said. "Now tell me what you're doing with Benson."

Selene's head shot up to search the hall for another clock. She found the red digits and sighed. *I've lost ten minutes.* Shifting her feet, she leaned to one side to stare down the hall. Taking a deep breath, she said, "I'm helping Uncle Benson with the VR bots."

Callum nodded as they set off again, turning into a narrower hallway. Lowering his head to look at her, he said, "That must be exciting."

Selene giggled. "I know everyone hates the bots, but I don't. I really really like 'em. They're cool. I mean, you get to control the robots, of course, but then you can see through the camera and . . . and, well, it's cool." She started walking as if her arms and legs couldn't bend. "I think it would be really cool to be a robot. You could lift whatever you wanted and even go out into space." She exhaled with a tremor.

Callum shook his head. They had arrived at a swinging hatch. "In that case, my dear, I shall leave you to your duties."

Selene bounced on the balls of her feet for several seconds before giving the man another hug. "I'll come see you tomorrow, Uncle Callum. And if it's okay with you, I'd like to hear the one about the princess and the dragon."

Callum smiled and glanced away for a second before saying, "Okay, hon. I can do that. See you later."

Her uncle disappeared around the corner, and Selene turned toward the hatch and looked back, nodding when Spike stepped around the corner. Benson was the only officer who let the dog roam freely in his presence, but in the Lab, Spike would be underfoot and that wouldn't make anyone happy. Like most of the Orphan's hatches, this one wouldn't let any of the bots through anyway, as it was designed to seal completely if there was a breach in the station's hull. Someone would even have to open the door for her, because she didn't have the authority to walk right in.

"Would you like to go in?" someone asked behind her as Selene stared at the door.

Selene shivered as she turned toward the approaching captain. Catching her breath, she narrowed her eyes and forced thoughts of bunnies into her mind. *You won't read my mind!* Her shoulders relaxed as she realized his smile suggested he was oblivious to her skulking through the utility halls yesterday. He even stepped close enough to bend down and pet Spike.

This close to the man, Selene noticed he had more wrinkles around his eyes. His hair had turned a lighter grey, and she even saw several stark white strands. He must still be visiting the exercise room, though; he didn't have the belly her Uncle Dallas and Hourev had managed to cultivate over the years. He wasn't wearing the same clothes he'd worn the day before, but he hadn't shaved his face. *He hasn't slept,* Selene realized. Then she scowled and hung her head as Captain Tulk reached up to press a control on the wall console beside the door. *You were waiting for me,* she thought.

With a chirrup, the door rolled open and she passed into the room, looking around. The bay was about a quarter the size of Sasha's Farm, but teeming with officers. Most walked with determination, focused on their goals. Others worked on various projects that Selene couldn't understand.

Someday, she thought as she recognized a dozen robots in mid-construction on one side of the bay. They were of different sizes, with multiple attachments. The humanoid forms, with arms of carbon steel and feet clad in rubberized resin to reduce their impact on the floor panels, were designed to lift large cargo containers. Beyond those stood massive robots designed for work outside the station. Selene had seen them from time to time, working on the hull or aft engines. They had a myriad arms for welding and cutting on the hull of the station or any of the docked ships. Her Uncle Benson had designed them because he didn't like sending any of the officers outside. Selene shuddered at the thought of floating through space without a tether.

"Hey there, kiddo," Uncle Benson said as he walked out of a small cubicle. His coveralls were dirty, his hair in disarray, as though he'd been working under one of the robots and it had blasted him with a pneumatic discharge.

Looking around cautiously to make sure nothing would careen into her, Selene stepped closer to salute the man. "Lieutenant Selene reporting for duty."

"Hmm. Someone has been promoted, apparently," Captain Tulk said behind her.

Selene whipped her head around, feeling her cheeks warm. She stared at Captain Tulk for several seconds before she realized the man was teasing. She sighed, averting her eyes before saying, "Um, maybe I did that." She looked up and added, "Uh, what rank am I?"

Captain Tulk cleared his throat, his gaze drifting to the officers nearby. He stood silent for several seconds before reaching up to pluck one of the insignia buttons from his collar. Squaring his shoulders, he said, "Mr. Selene Sotana, do you recognize the Terran Government as your liege?"

Selene straightened her back as the room quieted, everyone watching the impromptu ceremony, something that didn't happen often. *They're all looking at me.* The officers weren't paid anything; all of their needs were met. Rank was only used to establish discipline. Being elevated to a new rank did nothing for morale. It didn't accomplish a better work ethic. *Until now,* Selene thought. "I do."

Stepping forward as though this had been rehearsed, Benson asked, "Are you willing to follow the orders of any ranking officers?"

Without shifting her gaze from Captain Tulk, Selene intoned, "I am."

After a quick glance from Captain Tulk, a master seaman stepped forward to ask, "Do you promise to lead with integrity, loyalty, and grace?"

"I do," Selene said, stone-faced. Her heart raced, making the blood pound in her ears. She tried to fix her gaze on every officer in quick succession.

Captain Tulk knelt to press the button into Selene's collar. "Mr. Selene Sotana, I invest you with the mark of your rank. You are now Sub-lieutenant Sotana."

Selene unclenched her jaw and planted her feet to turn in place, just like Captain Tulk. Bending at the waist in a low bow, she then straightened her back and thrust her chest out so everyone could see her new pin. She saluted and held every officer's gaze for at least a second, holding her arm long enough to show superiority over the junior officers. There was no need to pretend she had a crowd of adoring fans; they were here and real. *I'm an OFFICER.* Her whole body trembled as she suppressed a smile.

Nodding, Captain Tulk said, "Congratulations, Sub-lieutenant; now we need to work."

Selene sighed, her moment of glory fading. Tilting her head back, she said, "Sub-lieutenant Selene Sotana, reporting for duty."

Captain Tulk threw a glance toward her Uncle Benson, who winked at her and said, "Ah, good; I didn't think I could handle having a pip like you as the same rank. It would have been depressing." Turning away, he yelled, "Alright, people, let's get some work done."

The congratulations kept coming as the officers moved by Selene. Most of the non-commissioned officers saluted before giving their best wishes and shuffling off to their own duties. It would be the last time most of them would ever speak in the familiar to her.

"Okay, Selene, you go over to that one," Benson said as he pointed toward a small cubicle with a low wall.

As she stepped into the cubicle, Selene caught her breath. The instruments filling the room dwarfed the chair at the centre. Even if Benson and his team had been working on making them more efficient, there had to be instruments for her feet and her hands. It even looked as if the chair would wrap around her torso and legs, so she would be controlling the entire robot.

"Don't worry about all that, kiddo. You won't even notice most of it, once you get in the seat."

Moving as if she were walking on eggshells, Selene crossed to the seat and climbed into it. Benson was there in seconds to help her set her feet and arms, then slide the helmet down over her head. He left the goggles up while he explained the mechanics of the robot.

"I'm actually quite glad you're going to help me," he said. "The rest of the guys are pretty sloppy with their work. Getting old does that. The last time you worked with some of this equipment, you looked pretty competent."

Selene studied is face as he spoke. He wasn't joking or lying as he praised her work. He wanted her to do the work. *He wants ME!*

"Now, remember when you are drawn into the VR, it will hurt your eyes for a second," Benson continued. "You will feel a little odd because what you see and what you feel will be different. When you knock into things—and yes, it will happen; the VR bots are bigger than you are, so it will happen—don't worry about it, because it will get easier. Anyway, you won't feel anything, but the seat will shake a bit."

Selene took several gulps of air to slow her breathing. Her heart still raced. *I'm here. It's really happening.*

Benson left, and less than two minutes later one of the technicians came in to make final adjustments. Smiling, the officer said, "Can I put your visor down now, sir?"

Selene stared at him for several seconds before saying, "Yes, please . . . Able Seaman."

The man shifted the goggles on the back of her helmet and drew them down over her face. Selene shuddered. She caught her breath as her vision blurred, then darkened. "Don't worry, sir," the officer's voice came through the darkness. "I know you won't screw up. You can do it."

Selene felt her stomach lurch at the prospect. Screw up? It was a possibility? *No, I can do it.* She would be fine. It was just a robot. She could *build* the robot, if she wanted to. She'd even recoded Cecile. Driving a robot was going to be a cinch. But then she frowned. She could screw up. She wasn't perfect. This was important. Why was her uncle even giving her the chance? *He believes in me.* He knew she could do it.

Selene cried out and forced her hands open, realizing she'd been clenching them so tightly, her fingernails dug into the scabs on her palms. She lifted her hands to wipe her eyes, but couldn't, with the goggles in place.

"Selene," a soft voice said in her ear. "Listen to me, Sub-lieutenant Sotana. It's time we got to work. We don't have time to worry about anything else."

Selene closed her eyes. She took a slow, deep breath before wrapping her hands around the handholds. *I can do this,* she thought, and waited.

Chapter 3

Though it felt like an eternity, the darkness lasted less than a minute. Silence reigned in her cubicle—the door must have been closed, though she didn't remember there being one. Perhaps it was a trick of the equipment.

The screen within the goggles flickered, then displayed a large storeroom filled with several crates of about her height.

"Hey, kiddo, what do you see?" Uncle Benson's voice asked in her ear. It sounded as though he was actually standing beside her.

Selene swung her head as if she would be able to see the man, then winced as the room spun around her. Her stomach lurched and she squeezed her eyes shut as her vision blurred.

Rubbing her temples, she took a deep breath and opened her eyes to stare at the complexity of her environment. Her cheeks burned a little as she envisioned how ridiculous she looked. *Are they laughing?* Anyone could have done a better job than she just had. She could have destroyed something.

Selene shifted her head again until she found a robot standing in front of one of the crates. *Oh, they're taller than me.* The crates were at least six feet tall. The robot was much like the humanoid ones in the Lab just outside her cubicle, with the skeletal makeup of a human, though its arms were much thicker. She could see the hydraulic cylinders that adjusted to move the robot's arms and legs in imitation of muscles. Though it didn't have a head, two small cameras were mounted on top of its neck, flanked by two small microphones.

Shifting its own cameras to gaze at her, the robot said with Benson's voice, "Everything is designed for ease. There are two eyes and two ears in roughly the same position as ours, so you don't get confused with spatial awareness. You should play around with the general controls for a minute until you can get the hang of it."

Selene accepted his suggestion, lifting her legs as though walking. There was a little resistance on the foot pedal, making her foot heavier as she set one foot down and lifted the other. After several seconds she skipped from one foot to the other, and though she had to lift her feet higher than normal, her steps were fluid. She moved like a ballerina, her toes outstretched. *They have rubber soles,* she thought as she cocked her head to the side to listen. She lifted her arms and waved them around for several seconds before pulling the hands closer. There were four fingers and a thumb, all providing a grip strong enough to crush her.

Uncle Benson cleared his throat. "Okay, once you get the hang of that, reach behind you and grab the hose that is attached to your lower back." His robot shifted as he spoke to pull forward the four inch hose that was latched to its back.

That looks easy, Selene thought as she followed suit. Within minutes she was wielding the hose like a vacuum. Still, she knew her movements so far had been rudimentary, and she was thankful she had the benefit of gravity to control the machine. She'd only have to get stuck outside the ship with the robot to would prove herself a failure. She shuddered again. Hopefully the robot was close enough to the ship being loaded without having to go outside. At least while she was within the station she could tell which direction was up. In the dark of space, she would be blind. For all her dreams of jumping around on asteroids and moons, space terrified Selene. It wasn't the cold or the silence or even the darkness; *everything* about space was lonely.

When her father had been alive, whenever he'd had to work on the hull of the station, Selene had waited for him to return, spending her time at the hatch, looking out into space. Being lost in space terrified her. She may be strapped in a seat at the centre of the station, but just the thought of seeing it on a video screen made her shiver.

"Alright, kiddo. Now that you have your vacuum I want you to step out into the hall. Don't worry, I'll be right behind you."

Selene followed the order, moving her robot to the door concealed beyond the first row of crates. *I know where I am,* she thought. She would have to take seventeen steps. Moving quickly, she set off down the hall.

After thirteen steps, however, she bit her lip. "Damn it." It took seventeen child-sized steps; the robots were not so small. As her robot careened into the wall, Selene felt her entire chair shake and then turn to the side as her vision twisted. Grimacing, she turned her head from side to side to gauge her position. She was on her side, the robot beached.

She waited several seconds, expecting to hear crass remarks or more laughter, but she heard nothing. Perhaps they knew they would have done the same, or Captain Tulk had shared one of his most determined scowls. She was unable to command the robot to look around for several minutes, but eventually her display showed the rotating room. Still no one commented on her near disaster as she finally managed to coax the robot to its feet.

As though nothing had happened, her Uncle Benson said, "You can join me in the bay when you are ready."

She wasn't long joining him. They stood overlooking a ship so large, only its tip had managed to enter the bay. The large doors had sealed around the ship to ensure no air leakage.

"Alright, kid—pardon me, Sub-lieutenant, you're going to enter this door while I take the one down there." Benson pointed to a large entrance to the ship.

The two took their robots slowly down the broad staircase and stopped in front of a pair of large double doors. Selene brought the clunky robot forward, waiting for Benson to continue his lecture.

He took a deep breath before saying, "The arks were designed to be boarded like this. In fact, there are two similar robots on the ship that will be emptying their cargo as soon as they touch down."

Selene followed his directions, shifting to open the door. The panels slid aside to reveal darkness within. "Are there any lights?" she asked. As she spoke, lights flickered on above her head. She smiled.

"Can I have one of these, Uncle Benson—er, I mean Lieutenant Benson?"

"Sorry, kiddo, they're pretty big. I don't think we'd get it into your room." He returned to business. "Alright, here's the deal. The first thing we have to do is scrub the air. We don't have to be too thorough; the vacuum is pretty intense."

Selene waved her apparatus around, sucking the air as though she could clean the whole ship. "Uncle Benson, why are we cleaning the air?"

"Typically the officers are locked in the fore decks, but when they come out they have to pass through these two corridors. We're scrubbing particulates that were left by the crew passing through this hall. When we're done we'll check the integrity of the sealed units on this level and then we'll get to work."

"What do we have to do?" Selene asked as she took another step deeper into the corridor.

"Who is that?" a new voice asked. "Is that a child?"

Selene froze, unable to recognize the voice. She furrowed her brows, glancing toward the voice and trying to imagine the speaker. *It must be one of the pilots,* she thought. He obviously didn't know about her rank and status.

"Is there a child in there? Where the hell did you get a child? Did she come from one of the other ships?" The man's voice rose in pitch and his questions came in quick succession, as though he didn't expect any answers.

Captain Tulk broke in. "Calm down, Lieutenant. You are speaking to one of my officers. That is all you need to know."

"The hell it is," the lieutenant said. Selene could hear him say something else, but it was muffled.

There was silence for several seconds before Captain Tulk returned to Selene's ear. Speaking slowly, he said, "Don't worry about that, Selene. You just keep working."

Selene huffed and sat back in her chair. The crew of the station believed in her, didn't they? Of course they did, or she wouldn't be strapped to this seat like she was. So why did it matter to the lieutenant? As long as his cargo was protected, wasn't that all that mattered?

As if her Uncle Benson could read her mind, he said, "You have to understand, Sel, that he hasn't seen another human except his crew for ten years, since he left Earth. He's been asleep for most of the journey at that, so the concept of a child is too much for him to understand."

Selene's shoulders slumped. *Ten years?* That was almost as long as she'd been alive. Of the rest of the time, he wouldn't have been able to stand up straight, and he would have had to live in zero gravity most of the time. *Living alone is bad enough,* Selene thought. She did that most days, but not being able to touch the ground? That would be devastating.

Selene wondered if the man had been awake long. Everyone she knew was cranky when they woke up. Waking up from cryosleep would be worse. *The long sleep.*

Finally her thoughts returned to her present situation. "I think I'm done, Uncle Benson."

"Alright, kiddo. On your left arm there is a screen with several buttons. I want you to press the button labelled Air Quality."

The screen on Selene's robot showed a transparent mock-up of the room. Selene pressed another button to project the image into three dimensions. After several seconds the tech that had tightened her into the seat said, "There is a small cluster down the hall about seven paces."

You must be able to see, too, she thought. Her camera lenses must be relaying to the officers sitting outside the cubicle. *Oh crap. You can see everything.* Selene felt her cheeks warm. They'd all seen her antics earlier. *I wonder how many of them wanted to replace me when that happened.*

Selene focused on her screen, finding the red blotch the technician had indicated. She pressed several other buttons until she knew what action each would cause. After a time, she set her robot off down the hall until she came to the section with poor air. When she was finished, she rechecked her system. *All green.*

"That's great, kiddo. Now put that tool away. I want you to go to the third door on the left. It opens the same way the main doors did. That's right. Now open the doors and step inside."

The technician's voice added, "The room is cluttered, Sub-lieutenant. You will have to be very careful with your movements."

With Benson, Selene stepped into a room as large as the Farm. It was filled with rows of large crates, each with a small screen flickering on the front.

"Okay Selene, I want you to go down that side and make sure all the screens test green. I'll start here and we'll meet—"

"Why?" Selene blurted.

Benson was uncommonly serious as he said, "We have to make sure there has been no radiation leakage into the cryo units. If they've made it through unscathed up here, then there are no problems below. It doesn't really matter whether we do it now or later, but it works for my system."

Not waiting to hear the rest of what he said, Selene set to work. Though the first crate showed a green light, Selene lifted her arm to view her own monitors. She moved quicker than she had expected, soon reaching the centre of the room. She scanned the rest of the room and smiled. *I win.* She chewed the corner of her lip for a second before continuing on into Benson's side of the room.

"Hey, who's been watching the new kid? I think she's been cheating," Benson said. His voice was light, and the others laughed.

"Somebody's a sore loser," an officer said, though Selene didn't recognize the voice.

Clearing his throat, the captain said, "The sub-lieutenant has given us the advantage of time. Perhaps we can play later."

Selene's heart raced at the praise, but then as the captain ordered them back to work, she floundered. She whipped her head around, causing her seat to rumble.

"Easy does it, Sub-lieutenant," the unfamiliar voice offered as her screen began to tilt sideways.

Selene twisted her torso, trying to shift the robot—too late; her robot tipped backward toward one of the cryo units. Everything was going to be destroyed, just because she was foolish enough to have a second of elation. She was so stupid! Captain Tulk had finally given her the chance to prove herself, and now she was going to wreck everything. Tears streaked her face as she closed her eyes. She couldn't bear to see the damage she was about to cause.

A last shudder shook the seat, and then it went still. When she felt another jolt in her seat, she opened one eye, then the other. *I'm still standing,* she thought as she turned her head. Beside her, Benson's robot stood tall, his arms supporting her back. Its upper torso shook as though laughing.

Whispering as though she were the only one to hear, Benson said, "Are you okay, kiddo?"

Her face burned as she stared at the robot. After a few seconds, she blinked and turned her head around to determine the damage. She shivered as a cold chill traced through her body. Her uncle's quick movements had saved her from calamity and the room from any damage.

"Hey, what are you two doing down there?" the unfamiliar voice asked as Selene felt the gyros in her seat shift, indicating that Benson was stepping away.

After a moment, Benson said, "I think we'll have to check the seat on the Sub-lieutenant's equipment when we're done."

Selene felt her skin tingle as the warmth faded from her face. She patted down her body and lifted her leg. "Um, so what do we do next . . . Lieutenant?"

"Now it's time for the real show," Benson replied, his voice full of energy. His robot seemed to bounce on the balls of its feet for several seconds before it beckoned Selene to follow. Selene cut short her laughter as she wondered whether it was her humour that got her the job. Was it even possible for anyone else to work with Benson? He was doing a perfect job of making his robot look human.

"Alright, kiddo. We have two more jobs. The first is easy. We drag a fuel line from the cargo bay to the ship and fill her up. The second isn't so simple. It's going to require a little more dexterity."

Selene cocked her head to the side. "Oh? What is it?"

"This ship was designed for long distance travel from Earth. She is filled with a whole bunch of wiring and equipment that she doesn't need, but we do. What we need to do is gut her without making it look like we've gutted her."

"Um, Uncle Benson how do we do that?" Selene asked as she followed him from the ship.

They needed both robots to pull the fuel line, eight inches in diameter and three hundred feet long, from the cargo hold. It was rubberized metal to reduce the risk of immolation. Benson moved quickly, taking the first portion of the line as Selene dragged it from the wall. Every ten feet, the man's robot bent to shift the hose, making sure the white dotted line ran along the top. When he was close to the ship, he waved his arm across the hull for several seconds before a cap fell from the hardened metal. He lifted the fuel line and shoved its end into the opening. Turning back to Selene, he said, "Okay, kiddo. Go back to the wall and open the valve."

The valve was gigantic, measuring over three feet. It even looked large when Selene put her robotic hands on it and tugged. It was tight, even for the robot, but after several attempts she managed to open the valve. The flood of fuel coursing through the line made it balloon out as it rushed toward the ship. As soon as it reached the ship, the pressure dropped.

"Alright, that's going to take a while," Benson said as he left the ship. "Now, it's time for my favourite part."

Moving her robot abreast of Benson's, Selene whispered, "How are we going to get all the wiring out?"

"Why, of course we get help," Benson replied as he clapped his hands. Before he dropped them, the door opened again. An army of doglike robots streamed through.

Smiling, Selene said, "Spike?"

Spike barked beside her in the cubicle and jumped on her legs. She shook with laughter and felt both her body and the robot moving simultaneously. She frowned and twisted to the side, far enough that the dog was forced to jump away. Selene shook her head, forcing the dual audio streams from her mind as she focused on her uncle's robot.

"We'll start with the wiring," Benson began as she shifted toward the doors.

Selene didn't have to question the need. The station couldn't afford to have a wiring problem. When the rats had infiltrated the station, Dallas had panicked. As soon as Benson's army of mechanical dogs had cleared the decks, Dallas had tested every line. He'd only had to replace a few lines, but enough to make him vow to have enough ready to rewire the entire station if the need arose.

Supply ships weren't exactly sent on schedule, so they had to improvise.

Benson took two short steps and reached into the ship to remove a steel panel from the wall. Before he could say anything, the army of dogs jumped into the panel and skittered down the wall. Selene could hear their pattering feet clicking for several minutes.

"In about three minutes," Uncle Benson said, "we'll be able to pull the wiring out as they clear it from the walls."

Sure enough, when Selene tugged on the wire a few minutes later, there was no resistance. Hand over hand she pulled, coiling it at her feet. After almost an hour they stood with their army at attention, the wiring wound onto several large spools.

"Uncle Benson," Selene asked, "why do they need so much fuel? Can't they just leave Earth with all they need?"

Turning, the Benson robot said, "The ships leave Earth with very little fuel because they have to travel light, so they don't have to worry about the acceleration. You remember physics, right? What velocity is?"

Nodding, Selene replied, "Velocity is mass times force. Okay, so the lighter they are, the faster they can go."

"Exactly, kiddo," Benson said as he bent to retrieve one of the rolls of wiring. Motioning for her to bring one of the others, he continued. "The fuel will allow them to navigate the system and to land on the planet. It takes a lot of energy to accomplish that."

"Oh, okay," Selene said with a quick nod. It made sense. Why would they want to cart all that fuel around? It was obviously flammable and there was an abundant supply here on the planet the station orbited. "They must have realized before they came here that they needed the fuel," she blurted without thinking.

"Indeed," Benson replied. Selene imagined his smile widening as he explained. "It was actually Callum who came up with the idea. That's why he's here."

"But what about the other stations? Aren't there others in Tau Ceti and Alpha Centauri?" Selene countered as she followed him up the steps. Although she wasn't actually carrying the wire, her movements were becoming sluggish, less refined. Was it just empathy for the robot, or had she been strapped to the seat long enough that the gentle resistance was taking its toll?

"Every system is different," Benson explained. "The one on Tau Ceti uses solar winds and the one on Sigma Draconis has a space elevator. It's in geosynchronous orbit over the colony."

Selene's eyes widened. *A space elevator?* Being able to visit the planet with the push of a button was fantastic. On the planet in the morning, fighting space devils, then on the station at night to sleep in her bed. *But then again,* she thought, *they live on the planet in the Sigma Draconis system.* "But why so different?" she asked. "Wouldn't it be easier to just make them all the same?"

Nodding, Benson said, "I guess that's not really an answer I could give you. Not a straight one anyway. Every station exists for a different faction, of sorts."

"Hey, what have you two been talking about for the last hour?" the unfamiliar voice interrupted.

After a brief pause, Benson said, "I've been giving her a lesson in physics, if you must know. I figured you would be bored."

"Oh," the officer replied. His voice trembled, as though the concept of doubting Benson was forbidden. "S-s-sorry, sir."

"Can I get back to it?" Benson asked with a dramatic sigh.

"Yes sir. The fuel gauge says it will take another sixty-five minutes," the man replied. Selene could still hear the irritation in his voice. She imagined a man wearing a constant scowl, then wondered if she could even recognize the man walking down a hall.

"Perfect. I think that's exactly how long it will take to finish her lesson," Benson said, his tone still even. He must have been cracking a smile deep within his own cubicle as he spoke. "Hey, kiddo, I have to teach you something. Whenever you want to speak to me only, all you have to do is press the orange button on your hand switch."

After a few awkward movements that made the robot look like it was saluting, Selene shifted the goggles on her face far enough for her to see the orange button. Closing her eyes, she found the button several times to make sure she could do it with the visor on. Confident it would be easy, she retraced her motions, making the robot offer salutation again. As she finished, the scowling tech asked, "Sub-lieutenant, is there a problem with the robot?"

Shaking her head, Selene said, "No. I . . . uh . . . just had an itchy forehead."

"Oh, if you just tilt your head to the side and then back, there is an automatic scratcher that can help you," the scowling man replied; Selene sensed genuine contempt in his voice.

Curious to see how the new toy worked, Selene did as she'd been told and found her forehead gently caressed by the device. After several attempts, the "hand" became more abrasive as it began to scratch. As she pulled away, the hand stopped.

"Alright, kiddo. Are you ready for your next lesson?" Benson's voice broke into her reverie.

Selene took a deep breath. "Uncle, why did you want me to do this job? I can't be the best at it."

"Actually, kiddo, the one thing the station is deficient in is manpower. I figured that if I could get you on board, someone else wouldn't have to do it. They can do their regular work and I can teach you what you need to know. Next time you can do it, and I might not have to. You get it?"

Selene knew her robot's cameras would be bobbing up and down as she nodded, so she didn't bother acknowledging her uncle verbally. He did make sense. She didn't know if anyone would mind and she, for her part, had been trying to get someone to notice her for a while. She wanted to help. Her parents would like it. If they were still around, they would know how good she was.

"Good," Benson said as his robot trudged on. "Now as soon as we get these rolls of wire into storage, the rest of the team should have everything else gutted."

Selene giggled. She was still having difficulty remembering that the voice in her ear was sitting in a chair like her own not ten feet away and what she saw was happening almost a thousand steps along the main hall.

Turning back, Benson asked, "What's so funny?"

"Oh, uh . . . I kinda looked up to see you when you said that, before I realized you were just a robot . . . Well, you know what I mean." Selene shrugged. *God, can we just get on with it?*

"Ah, you should see the rest of the guys when they try. Trust me when I say I'd rather have you here any day."

The praise was enough to straighten Selene's shoulders and lift her head high. She was important and nothing anyone else did could match her prowess with the robots. She would become an expert at the chair—*Even better than Benson.*

The two robots shuffled into the storage room, sliding their cargo before them, then returned to the bay where the small army of Spikes had managed to tear several new parts from the ship. The pile had been neatly stacked on two large pallets.

Selene thought her robot's movements were smoother as she followed her uncle's example and lifted the pallet up chest high. As she did, one of the ratdogs scrambled from the ship, tugging on a large box that was too big for it to handle. She knelt, waiting for the little creature to reach the others. "Come on, you can do it," she whispered as the others bent to help the first lift its cargo onto her pallet.

Watching her, Benson said, "The arks never have much to take. They weren't built for people to be walking around, so they don't have the modern toys, and fewer toys means less wiring. It's a shame, really."

Following him from the room as he retraced his steps to the storage area, Selene asked, "Why don't we just ask Earth to send more supplies—or, even better, have the ships sent back from their destinations?"

"Weight, hon. There isn't enough room to send extra supplies, so we have to make do. We use the wiring and the plastic as-is, but most of the steel is re-smelted down here in the Lab."

Smelted? That meant heat, tremendous heat. "Can I see that sometime?" Selene asked. A smile had crept onto her face as she imagined herself a blacksmith, pounding on an iron forge: Bang, bang, bang.

"Sure, kiddo," Benson replied.

Their worked for another hour, retrieving various articles the ratdogs had dragged from the ship. Benson only had to scold the dogs once for removing something they shouldn't have. Selene giggled as the dog in question hung its head for a second as Benson raised his voice to scold it. When he spoke, every creature jumped to attention and scrambled to lift the computer terminal from the pallet. As one, they trudged back into the ship, carrying the terminal as if it were a sacrifice for a pagan god. Selene counted to fifty-six before they returned triumphantly with another terminal. They nattered at each other for several seconds, as though they had a hierarchy, before one of the creatures lifted the terminal onto the pallet.

Benson paused his whistling now and then to offer information about one of the treasures the creatures removed. She was happy for the experience, but as the time dragged on, her chair began to chafe. Her robot must have looked ridiculous when it began to shuffle from side to side as she scratched her back.

At the end of the sixty-five minutes allotted for the fuel, Selene yelped as a cramp coursed through her leg. She scrunched up to rub her calf. "Oh, hell," she said as her robot punched itself. It teetered for several seconds before falling forward. With a clang that resounded through her audio, the robot collapsed to the floor. "Son of a—"

Selene paused. Her robot rolled around on the ground until she found one of the tiny ratdogs underneath. "Oh, I'm so sorry. Uncle Benson, I'm so sorry," she cried as she tried to push her robot back to its feet.

As she regained her footing, Selene shifted to grab the creature. Unfortunately the weight from her robot had crushed it so flat, there was nothing left to grab. She was in full tears when Benson reached her side.

Bending down, he said, "Oh, kiddo, don't worry about that thing. I can make a dozen more this afternoon. We're pretty much done here, though, so why don't we pack up. You take that last pallet down to the storage area and power your bot down. The techs can lead you through it."

Selene sighed as she glanced at the flattened creature again. Her lips puckered as she gulped for air. *I'm so sorry.* Her goggles misted from her tears and she closed her eyes. When they'd cleared, she turned to the pallet. Her robot's shoulders drooped slightly as it bent to lift the pallet into the air. With sluggish steps, Selene guided it to the storage area.

Clearing her throat, she said, "Um, can anyone hear me?"

"Oh, sorry kiddo, you have to press the button again to talk to everyone," Benson's voice said.

How could I have missed that? Of course it was because she was just a child. That's what he'd said wasn't it? *The concept of a child is too much for him to understand.* Even Benson thought she was a child. Why else would he call her kiddo? And now he just dismissed her like that?

Pressing the button, Selene repeated her question. "Can anyone hear me?"

"Yes, Sub-lieutenant. Are you ready to disembark?" the grumpy tech asked.

"Yes please," Selene replied. There was nothing else in the world that she wanted except to disembark. *I have to go. Get me out of here.* She didn't want anyone to tell her how bad she had done. She just wanted to be alone to dream of the good things, like space elevators.

Within seconds Selene felt her safety straps being removed. Her goggles were lifted and immediately the vision of the cargo room was replaced with the face of a middle-aged man with a week-old beard. The man smiled, bending to remove the rest of the seat's attachments. He stepped aside almost too slowly as Selene bounced from the chair and bolted through the door.

The main bay was quiet as she entered. Most of the officers had left, though a few remained working on the main computer terminals. Only one looked up at her, a smile on his face. Selene could see it was one of pity as his gaze softened. He didn't have to say anything to tell her he was sorry about her mistakes.

Selene felt her face heat up as she broke eye contact with the man to look at the floor. She stood for several seconds tapping her hand against her leg as she waited for her Uncle Benson to disembark from his own VR machine. Finally, as she realized he wasn't coming, she thought, *He's still inside laughing at me. And why not? I screwed up royally this time. Captain Tulk is going to kill me.*

Selene huffed and caught her breath, bending to scoop Spike from the floor, then pausing to hitch him higher when he slipped through her moist hands. She turned and ran headlong into an officer stepping into the bay. She stared straight at his sweat-stained shirt for several seconds, then glanced aside and mumbled breathlessly, "S-s-sorry," before darting around him and out the door.

Chapter 4

Selene's focus was locked forward as she moved through the crowded halls, unable to meet anyone's gaze. She passed from the well-travelled section into the lesser known halls used by the engineers maintaining the electrical and hydraulic systems. Thankfully, they were all employed in the Lab, or she would likely have lashed her anger out on them. *Stupid engineers.* It would have been better if they'd said something instead of throwing pity at her. Selene balled her fists and pounded the wall. "Damn engineers. Damn it, why couldn't you just say something?"

It would have been better if they had. Get it over with—that's what her father had always said. At least then she wouldn't have to worry about having to prove herself all over again. It had all been for nothing. Those looks. *Oh, I hate them.* Selene pounded the wall again.

Visions of meeting the officer's pitying gaze plagued her as she moved farther into the station. Her shoulders slumped and her steps dragged. Nothing would have stopped her from tearing into the man with her teeth and nails. Within the hour everyone on the station would know about the creature she'd fallen on, not to mention the damage to the robot itself. They would be talking about how she couldn't even keep the robot on its feet.

How could she have been so stupid? Even her Uncle Benson would be sitting in the Lab, laughing at her mistakes. He'd be saying, "Oh, and then she tripped. Was that ever funny!" The others would be asking for the footage, and then all her mistakes would be on display for everyone to watch for the rest of her life. She wouldn't be asked to do another thing until she was twenty, and maybe not even then.

Selene ground her teeth, then winced and pressed her fingers against the chipped canine tooth that had gashed the inside of her cheek. Blood covered her fingers as she pulled them away. Tears sprang to her eyes and she sniffled. The captain was likely laughing at her now too, throwing back his head and laughing with an open mouth. He would be slapping his thighs as he re-enacted her crashing robot. Captain Tulk had never laughed to her face, but she'd heard his deep baritone laughter that came from deep in his chest, and his shoulders shook when he laughed. Maybe he laughed at her expense every night. *The kid who couldn't do anything right, given her last chance and she fails.*

Selene fell to her knees, pressing her palms hard against her eyes. Shudders wracked her body as she cried. "I hate you. I hate you." *I wish you hadn't seen.* She punched the grated floor. It didn't matter. It was all caught on video anyway.

Spike nuzzled her elbow. He tried to push his way onto her legs, but she pushed him aside. "Not now, Spike. I can't deal with you right now." In response, the creature's front legs dipped as though he was looking to the floor. After a moment the robot shifted again to rub his head on her knee.

After what seemed like hours, Selene fell back to a sit flat on the floor. Her shoulders shuddered, but the tears had gone dry. Though tender and puffy, her eyes were able to focus. She laid her hands on Spike's back as he nestled in her lap. Spike shoved his head neatly into the crook of her elbow, sighing as she stroked his head. Selene blinked the tears out her eyes. "You're right, Spike. None of it matters. Dad wouldn't want me crying like a child, would he? He'd tell me to wake up. Uncle Benson isn't making fun of me. He helped me. He lied to keep my secret safe."

Though he made no sound, Spike squirmed as he tried to push himself further into her lap.

Selene knew her words were true. She *was* being childish. Crying was unacceptable to her uncles and Captain Tulk. Her father would have scolded her the second she ran from the Lab and told her to rethink her fear. He would have her doing math or writing new code for Cecile, to forget the event.

A sudden shudder rocked Selene's body. That was all before he'd died, before he'd been found in the Lab. She'd managed to mask her fear when she had entered earlier, but now nothing could keep the image from joining that of the laughing officers. Soon it replaced the laughing officers altogether.

Selene wiped her tears away again and took a deep breath. "One, I woke up on time," she said. Spike lifted his head at the sound of her voice, but then relaxed as she continued. "Two, Cecile's programming is working better than I thought it could. Three, I got asked to work with the robots."

Selene's brows relaxed as she thought about the robots. Her trembling stopped and after several minutes she dropped her hands and fell still. It may have been work, but using the robot had been like a dream. She'd experienced using the virtual reality matrix when she had taken classes, but in the Lab she had felt like the robot. *I actually did it.*

She stood, back straight, and swivelled her head from one side to the other, imagining herself the robot. Her steps were long and straight as she moved down the hall, not moving her elbows out or bending her knees. Nothing stood in her path as robot Selene walked down the hall, her army of Spikes in tow. She was clearing the ark for transport, pulling wires and terminals. She was going to save the station with her work. She was going to take her robot and work in the station next. She shivered. *I'll have to go out into space.* It was the only way to fix the station.

She had to stifle her giggles. "No Spike, you're right. A robot doesn't laugh. Come on, we have to save the planet." She took several more steps as her robot landed on the planet. The gravity was heavier on the planet, however, and she was forced to take lower steps. Spike danced around her. She even managed to count through her multiplication tables in the process. Why not study while she daydreamed? When Captain Tulk came later to test her, she had to know the rules.

Selene paused as footsteps echoed through the hall. They were heavy, one foot dragging. *That isn't an engineer.* They travelled down one hall and then returned before going down another. As she continued her game, however, the footsteps stopped. She shivered, feeling someone's gaze on her back.

Though she didn't understand why, a shiver ran down her spine when she turned. *The sweaty shirt man.* Though he smiled, his eyes weren't scrunched up like her uncles'. Even her grandfather smiled with his eyes. This man smiled with only half his mouth and he licked his lips like she was dinner.

Selene tensed, her gaze darting to either side of the man, searching for an escape. *I can make it,* she thought, but then paused and glanced back to Spike. *But Spike can't. S*he turned to look down the hall behind her, seeking another route. *Nothing.*

It wouldn't matter, though; she had to force her feet to respond. *Come on. Please. PLEASE!* She clenched her teeth, wincing again as the chipped tooth cracked.

"Hey there, kid. My name is Jameson. I'm from the ark. I wanted to thank you fer doing what you did. You were a class act."

Selene bunched her fists as the man stepped closer. Her nose scrunched up and she scowled as the putrid odour of his sweat and something else on his breath wafted closer. He made her want to retch, but even the contents of her stomach wouldn't bend to her will.

"Why don't you jes come over here fer a minute," the man said, then wiped his mouth with the back of his hand.

"I-I-I don't want to," Selene said softly. Her eyes darted from one side of the hall to the other. *Please, Uncle Benson, Uncle Callum . . . I'll do anything. I'll scrape the floor.*

"Why don't you come here, little girl? But you're more like a woman, aren't you? Is that how they justified it?"

Selene's stomach churned as she caught another whiff of his foul breath and body odour. Sweat sprang out on her forehead and she shivered as the man reached out to gently rest one hand on her shoulder. She could feel the vise-like pressure of his grip as he squeezed.

"Why don'ts you come with me, Sub-lieutenant?" the man slurred.

"Uh . . . I . . . I think I should go back to . . . to . . ." She could feel his hot breath on her ear. Her face contorted as bile rose in the back of her throat, and she started to tremble as he entwined his fingers in her braid and sniffed her hair before shifting back on his heels. Selene's neck tensed.

She wiped the sweat and tears from her face with shaking hands, her eyes still darting in every direction. How long had it been since she'd seen a station officer? They must be close by. *Please,* Selene silently screamed. *Let me go.* She pulled against his iron grip.

"Why don't we just take a seat right here?" Jameson asked as he stumbled toward the wall.

As the man staggered away, Selene found her courage, managing to push his hands away and take two quick steps back.

Jameson moved so fast that Selene didn't see him move. In a flash his hand was on her braid; he yanked her closer and whispered, "You were good with giving orders to that robot. Why not take some now?"

"Please, let me go," she said through clenched teeth.

"Do you know what they did when I asked about who you were? You must hold some special position here, Sub-Lieutenant," Jameson said as he tugged her closer. "Does your daddy know you're here?"

Selene stiffened and gasped. "Don't you dare talk about my father."

"Oh right, I heard he died. Didn't have anything left to live for, eh? Did he tell you why they don't let women on the station? Because all the women want to do is screw. I bet your mother—"

"Shut up, you goddamn—" Selene said through clenched teeth, lips twitching, eyes staring forward at the bulkhead. Her mother had built Orphan Station. She was a hero. Captain Tulk and all of her uncles only told good stories of her.

"Did your father like your mother? Or were you just a mistake?" The man's voice boomed in her ear and his hot breath smelled almost sweet. It reminded her of a glass of juice that had turned rancid.

Selene's body stopped shaking as the man cuffed her once with his palm and then with the back of his hand. An explosion of stars erupted in her vision as she leaned over to throw up, blinking as sweat and blood stung her eyes. She gasped as the man's grasp on her hair loosened, tensing in anticipation of the inevitable blow. An eternity passed. Then, a dull clicking sound of metal on metal, and she was rocked to the side. She opened her eyes to an explosion of light.

Beside her, Spike lunged at the man's feet. As the robot connected, Selene was thrown to the floor. She landed on her knees and stayed there, whimpering. *Get him, Spike,* she thought, wishing the man was a rat so Spike could eviscerate him.

The man cried out in pain, turning to kick the creature. Like a ball, Spike skidded across the floor. That didn't slow him down; he was soon nipping at the man's ankles, darting between the man's legs and turning so fast that Selene couldn't register his movement. Spike paused. As if by magic, two serrated blades appeared between the robot's upraised front legs. These shot forward, puncturing the man's flesh.

The man screamed again and grabbed the robot, lifting Spike up by the back foot. He swung his arm so hard that his biceps bulged as he bashed the creature into the wall. Then again, and several more times. Spike shattered, pieces flying in every direction.

When he was finished, he again wore his fake smile, though sweat drenched his shirt. He looked at her with narrowed eyes.

"Spike!" Selene cried, pulling as hard as she could against his grasp.

"Spike's dead," the man said, his spittle hitting her face. From somewhere at his back, he retrieved a short blade, its smooth, shiny metal glinting in the overhead light as, holding it like an extension of his hand, he pointed it at Selene's eyes one at a time. She could see traces of something dark coating part of the blade.

Selene closed her eyes. *Papa, please help me.* She was never going to see him again, she realized. She wasn't going to go to the planet. When she opened them, her eyes fell on Spike's body, the scattered pieces as broken and tangled as the robot Selene had crushed earlier in the day. She was going to join him. She wasn't going to be asked to work in the Lab anymore.

"They should have sent you away, like they made me send my boy. You know you aren't supposed to exist, right? Your mother wasn't supposed to be on this ship playing house," Jameson said as he waved his blade around.

Selene dry heaved several times. When she could stand, she kicked the man deep in the shin where Spike had made his mark. He yelled and stumbled back, pulling her closer. Selene drew breath and screamed, *"Help! Please help me!"*

Silence, but for Jamison's laboured breathing. She glanced around the man. *Please, someone come.*

A voice called out in the distance. The echo of footsteps bouncing on the grating followed—not the plodding steps of an engineer or meandering steps like Jameson's. These were deliberate, approaching fast. Selene almost collapsed with relief.

Something heavy hit Jameson from behind. Still held tight in his grip, Selene stumbled as he staggered. When Jamison swung to one side, she saw the security officer, Ray, staring down at her. *Uncle Ray?* His eyes narrowed and his face flushed beat red as he lifted his head to stare daggers at Jameson. Grabbing Jamison by the arm, Ray flexed both his arms. Jamison struggled, but Ray was stronger—his movement pulled Jamison forward and he crashed to the floor.

Jameson maintained his grip on Selene's hair, and still clutched the knife in his other hand. Ray grabbed for the knife hand, snagged the man's wrist, and beat it several times against the bulkhead. The knife clattered to the floor beyond Selene's reach.

Grunting, Jameson punched Selene's chin. "You little whore."

Pain exploded through her face, and her world spun. Selene opened her eyes and took a deep breath, trying to find her footing. Though locked in battle with Ray, Jameson still had a white-knuckled grasp on her hair. The man landed several more blows in quick succession. Her face and chest throbbed and she felt blood running down her cheeks. *Oh God, that hurts.* This was far worse than the scrapes she got when running from the captain.

Selene glimpsed the shiny blade lying on the floor as she was dragged from one side of the hall to the other. She reached for it several times, but her fingers never connected. Then Ray punched the man in the stomach and he doubled over, giving her enough reach to grab the blade.

At first Selene pulled the weapon back, thinking to stab the man. But she paused as Jamison landed successive blows on Ray's bloodied face. *He's winning. I have to get away.* She lifted the blade to her head and sliced the braid free.

Selene fell to her knees and scrambled between the two men as they fought. With her head no longer in his grasp, Jameson was teetering backward, his legs flailing underneath him. Unaware of her position, Ray kept close to the crazed attacker. There were a few frenzied seconds as Selene sat back against the wall, watching the two officers exchanging blows. When Ray realized Jameson had use of his other hand, he bellowed, "Run, Selene. *Go home!*"

Her legs were gelatin, refusing her command to stand or even crawl to safety. She could only sit, her eyes glued to the fight—until she heard Spike whimper. Only two of his legs remained and half of his body, the rest had been spread across the floor. Now, rather than try to come to her side, the creature was pulling itself toward the fight, unwilling to let the man go unpunished. *Spike. No.*

Move. MOVE! Her legs accepted her command. She was on her feet, tottering away from the fight. Then she turned back to grab Spike, but too late; he had managed to rejoin the fray.

"Go, Selene. Go!" Ray yelled as he balled his fists to punch Jameson in the chest. Blood ran down Ray's neck. His blows were fierce, but the other man had regained his balance and soon redoubled his efforts.

I have to go.

Selene willed every muscle to move her down the hall. The pounding in her face matched the ache in her brain; she struggled to stay awake. *I can't stop. I have to get help for Ray. Jamison's going to kill him.* And then, if she didn't move fast enough, Jameson would be free to find her and do what he wished.

Swallowing the lump in her throat, Selene scrambled fifteen paces down the hall before reaching one of the access holes for the utility halls. *I'll be safe here. He won't find me.* She threw the door open and fell inside. Her heartbeat pounded in her ears as footsteps approached. *Oh, God, don't be him. Please let me get away.* She paused to listen, but the pounding in her ears obscured everything. She wiped her face to clear the blood and sweat from her eyes and pushed off the wall.

Navigating her way through the internal system, she reached the hall by her own quarters. Chest heaving, she peeked through the grate, making sure no one was watching as she entered the regular corridors. When she reached the door to her quarters, Selene pounded on the security pad, her hands shaking so much that it took several attempts. Just as she was about to scream in frustration, the door swung open and she tumbled inside.

She glanced back toward the hatch before shutting the door, tears streaming down her bloody face. *Where's Ray? Please don't die. You have to win.* Ray was the stronger fighter. He was the one trained for fighting.

Selene managed to drag herself to the couch before she collapsed onto it and lay there, curled into a ball, hiccupping uncontrollably between spasms that culminated in vomit. After several minutes she wiped the bile from her lips with the back of her hand, moaning as she touched the bruises on her face.

Her hands fell to her chest and arms. It felt like bugs were crawling under her skin where Jameson had touched her. *So dirty.* She began scratching. Her ears burned at the memory of his words: *Why don't you come here, little girl? But you're more like a woman, aren't you? Is that how they justified it? Does your daddy know you're here? Oh right, I heard he died. Didn't have anything left to live for, eh?*

What if it's true? Her father had refused to see her before he'd gone. It was possible that he'd left because of her. It was possible he didn't want to see her grow up because of what she would become.

Selene shook her head and rolled off the couch to her feet, her gaze dancing around the room. Her fingernails drew blood on her arms as she shuffled into the latrine.

She stopped, staring into the mirror. Then she shuddered and looked away, tears streaming down her face. She fell to her knees and hurled again before calling out, "Shower water. Hot . . . hotter."

The showerhead burst into life, raising a fog as she tottered to the shower cubicle. The water was a searing fire on her already burning skin, but she had to cut Jameson's grasp from her arm, burn his odour from her nose. She had to clean her hands to remove the thousand needles pushing through. So she pulled herself up against the wall, welcoming the near-scalding water.

Oh Spike, she thought. Though he was an artist when it came to his robots, Benson would never be able to fix the tiny creature. Spike was dead. "I'm so sorry, Spike; please forgive me."

Selene fell asleep with the shower still running, the last of her reserves spent whimpering, "So sorry, Spike. So sorry."

Chapter 5

Selene gasped and yanked her head away from the wall of the small shower cubicle. Thrown into consciousness, she sputtered the water trickling down her throat. The water washing over her bruises was electrifying, cold and hot at the same time.

She lifted a trembling hand to investigate the puffy contours of her face, and winced. Her cheeks were swollen, her eyes nearly swollen shut; she gasped as she touched her nose. She could feel the sharp edges of a few broken teeth cutting into her lacerated lips, and her chin had two long gashes down the right side where Jameson had connected with his knuckles.

She tried to speak, but her voice eluded her summons. Her legs wouldn't hold her and the warm stream falling on her skin was almost soothing as it pooled around her. She curled into a ball.

She didn't know how long she slept, or whether it was sleep at all. She knew there were dreams at first. She rolled for several minutes as she attempted to keep the water from her mouth, imagining she was covered in blood and dirt and living under the pounding rain for several days would cleanse her of the taint.

When she awoke, Selene was curled up in her bed. *No,* she thought; not her own bed. She slept in the one her father . . . the one her parents had used. She sighed. One of her uncles must have found her in the shower. *What will they think? Do they even know?*

Did Ray put me here? No, he doesn't know where I sleep. She didn't even understand how Ray had been the one to come to her rescue. *He only cares when I'm in the utility halls. Why was he even there?* It was possible that Ray had called for help. *Maybe he's still beating him.* "I hope he spaces you," she said to her attacker, certain she spoke the words aloud, though she couldn't remember hearing her own voice.

Her lips were still cracked, but more from being dry. She tried to lick them, but her tongue was stuck to the roof of her mouth. She rocked back and forth and opened her eyes wide as she let out a deep breath. *Open, damn it.* Selene quit her silent screaming and forced her tongue out far enough to moisten her lips.

As she stirred, a soft voice said, "Don't move, child. Here is some water."

Selene shuddered and then went still. Was that Jameson's voice? Was she dreaming? *No, he's gone. He has to be gone.* The voice was deeper than the one that haunted her nightmares. It was commanding, leaving no room for choice. "Captain?"

Selene felt firm hands under her shoulders, elevating her, and then the cold taste of steel pressed against her lips. After several futile attempts that sent water trickling down her face, she managed to gulp down a few mouthfuls. She fell asleep again as soon as the cup left her lips.

Her dreams were filled with voices she couldn't understand and the sound of distant crashing. *Maybe I dreamt it all.* She'd kept a glass of water beside her bed since her father had left. She could have dreamt that the captain had come to help her. For that matter, she could have dreamt it all. *Maybe Jameson didn't exist. Maybe he was just part of my imagination.*

"Sir, we're coming out of the dark side." That voice was familiar too, and not the same one that had offered her the water. "The ark is ready to depart and we need your presence on the secondary bridge."

"Uncle Dallas?" *Why didn't you come and see me?*

"I'll be there soon," Captain Tulk replied. His voice was even, as though he didn't have the energy to speak.

"You've been here for four days, sir. It's time. The medic comes every hour to check on her." Dallas must have moved closer.

Don't come closer. Selene shook her head. *I don't want you to see me. I don't want anyone to see me.* She was bloodied and bruised. Her chest heaved as she rolled to her other side.

"What would you have me do, Commander? I've already failed her once."

Captain Tulk had obviously read her mind again. She'd called for help and he hadn't come. He was the captain. *The goddamn captain.* He'd disappeared after she'd been strapped into the VR seat. Jameson had found her fast enough. The others had no reason not to do the same. *Why?*

"Sir, you did what you could. No one knew how bad Jameson was when he came on board. I know we lost Blair and Hayward, but Ray has left the infirmary and Selene will survive."

Selene could hear a reticence in his voice, as though he'd wanted to say something else. She imagined him saying, "I think you should leave, Captain. You failed her and the rest of us." *You should say that,* she thought.

"What did you do with . . . ?"

"He was on some drug. We've sent him back to the ship with the others. I can say that our people didn't supply the junk. He had his own."

"He should be spaced," Captain Tulk growled. "He should be thrown into the air lock so Selene can watch him . . ." His voice trailed off. There was a sharp intake of breath, then the mattress shifted as someone sat on the end of the bed.

Are you crying? Selene thought in surprise.

There was a pause before Dallas said, "He's been dealt with, sir. You don't have to worry about the repercussions."

"What did you do, Dallas?" Captain Tulk asked. The mattress shifted again; he must have jumped up from the bed.

Selene cursed mentally as a cramp seized her leg. She tried to ignore the pain, but she was forced to shift her position to relieve the tension. As soon as she moved, the conversation above her stopped. She imagined them looking her way, just as they had when she was in the air system. There was no anger now, though; just pity. She hated that look; she'd seen it too often on people's faces when she was younger. Oh, you're just a kid; Let me get that; Oh, your parents died; Let me help you or teach you or whatever. *Leave me alone!*

The room was empty when Selene forced her swollen eyes open. Everything was blurry. She could only see shapes. She lay there, lifting a hand to scratch her shoulder, then wincing as she pressed too hard. The bruises ached as though Jameson still held tight to her shoulder. She moved her hand to tenderly probe her face. Her nose had been reset, though it still felt out of place. *At least I can breathe through my nose.* Though some of her teeth seemed capped, several others felt jagged and sharp under her tongue, and they throbbed when she pushed on them.

Selene dropped her hands back to the bed and patted it for several seconds. She licked her lips, then called, "Spike?" Then, remembering, she caught her breath and closed her eyes. *I'm sorry, Spike.*

When the tears stopped, she opened her eyes and shifted to the side of the bed to drop her feet to the floor. She paused, shaking her head, and rocked back and forth several times to gain the momentum to thrust herself off the bed, muttering, "I . . . I guess I'm still—"

She stood, her back perfectly straight—which made her scowl. She must look like a robot. At her first step, her knee buckled and she crashed to the floor. "Damn it," she hissed.

"Selene?" Cecile asked. The computer's voice was subdued, as if it didn't know how to speak to her.

Selene sighed and frowned at the ceiling, lips pursed. After a few seconds she said, "I'm here, Cecile."

"I cannot see you, Selene. Why is that?" Cecile asked.

Is that concern? And the voice sounded more human. It didn't sound like it was speaking through a can, either. "I *am* here, Cecile," Selene replied, wiping her tears away.

Unaware of her condition, the computer fell back into its routine. "Good morning, Miss Selene. Do you require any assistance?"

Selene grimaced as she shifted awkwardly into a sitting position on the floor. She had to pause and close her eyes briefly, then blink several times. *I'm still wearing the clothing from before,* she noticed for the first time. Whoever her benefactor was, he'd been kind enough not to violate what little dignity she had left.

Her body trembled as she pushed herself back to her feet and tottered toward the bathroom, every step short, cautious. She balled her hands into fists and clenched her jaw, determined to make it. As she passed the couch, she saw blood smeared on the floor. Someone had tried to clean up the mess, but not well. There was more blood smeared on the floor and walls.

At last Selene crossed the threshold into the latrine, and tilted her head to look into the mirror. Only the day before she could have imagined her movements were like those of a robot, but now she saw the truth: she was a broken little girl.

She didn't care that her Uncle Dallas and Captain Tulk had said the man had been on some drug. "I'm not a mistake." *I'm not.* Her father had loved her. He'd told her so many times, and that she was all he and her mother had ever wanted.

Selene fell forward into the counter. She couldn't recognize herself. Although the blood had been cleaned away, the bruises covering her face were there. There wasn't an inch of clear skin and the swollen flesh made her look puffed up like her Uncle Dallas.

It didn't matter if Selene Sotana was a mistake; the girl standing in front of the mirror wasn't her. She wasn't Sub-lieutenant Sotana, either. The girl or woman standing in the bathroom was no one. She couldn't even breathe without hearing the proof of Jameson's words. She wasn't supposed to exist.

"Cecile?" she whispered.

"Yes, Selene," the computer said from the other room.

"Why am I here?" Though she was sure of the answer, Selene didn't want confirmation.

"I am sorry, Selene. I don't understand your question." It was a standard result, one that Selene had programmed for any answer the computer couldn't compute. The computer could answer questions on math, fact, even logic, but it had no capacity to explain what was or wasn't possible.

"Cecile, access the mainframe. Explain why Selene Sotana exists."

"Selene Sotana was born to Savir Sotana and Robyn Sotana on Orphan Station," the computer replied.

"Why was I allowed to be born?" Selene asked. Her voice cracked.

"I am sorry, Selene. I don't understand your question."

Of course not. There it was. There was the proof. She shouldn't have been allowed to exist. She knew that she shouldn't have. She had always known it, but the station was her home. Her uncles were just officers. She had the run of the ship because no one knew what to do with her. Her breathing was shallow as she asked, "Cecile, why was I allowed to stay when . . . when my father . . . died?"

"A child can only be kept by her kin."

Kin? What the hell does that mean? And is that a hint from a computer? "Cecile, do I have kin on the station?" Selene's heart thrummed in her ears.

After a pause, the computer replied, "The officers of Orphan Station are all your family." The voice seemed more baritone.

Selene stepped back, her brows furrowed. "Cecile, disconnect from mainframe by order of Savir Sotana, call sign beta-alpha-niner."

There was a pause as the computer executed her order. When it returned, the voice asked, "Would you rather have porridge or—"

"Cecile, has anyone attempted to hack into your code?" The computer's response was no different from the last time she'd asked, but Selene wasn't expecting anything else. "Cecile, has anyone been listening to our conversations? Has someone other than me been stopping your program?" Her voice cracked, and her grasp on the sink had turned her knuckles white. She staggered out of the bathroom and retraced her path to her bed.

As she neared the bed, the computer said, "My programming has been paused seven times in the last week."

Selene stopped and stared up at the speaker. *Seven?* She shook her head and sighed. Selene didn't even want to know when it had happened. They had no idea what they'd done. *They don't even care.* Cecile wasn't just a program. They couldn't just press a button and make her stop. She'd be no different than Spike then—broken.

She shuffled closer to her bed, her shoulders slumped, her eyes on the floor. She'd half hoped that the new questions had been of Cecile's own choice. It *was* possible for the computer to learn. It was possible for the computer to become self-aware. Its programming was complex enough to run the whole station, so becoming self-aware wasn't a stretch of the imagination. *It's not pretend.*

There was no leap in sophistication or self-awareness for the computer, though. Someone had hijacked her program and pretended to be Cecile.

"Cecile, can you push your code to the computer screen at my bed?" Selene braced her hands on the bed and crawled under her covers. She was asleep before she heard if the computer had complied.

Again her dreams were haunted by Jameson's face. He came forward and hit her repeatedly on the face. As he stepped back to throw curses at her, Selene would wake for a minute, then fall back asleep.

When she woke long enough to keep her eyes open, Selene realized that her stomach didn't feel like a punching bag. The ache in her shoulder had subsided and her nose no longer felt as if it was floating away from her face. She patted the bed where she knew Spike was lying, but found nothing. "Ah, hell," she said, shaking her head.

"Selene?" The voice was familiar, but Selene couldn't place it. Someone waited in the living room. She rose and walked out to greet her guest.

When she arrived, Selene realized it was *guests*. Captain Tulk sat in the single chair and her Uncle Dallas occupied the couch. Dallas stood when she entered, nodded to Captain Tulk, and moved toward the door. He paused there and bowed deeply to Selene. "My dear, I will be back later for your session."

Selene knew he was trying to make things normal for her, but there was no way she could leave her quarters. *Normal?* The fact that Jameson had been sent on his way was little relief. He had done his work. *He SHOULD have been spaced.*

Sighing, Selene said, "I think I might need a day before I can type, Uncle Dallas."

A smile touched his lips as he nodded. Although his eyes did not smile, they were not like Jameson's. They spoke of concern for her. It was that pity she saw in the faces in her dreams; the pity people had for her because she was a child.

"Sub-lieutenant Sotana," Captain Tulk said stiffly as the door clanged shut behind Dallas.

Selene turned quickly, wincing as she saluted. She stood still for almost a minute before Captain Tulk stood.

He cleared his throat as he looked down at her. "I need to know that you will be okay, Selene," he said softly, though she imagined he was actually yelling, "Get out of here, Selene. There's nothing wrong with you."

Which was wrong. It was a lie. She was broken. She wasn't even supposed to exist and he knew it. He knew the rules, had even let them be circumvented. But then, why would he do that? Staring up at the man through narrowed eyes, Selene asked, "Who are you?"

Looking down his nose, Captain Tulk replied, "I am the one asking the questions, Lieutenant."

"Lieutenant?" Selene asked in a strained voice; she was grateful it hadn't cracked. "I am no more a lieutenant than you are just a captain."

"Explain yourself, Lieutenant," he said. He planted his fists on his hips and glared down at her. His jaw began to twitch as he waited for her answer.

Stepping as close as she could, Selene said, "*Okay?* He hit me like I was nothing and you weren't there."

"There?" he said through clenched teeth. "Ray was there within seconds, Selene. I commend him—"

"Commend him?" Selene screamed. "For being there first?"

Wiping the spit from his shirt, he said, "For finding you at all, Selene. You ran from that room and disappeared. I commend him for stopping Jameson from doing worse."

"Worse? Like what? Killing me? Why does that matter? I'm not even supposed to exist," Selene screamed, punching the air between them with her fist. She winced as she connected with his chest. Pulling her hand back, she rubbed her arm, sputtering for a few seconds, opening then closing her mouth several times.

She pushed past him and marched through the hatch into the main hall, Captain Tulk bellowing behind her. *You can burn if you think I'll trust you again.* He had said he was glad Ray had saved her. He wasn't glad that she was alive. *You're just glad that you don't have to deal with the consequences of a little girl dying.* Then he would have to explain to the crew how he'd failed.

Even with her injuries, Selene navigated toward her entrance to the utility hall with ease, seeing no one else in the hall. *They probably don't want to be seen near "the child's" quarters.*

54

"You get back here, Selene," Captain Tulk roared as she reached the entrance. She didn't look back as she threw the grate open and jumped inside. It clanged shut behind her.

"I'll show you how I shouldn't exist," she said as she moved along the utility hall. Out of habit she stopped several times, only to realize that Spike no longer accompanied her. She hung her head and closed her eyes as tears welled, then pushed onward.

When she stopped, Selene didn't know how far she'd gone. Within the utility halls, everything looked the same. And her vision was still blurred, so she could see nothing beyond ten paces. She looked around, trying to gauge her position. *I'm in the lower section, not far from the Farm.* She wasn't going there. Sasha was only slightly above the captain on the list of people she didn't want to see. *Goddamn officers. Glad he saved me?*

Selene drew a deep breath and sighed, "I can't do this anymore. Why . . . why did you let him hit me?" Her lips puckered as she struggled not to cry.

She thought about what Dallas had said when they thought she'd been asleep as she set off again, moving toward the upper system. She could get lost in the halls of the outer system, and no one would find her then. "Ray was the only one there," she said to herself. Ray had come to her rescue. The man barely tolerated her, yet he was the one to save her. Why would he? Was it just his job? The look he so often gave her wasn't all that different from what Jameson had given her. Ray's eyes radiated anger and resentment, not love and acceptance.

To leave the old section, Selene had to open a large hatch that was usually locked from the other side, but when she tugged as hard as she could on the circular handle, it released and the door slid aside. Quickly stepping over the bulkhead, she turned to close the hatch before an alarm in the operations room told them where she'd gone.

Several direction changes later, she knelt in the corner of a storage cubby overlooking Ray's office, watching him through the grate. The man sat in his chair, his back straight, his arm in a sling. She saw several gashes on his face and hands. If there had been any bruises, they'd long since faded. He was speaking in a hushed voice into his radio: "I understand, Captain. I know, but you have to understand how bad it was for the girl. If nothing else, I would offer her my congratulations. Those two dead seamen could have used her courage."

He paused while the captain spoke. His body was tense and he drew breath several times to speak, but didn't interrupt. Though his shoulders were relaxed, his legs bounced under his desk. "I've seen it before, sir," he finally said. "She needs time."

Pressing the Disconnect button on the radio in his ear, he stood slowly, wincing several times, then began to pace the room. After several minutes he stopped long enough to tip a pill from a small vial on his desk. He threw it into his mouth and swallowed hard, not bothering with the water pitcher sitting beside the vial.

"Computer, record personal entry March sixteenth, year twenty-seven. Oh hell, I don't even know why I still do this," he groaned, "but the doctor says it gets things off my chest."

Ray turned away from the door and stared at the wall for a few seconds. *Can he see me?* Selene shifted away from the grate and held her breath until he turned away. Only then did she release the pent breath. Chest heaving, she watched him pace away, then shuddered at his first words.

"Lieutenant Jameson has been sent on his way, though I tend to agree with the captain. My wounds will heal, but the damage he caused may never be reversed." Ray sighed. "I think I might try to go down to see the kid today. She'll have to return first, I guess. The captain says she just ran away."

Selene felt her strength drain and she sagged back against the bulkhead, her legs flying out from beneath her as she listened. She knew she shouldn't be listening, but she had to know why he'd done it. Why hadn't he just let her die? It would have solved so many of their problems, if she weren't around. He didn't love her. The look he'd given her in the Farm was enough to give her the shivers.

"I don't think I'd envy her position," Ray said. "She's got more courage than I've seen in a lot of people twice her age. Hell, I couldn't have stayed alone on a station like this after my parents . . ." He fell silent for a while.

Tears flowed down her face as Selene listened to the man speak. She had never realized Ray had ever thought of her like that. All she'd ever seen him do was scowl or swear at her under his breath.

He'd even called her a feral child who needed discipline. That had been after her father, Savir, had gone away. Ray had caught Selene running through the halls while a large passenger ship was docking. She'd sworn at him for several minutes before Captain Tulk managed to dislodge her from the man.

Selene stood and turned to leave. Ray did care for her. He had meant to save her. *You cared.* A smile crept onto her battered face as she shuffled away. Ray was the only person to come to her aid. He was her true family. Everyone else had failed her. Captain Tulk had failed her, and Benson had failed her. Who cared if they weren't laughing? They hadn't come when she cried out and needed them most. Only Ray had. *Maybe you're family.* If she could, Selene knew she should stay close to the man. *You're the only one who can protect me.*

Looking around the cubby where she stood, Selene frowned. Though it was spacious, there were two exits from the room. Without dragging a welder into the room to seal one off, she couldn't defend it. "Maybe I can lock the door," she mused aloud. "I can guaran-goddamn-tee that I won't be going home again."

It was just an ark that Jameson had come from—what about a full ship? There could have been a dozen or a hundred Jamesons on a ship like the *Orient*. She wasn't safe anymore. There was one thing that Jameson had proven: she was growing up, and that meant more people would notice her. She couldn't blend in anymore. She had to stay away and there was only one place that was safe—close to Ray. Ray was the only person who would protect her. She didn't care if she saw any of her uncles again. They'd proven how much they cared.

It took Selene hours to collect the items she needed. She dragged five armfuls of pillows and blankets alone to the cubby outside Ray's office. When she was finished, Selene looked around at her new quarters and smiled. Moving to the makeshift bed she'd made from the pillows, she lay down, grimacing as she shifted on the bed until she was relaxing with her head against the wall. Then she reached for the computer plate that Cecile had downloaded for her.

"Cecile," Selene whispered.

"Yes, Selene," the computer replied from the plate she held in her hands.

"Lock utility doors to A9572, please." She was too far away to hear the doors lock, but Selene set the plate down, confident that Cecile had complied. Her breathing was slowing and she was having a hard time keeping her eyes open. Several times her eyelids drooped before she flashed them open. "So sleepy," she murmured.

The next time Selene opened her eyes, she groaned, her body stiff again. Blinking, she sent her eyes from one side of the room to the other and gasped. *Where . . . ?*

She was surrounded by pillows. There was a small air conditioning unit near one of the doors that led from her lair. Beside it stood a stack of her clothing, folded exactly the way her father had taught her, though the stack itself was less than perfect. A sheet hung from the ceiling in the corner, partitioning the room into two.

Then Ray's voice came through the grate behind her and she sighed, continuing to blink away her blurred vision. Pushing herself to her feet, she wandered around. Her frown softened when she found the small cooler hidden in the second room. She shuffled over and opened its lid. *Crap, there's nothing in it.* "That won't do," Selene whispered. Though her body throbbed painfully again, the growling in her stomach was her first priority. She had to eat—and pronto, as her father would call it—or Ray was going to hear her through the wall.

Selene crept into the main hall, glancing in both directions before she closed her eyes and walked ten steps to the right and fifty-seven to the left before she took another right into the Mess hall. Even with her limp, she made it without running into any walls and no one passed her, so she didn't have to explain anything. She didn't want to explain anything.

When she entered, Selene shifted her gaze to the few officers present, all intent on their own meals. *It's between meals,* she thought with a sigh. They weren't in the dark side, so the officers would be out working, checking the wiring in the outer ring or preparing for the next wave of ships. She might even get in and out of the Mess without the officers present noticing her.

Tearing her eyes away from the officers, she walked over to the counter. It displayed far more than she expected, but only one platter that appealed to her; it was filled with grilled cheese sandwiches. She snorted. *Who else eats these?* As far as she knew, her father had been the only other person to care for them. She wondered if she could lift the whole platter to take back to her cubby. *It wouldn't fit in the cooler, though.* She sighed. *And if I drop it, everyone will look, and Captain Tulk would come.* After a surreptitious glance back at the occupied tables, Selene searched for a bag and found one under one of the platters. She stuffed a dozen sandwiches into it and, satisfied that she now had enough to eat for several days, wondered what else she should eat. She smiled when her eyes fell on a large bowl of macaroni and cheese at the other end of the counter. She'd missed it in her first perusal. *They must have been expecting me.*

She didn't see any sealable bowls so, shrugging, she found another bag and stuffed it full of the pasta before tying off the top. Then she grabbed a large bottle from the table and turned away, only to freeze at a resounding crash on the far side of the Mess. Dropping to one knee, trembling, she looked across the room. She had to hold her breath so she wouldn't hyperventilate. The bags slipped through her suddenly sweaty hands. Then she relaxed with a sigh. *It's just one of the officers,* she thought, watching a man crouched on the floor, picking up the scattered contents of the tray he had dropped.

She headed toward the exit, turning back only long enough as she left to make sure no one had seen her. Confident that she had gone unnoticed, Selene retraced her steps to her new quarters. Once there, she stuffed the food into the cooler. Three sandwiches beyond the one she ate wouldn't fit. *I'll have to switch them out,* she thought as she sat back.

Her eyes drooped again. The pain had become a dull ache. Sleep was calling her. *Come to my arms,* it said as she moved to lie down. She was asleep before her head hit the pillow. Her dreams were filled with dark shadows pulling at her hair. After a time, however, her dream Ray came to her rescue, quicker every time, until finally he pre-empted the attack and kicked Jameson in the groin as soon as he entered the Lab where Selene was working with the robots.

Chapter 6

When Selene woke, it wasn't sudden. She felt encased in steel, her entire body ignoring her demands. She couldn't force her legs to move or her eyes to open. *Move. Move, damn you.*

Selene remembered where she was as her eyes fluttered open. She looked around her new home for a few seconds before she stood. As she moved, her heart quieted its thundering in her ears. *I'm fine. I'm safe. No one can follow me in here.* Dallas was too fat and Sasha wouldn't dare degrade himself to crawl in to find her.

Ray wasn't in his office yet. She looked at the small clock she'd set on the wall, nodding. *Soon.* Ray was a meticulous man, keeping his office in perfect order. He polished his small shrine at the same time every day, using the same quick movements and saying exactly the same words. *Has it been a week yet? No, five days at most.* Although her food was almost gone, she did have a couple days left.

Selene reached for the bag of toiletries that she'd bought from her rooms while Captain Tulk wasn't looking, and pulled out a hairbrush. She looked at it for a moment before grabbing for her hair, then froze, nostrils flaring and tears flooding her eyes as her fingers clutched at the shorn stubs of her hair. Not for the first time, she rested her hand on her neck and sighed before patting the back of her head. *Stupid Jameson.* She curled her lip and spat.

Several minutes passed before she lifted the brush to pull it through what was left of her hair. Her face contorted with every stroke as images of Jameson throwing her into the bulkhead assaulted her. He'd taken three feet of her braid, leaving her hair as short as

60

she'd ever remembered it. Patting her hair again, Selene lowered her hand to where the end used to be. *Five years' worth,* she thought with a sigh. It would take forever to regrow now. Everyone knew that hair slowed its growth when you became an adult. Though they tried to hide the fact, many of the officers were actually bald. *Bald.* Her mother had had long blond hair. She'd said it had taken a lifetime to grow it that long. Then again, Selene thought, Savir had said she'd refused to cut it and instead swore at herself every time she had to wash it.

Selene paused as the door to Ray's office creaked open. Her shoulders relaxed as it clanged shut. Her breathing slowed when she returned to the chair she sat in all day.

After a few seconds, Selene reached for the computer plate that Cecile had downloaded for her. It was connected to the main system, but Selene had made quick work of the positioning system. She wasn't ready to let anyone know where she was staying.

"Where are you, Selene?" Ray asked from within his office.

It was the same every day. He would start with his hypothetical question, as though he knew she waited outside his office. Of course he couldn't know that. Selene had made sure to clear every piece of technology before she'd dragged everything back to her new quarters.

After he spoke to the walls, Ray would go through his prayer, then start into his reports. Selene watched him for days, learning that his job was tedious and boring. Protecting her had been the only real action he'd seen beyond reprimanding her for months. There wasn't any need for policing during the dark side, and rarely was there anyone awake enough during the other times to need it. Usually he had to make sure no one entered one of the restricted areas.

Ray wouldn't be staying in the office long today. There was a ship approaching from Earth. Selene hadn't decided what to do when he left. The first time she'd followed him, but the risk of discovery was too high with a larger ship. She wouldn't be able to pass from one section of the utility hall to another without being noticed.

"I need you to come home soon, Selene. Everyone is worried about you," Ray said.

Selene frowned. She was sure she'd removed all the electronic tags, but his pleas were becoming more insistent. It was as if he knew she was watching. Was it possible the station itself had been upgraded to see her? *No.* "They don't know squat," she murmured. "You can't see me and you can't hear me."

Even so, Selene stared at the grate for a moment before shaking her head. She knew the technology that kept the sounds in the utility halls from leaking out into the public sections. It couldn't be shut down. She was safe.

She looked away from the hole and wiped sweat from her forehead. *Why is it so warm? Why is it warm at all?* When she'd explored the utility halls, they'd been as cold as space. Now, every day since she'd run from Captain Tulk meant another sweater removed. "Damn, it's *hot*." She shifted in her chair. "Maybe they screwed up the environmental systems." It wouldn't be the first time. The environmental system was complex enough that slight changes in one section could cascade through the rest. Selene had seen the officers who worked on the internal environmental systems. They were smart; almost as smart as her mother. They had to be.

"Ray?"

The voice broke Selene's reverie. Instinctively ducking, she looked lower to peer into Ray's office. He sat in the chair staring at the wall, as he usually did in the afternoons. Dallas stood in the doorway, tapping the frame with his beefy fist. He shot a quick glance toward the air regulation grating, as though he too knew she was there. *Could he know? No,* she thought. They all knew she was in the utility halls. There was no other place she could be. *They must all be talking to the ducts.* Selene covered her mouth to suppress a giggle as she envisioned Dallas and Sasha talking to the walls. They were about as emotionally aware as Ray seemed to be. Dallas would likely end up pounding the grate and trying to stick his large head in and Sasha would stick his nose in the air as he uttered, "Zat is unacceptable."

"What do you want?" Ray asked from his chair, steepling his fingers as he spoke. It made him look like he was plotting the large man's demise. Savir had once said Ray had been sent to the station as punishment for trying to take over the world. Selene scowled. *At least he isn't looking down his nose at Dallas.* He would have been doing that if Selene were in the room. It didn't matter that he'd saved her. He would still treat her like a child.

Selene crawled closer to the grate to hear what her Uncle Dallas said. He was sweating, even more than he normally did. *The temperature must be higher in the public section too,* she thought.

"We have a ghost ship," Dallas blurted. His eyes danced around the room, unwilling to lock with Ray's. Perhaps the security officer did look down at the others and Dallas wouldn't let him succeed.

Leaning forward, Ray asked, "What exactly does that mean?"

Dallas also leaned forward. "We have a ship coming toward us on autopilot, showing no signs of life."

Autopilot? Why would a ship have autopilot? Wouldn't that make the pilots unnecessary? Selene started to breathe faster. No pilots would mean that Jameson wouldn't have been on that ark. Jameson wouldn't have done what he did to her. He couldn't have done what he did.

"Is she going to stop?" Ray asked as he pushed away from the desk and stood, shifting his shirt to cover the unhealed gashes. He waited for Dallas to reply.

"I think so, but I don't really want to enter the ship without someone close by, to—you know . . ." The man fell silent, as though what he had said was sufficient to scare Ray into action.

Ray leaned back and crossed his arms, staring into the middle distance for a minute before reaching into his desk to retrieve a small handheld device. Selene couldn't see what the device was, but she expected it to be the famed pistol no one had ever seen, but talked about incessantly in the Mess. "Ray has a gun," one officer would say. Some of the others wouldn't care, but others would lean in, hoping to hear more. Weapons weren't allowed on stations, especially ballistics weapons. They needed neither the damage from a bullet nor the cascading effect of an energy discharge to destroy the wiring or worse, start a fire. The mere fact that Ray had managed to bring a weapon to the station meant that he had at one time expected danger from the passengers.

Cool, she thought. She would have snuck in to look if she'd known it was there. *Maybe tomorrow.*

Her Uncle Dallas stared at the black thing Ray held in his hand. "You don't think you'll need that, do you?"

I have to get a better look, Selene thought. She shifted from one end the grate to the other.

"Hopefully not," Ray replied as he shoved the weapon into his pocket. It was gone before she could see it. *I have to see it,* she thought. Was it energy or ballistic? If it was energy-based she could easily recreate a smaller version to protect herself from people like Jameson. She wouldn't need any guardians then. *Definitely tomorrow.*

Within the room Ray motioned for Dallas to leave, saying, "Lead the way."

Dallas shifted his bulk and left the room. The man had been thin once. Selene remembered that before her father had died, Dallas had been almost as thin as she was. Savir's death must have hit him hard; when he was forced to take over her father's position, he'd gained the weight.

Selene leaned back and scratched her head. Her options were few. The ghost ship offered more danger. She could be caught out in the open. She could be seen by passengers. On the other hand, Ray wouldn't be near if someone came through the utility halls. *It's only fair that I keep Ray safe. I can call for help with Cecile if there is a problem.* And it wouldn't hurt to be close by in the odd chance that he brought out the weapon.

She glanced around her quarters, then retrieved a couple of sweaters. It was possible that only the local network of utility halls had had a temperature increase; she had to be prepared to enter the cold confines she was used to. She contemplated her cooler for a moment before reaching in and grabbing a sandwich and stuffing it in her pocket. There was no telling how long she was going to be away. "This would be way better if Spike were still here," she sighed.

It was possible that Dallas or Benson would fix the creature, though Selene held out little hope. By the way the pathetic creature had been crawling forward to attack Jameson, Selene wasn't sure it could ever be fixed. And just grabbing another from the shelf wouldn't be the same. He wouldn't have the same memories or know the same commands.

Shaking her head to clear those thoughts, she left her makeshift quarters and crept down the utility hall, shadowing Dallas and Ray as they made their way up to the docking bay. She had to cross the main hall twice, each time her heart pounding in her ear as she listened at the door for several seconds before cracking it open. She knew she didn't have much time before the two officers disappeared around a corner, so she had to ignore the butterflies in her stomach and just burst into the hall and cross before anyone could see her. After several minutes of skulking down the hall unconcealed, she felt her shoulders relax, and she was able to soften her footfalls.

When they reached the docking bay area, Selene ran out of hall to hide in. She sat at the grate staring at the two officers as they meandered down the hall away from her. They spoke about the ship, but few words made it far enough for her to hear. She had to find a way to get closer without disclosing her position.

Ray glanced over his shoulder as the pair spoke, as if waiting for someone to join them. Selene could see that he wasn't looking at her, but each time he checked, she shrank back into her hideout, feeling as if his penetrating eyes could see her through the wall.

"Ray?" A voice called, sounding as if it came from right beside Selene and causing her to backpedal farther into the shadows, heart racing.

She tripped over her own feet, falling against the bulkhead and grazing her temple. Sighing, she told herself, *He isn't in here. Just outside.* She leaned forward to see. He now stood facing Ray and Dallas, his back to her. Another set of legs stood beside him, but Selene couldn't recognize the pants.

"Is it done, Ray?" Captain Tulk asked. Selene heard concern in his voice. He sounded like he had on the day she'd run away. Selene sniffed. *Serves you right.*

Ray nodded. "Yes sir."

"Good," Captain Tulk said before shifting out of Selene's view.

As he moved, Selene could see that the fourth officer was carrying something above the level of the grate. It was a cage, but Selene didn't recognize it as coming from the Farm or Lab. *Maybe it's for the ship. Can they take over the autopilot?*

She crept closer to see the cage, then retreated as one of the officers shifted his footing. On her second attempt, Selene realized, *Oh, it's Sasha.* She scowled. As Sasha stepped away from the grate, the crate he held swung, as if something moved within it. Selene brought her head up as a dog barked. "Spike?" she gasped, then slapped her hand over her mouth. This wasn't just a grate, but a door to the utility halls. It was possible for the sounds to escape.

It was too late, however; the four officers all moved away from the grate and Uncle Dallas bent low, saying, "Hello Selene."

Selene ground her teeth, shuffling farther away from the opening. "Stupid, stupid, stupid. I should have known," she berated herself under her breath. She'd almost made it; now she was caught in the open, so close to the main hall, they could grab her before she managed to turn, let alone travel back into the depths of the station. *How could I be so stupid?*

"Why don't you come out and join us, Selene?" Dallas asked as the grate swung open.

Selene sat in silence for several seconds before saying, "I don't wanna." *You'll lock me in my quarters. To hell with you.*

The officers shared a look so brief that Selene wondered if she'd imagined it. They were communicating somehow. Was Captain Tulk reading their minds now? *No, that isn't possible.* He couldn't actually do it, even if she imagined that it could happen. *You all have a plan or something.* A plan she had to figure out.

Nothing came to mind. So she had the choice of trying to trick them, or cutting her losses and running back through the utility hall. That wouldn't do any good. That would leave her farther from Ray than she had been since being attacked, and there was at least one ship other than the ghost ship docked to the station. That meant there were more potential Jamesons wandering through the halls. Selene shivered and held her breath as she looked around the hall.

"It's okay, Selene," Captain Tulk said as he knelt beside Dallas. He looked like Savir had, near the end. He'd let his beard grow scraggy and his eyes were sunken and haunted.

"It's not okay," Selene retorted. They were trying to get her leave her new home. She couldn't let them win, not when she couldn't protect herself. *I hate you.*

"Selene," Dallas began, "it's time you joined us. We can—"

"You can't do anything," Selene screamed. "You can't do anything, just like you didn't do anything before."

Captain Tulk's face flashed white as the colour drained from it. His jaw twitched and the corner of his lip curled. *Who's the feral beast now?* she thought. *I don't give a damn. You can go to hell.* He'd left her to Jameson. He could have saved her. He could have supported her when she was helping her Uncle Benson, kept her from running.

Tears welled in Selene's eyes as she tensed her legs, ready to run back into the darkness behind her.

Throwing out his hands, Captain Tulk said, "Wait, Selene."

"Wait for what?" she asked as she edged backward.

Looking up to the others, Captain Tulk said, "Clear the deck."

There was a flutter of movement beyond Selene's field of vision as the officers all stiffened, then whirled and left. Sasha kept the cage from her view as he moved away.

"Selene," Captain Tulk said before sighing, "You're right."

"That's what you sent them away to say? You didn't want anyone to know how you screwed up?" Selene surprised herself with the accusation. She wasn't even sure why she'd said the words, but now that she had, she didn't feel guilty. The man wouldn't even let the others know how he'd screwed up. She ground her teeth. She could hear the blood pounding in her ears and her lips twitched. *I hate you!* The only thing keeping her stationary was the growing desire to punish Captain Tulk.

"Stop it, Selene. Robyn did the same thing and it was unacceptable then, too."

The invocation of her mother's name rocked Selene back on her feet. *How dare you? You rotten . . .* The man had no right to invoke her mother. It wasn't fair to do so. So what if he knew the woman when she was younger? He wasn't worthy enough to talk about her. He'd failed her, too.

"Oh Selene, I have failed you," Captain Tulk continued, his voice heavy. "I see that now. I did you a great disservice—first when Robyn passed away, then when Savir joined her."

Selene swallowed hard before whispering, "Don't you dare talk about them. You have no right. You aren't family. They're just gone and I'll see them again."

Captain Tulk fell forward onto his hands, trembling. His arms shook so hard that he appeared ready to collapse. His eyes were closed, though Selene could see tears flowing from them. "I—I a—I am family, Selene. That's why I have failed you. I am family and you didn't know."

Family? What do you mean? The officers were all family. He was the least family. Selene shuddered and went still. Cecile had answered the question several days earlier, however. *I can't be here, except with family.* If nothing else, Captain Tulk wouldn't disobey an order. Order was everything to the man. That meant there was family present and he was admitting that it was him. *All the stories . . .* Stories of her mother before she'd met her father. Stories of her mother when she was a child. There was only one way he would have known.

Captain Tulk was her grandfather.

Selene bunched her legs and ran for the door. She burst through and jumped at Captain Tulk, her upturned fist connecting with his face. She didn't want him to recover. *I want you to hurt like I did,* she thought as she punched him again. "You are not family, damn you. You are not!" Her high-pitched voice sounded more like a shrieking bird.

He accepted the pummelling without comment until her arms tired and she dropped them to her side. She'd managed to draw blood over his eyes and lower chin, but he didn't seem to notice. His tears still flowed unabated as he stared at her. He sat back on his knees, gulping for air. "You are so much like your mother, Selene."

"Stop it. Stop it. Stop it!" Selene screamed, pounding on his chest.

"Please, Rob—Selene." Captain Tulk fell silent for a second. "Selene, your mother . . . Robyn is . . . was my daughter. You are my granddaughter. We are family."

Selene paused for a second with her fist clenched, ready to punch again. *Family? Grandfather? What are you saying? How could YOU be my grandfather?* The thoughts came in quick succession. She couldn't finish one thought before another replaced it. *Goddamn it.* "You're lying," she whispered as she dropped her arms. *It can't be true. It must be their plan.*

"No Selene, I am not lying. I am your grandfather. My transgression was not telling you, but—"

"*Nooooooooo!*" Selene screamed, her face contorted. She felt her lower lip trembling and opened and closed her mouth several times before she sat still.

"Selene," Captain Tulk said, gazing into her swollen eyes. "I . . . I'm sorry." He had controlled his tears enough to see her, though she knew it wouldn't be for long. His eyes still bulged as if they were about to pop from their sockets.

Good, she thought. *You deserve to hurt.* She found her voice and said in quick succession, "You can't be my grandfather. Why didn't you tell me? Why didn't my father tell me? Why didn't you save me from . . . from *him*?"

"I . . . I didn't know, Selene. I didn't know he was after you," Captain Tulk said, wiping the back of his hand across his eyes. "I had to leave the Lab. When I . . . when I found out, I tried to find you, but Ray got there first." He leaned forward, as if he were praying. He gasped for the air to say, "I found you in your shower. I didn't know what to do. You . . . I'd never seen it before. I t-tr-tried to help, but you were asleep. You fell . . . I watched over you . . . for days. Oh God, your face, your beautiful face."

Selene blinked. Her world spun around her. She caught her breath and lifted shaking arms to cross them over her chest. *You tried. You . . . love me.* He hadn't left her to die. He'd been looking for her. The station was large enough to get lost in. *I've been hiding for days.* He'd tried, but failed. *Is that any different?* she thought, and rocked back against the wall. He *had* still left her to fend for herself.

In his uncanny way of reading her mind, Captain Tulk said, "I did fail you, Selene. If you are angry, be angry because I wasn't fast enough, not because I didn't try. I ran so fast, but I couldn't do it. My heart was beating so hard; I couldn't—"

"You came?" It was more question than statement. He'd tried, but he was just a man. He wasn't God. He couldn't read her mind, even if it seemed like he could. He couldn't run faster than Jameson. *Of course,* she thought as she balled her fists. Jameson was half Captain Tulk's age and he'd had a head start.

She stared at Captain Tulk. Selene's legs were like jelly. Her knees buckled and she threw out her hands to stop herself from falling forward. As she did, she felt his arms wrap around her back. She tensed as she felt his embrace. Sweat broke out on her forehead as visions of Jameson's sweaty hands twining into her braid sprang into her mind. Bugs crawled along her skin. There were marbles in her mouth as she said, "You are my grandfather."

As if the words alone were enough, Selene felt her skin calm, her shoulders relax. Her world hadn't been destroyed, but recreated. Her family of uncles had a father. She had a grandfather.

She shivered. At that acceptance, Selene's focus returned to the man's embrace. What he offered was more than that of a saviour. He'd been the one to care for her when she was in pain. But was that enough? Could he prove he was family? She knew her thoughts warred on her face as she frowned, then softened her gaze, then again frowned. Through it all, she clenched her jaw until she felt several teeth shift.

"You are so much like Robyn," Captain Tulk whispered. "She got so angry when I took my first posting that she ran away from home."

"Why . . . why didn't my father tell me?" Selene mumbled in the man's ear.

Captain Tulk shook his head. Pulling back, he said, "When Earth first chose Robyn's design, I forbade that she join the mission. Mixed genders on a station like this don't work well. Some of the other stations have all men, some all women. I didn't want her here on a station filled . . . filled with men. It wouldn't work."

He paused and took several deep breaths before continuing. "Robyn was the shining star on this station. Everyone loved her from the beginning. When . . . when she and your father married, I was beside myself. Everyone on the station is supposed to take their supplements to reduce the need for . . . They weren't supposed to have children. I didn't want—"

Tensing, Selene said, "You didn't want me?" *He hates me.* She felt her face warm again. How could he not want her? He was her grandfather, not just a random man. What kind of monster wouldn't want to see, to know, his family? *He's no better than Jameson.*

"No, wait—it wasn't like that, dear. You know how difficult it has been for you. Space is bad enough for adults. Children should grow up on a planet with proper gravity and . . . and . . ." Captain Tulk fell silent and closed his eyes, sniffling.

"You were such a beautiful baby when you were born. I loved you instantly, but it didn't matter. Neither Robyn nor Savir would let me see you because of what I'd told them. I tried . . . I tried to tell them I was wrong. But then when your mother . . ."

Captain Tulk had to pause again. Tremors wracked his body. After a time, he said, "Savir felt . . . felt that I had caused her . . ."

Selene's face contorted as she pulled back to stare at Captain Tulk. She opened her mouth several times before asking, "Did you?"

Shaking his head, Captain Tulk said, "No, dear. Robyn's . . . your mother's death was an accident that no one could have foreseen."

Selene felt her body relax. There were so many questions, and her grandfather had the answers. She had to know the truth. Why had her mother died? Why didn't she know about her grandfather?

"I tried so hard, but we couldn't work it out. Savir was a great man, we just . . ."

Selene frowned and pulled back far enough to look at his face. The truth was a mistake. Everything she didn't know was because two men couldn't get along, and her grandfather sat there explaining how they shouldn't have allowed women aboard? It was ridiculous to think that the rules were at fault. If her mother had lived, Selene knew everything would have worked out. *She'd make everything right.*

As these thoughts coursed through her mind, others followed. Did that mean Jameson was right? He'd said Robyn was playing house. Had Jameson only parroted her grandfather's words? Would that be her own fate, everyone looking on her as if she shouldn't exist? Or worse, was she going to be everyone's punching bag?

As her mind raced through these questions, Selene felt her grandfather shift. In one swift movement the man stood, lifting her into his arms. He didn't wait for her to give voice to her silent protest, but stepped toward his waiting men. The man's uncanny ability to follow her thoughts presented again as he said, "Jameson had taken very powerful drugs, Selene. His actions are neither typical nor acceptable. Please don't think what he said was true. You are the shining example of why the rules are wrong."

Selene sighed as she nestled into his shoulder. He felt right. He didn't have the sweet stench that Jameson had. Captain Tulk didn't make her feel like throwing up her food or shivering as if the hall had gone as cold as space. For a second, it almost felt the same as it had when her father carried her to her bed.

Selene's breathing evened out as she glanced at the other officers. His love wasn't like that of her uncles. The jokes her uncles told her were always aimed at getting a smile. Even when they reprimanded her it wasn't mean, or even stern. That was a game she played to make them feel comfortable; a game they all played. With her grandfather, whom she'd known only as Captain Tulk her entire life, she was safe. He reprimanded her the same way her father had— always firm, and always with a tear in his eye. *You weren't reading my mind.* He was only thinking of what Robyn would do.

Resting her head on her grandfather's shoulder, Selene drew a deep breath, letting her eyelids droop and feeling tremors run through her body as her tension eased. A cramp was growing in her leg but she ignored it; her arms were relaxing their grip on his neck. A screech of metal on metal signalled a door opening. She felt herself lowered as Captain Tulk stepped through then stopped to wait for his officers.

"We can return now," she heard him say.

"Captain." Sasha's voice.

Captain Tulk sniffed before saying, "Go ahead."

"What, *exactement*, did you want *moi* to do with this?"

"I don't know. Perhaps we should ask Selene." He set her back on her feet on the floor.

Selene's eyes snapped open. Sasha approached with the rectangular cage in his arms. Something scratched within the cage as he set it on the floor and lifted the latch on the front door.

Leaning closer, she asked, "What is it?" Holding her breath, she knelt and squinted into the dark interior. Her eyes widened and she skittered backward on her knees the instant the creature emerged from the box. "Wha . . . what is it?" she asked again, her voice quavering as she cocked her head to the side.

The fluffy creature bounded several steps toward her before skidding to a stop inches from her hands. It lifted its dark nose and mirrored her stare for half a second before offering a low growl, then a bark.

"It's a Spike," Selene said with a short laugh before covering her mouth with both hands. *A real Spike*, she thought. A dog. She rested her palms on his soft coat. "Ooh . . ."

The brown puppy was already showing signs of his potential size. His long legs seemed disproportionate, as if someday, if they continued to grow along with his body, he would be able to step right over Selene. His dark eyes were hidden by a droopy forehead and foamy slobber dripped to the floor unabated. "He's so beautiful," Selene said breathlessly as she petted him. *So soft,* she thought. His skin was wrinkled and folded, as if his body had been shrunk from twice his size.

Selene wrapped her arms around the puppy, pulling him into her lap. She hummed as she squished her nose into his soft coat and nuzzled him. When she was done, she cooed and pulled back, smiling as the puppy turned to slobber all over her face. "Yee-uck," she said before erupting into a high-pitched giggle. She looked at Captain Tulk, light-headed with elation, and asked, "Is . . . is he mine?"

Smiling down at her, Sasha said, "I found him on one of the arks awhile back. He's yours now."

"Really?" Selene asked as she wiped her nose on her sleeve.

"Yes, hon," Captain Tulk said. "But you have to keep him safe. He can't go into the utility halls like Spike did. You'll have to stay out here and keep him safe. You understand that, right? You have to be like a mother to him. You have to be an adult."

An adult? That was something else Jameson had harped about. *NO*, she screamed in her head. Jameson held no sway over her actions. Captain Tulk himself had said as much. Jameson may have been a parrot, but that didn't make his actions acceptable. She could be an adult. She could keep the dog safe. She didn't have to be what the man called her. *I am not a whore.* She knew what the word meant. Every once in a while a woman would come through the station and sleep with more than one of the officers—sometimes at the same time! Captain Tulk would bellow as if about to breathe fire when it happened. That was how she'd heard the word the first time. He didn't speak like Jameson, though. He was always angry with the officers. He called *them* the name, not the women.

The puppy in her arms nuzzled her again. Nodding her head in acceptance of her duty, Selene asked, "What's his name?" She didn't want to think about anything else but the puppy.

"You'll have to ask him that," Sasha replied.

Embracing him, Selene whispered into the dog's ear, "What's your name?"

In response, the dog began to lick her face with his long, warm tongue. Selene pulled away, giggling.

"Look how he bends his neck," Selene said, giggling again. "He bends his neck almost backward."

"Why not call him Bendy?" Sasha asked with a laugh.

"Oh Uncle Sasha, that won't do," Selene said, shaking her head. "That's not a real name. It would have to be like . . . Bendal . . . no . . . Benton . . . no. It's Bentley. His name is Bentley." She clapped her hands.

Captain Tulk knelt, lifting a tentative arm to her shoulder. As she shivered, he reluctantly let it drop. Of course he didn't know the details of her attack. There were no cameras to show how Jameson had done just that before smashing his hand into her face. Taking a deep breath, Captain Tulk said, "Hon, why don't you go back to your room now?"

"No, I don't wanna," Selene she said, shifting to look up at him. "I want to play with Bentley."

Stepping away, Dallas said, "Well sir, I have to return to the Lab."

Selene looked up at him with narrowed eyes. "But what about the ghost ship? Shouldn't we be looking into it?"

At mention of the ship, the others shifted their feet. None of them could meet her gaze as she searched their faces for an explanation. Finally she looked at her grandfather.

He shook his head, smiling with both his mouth and his eyes. "I'm sorry, hon. There is no ghost ship. It was the only thing we could think of that would get you out of the damned utility hall. I didn't want to lie to you, but . . . ."

It didn't matter, though. Selene looked around at the others. At Captain Tulk's admission, they were able to share in the responsibility. Even Ray, who she didn't think knew how to lie, blushed and glanced down the hall. They had told a lie. It was something she'd been told never to do. *But then I wouldn't have learned about Captain Tulk. About my grandfather.* She understood they'd done it was because they couldn't talk to her—they'd had to do it. She had to act like an adult now. She had to accept that sometimes it was acceptable to tell white lies.

Selene's thoughts became muddled as she tried to work through them. There was no ghost ship, but she had a bigger, stronger family. Her father was gone, but she had a grandfather. Spike was gone, but now she had Bentley. *I'm sorry, Spike. I won't forget you.*

Her eyelids drooped, and she felt her grandfather scoop her into his arms again. The puppy in her arms wriggled and whimpered. "He was a bad man, Selene. Do you understand that?" her grandfather said in her ear.

Selene's face contorted at the thought of the man. Looking up to her grandfather, she said, "I know."

"I hope so. I don't want you to think that everyone that comes along is like that. He was sick. It was a terrible thing and it shouldn't have happened. Not everyone is like that." She felt him shiver.

She was fast asleep before she remembered to ask whether she had to collect her pillows. They wouldn't know she couldn't sleep without the special ones her mother had sewn for her.

Chapter 7

Selene woke up in a strange room. She rolled her head around on the pillow to see everything, and frowned. The room was new, but all of the things that she'd carted to her temporary lodgings outside of Ray's office were piled around her. There were things she'd left in her old quarters as well.

Rubbing her eyes with her palms, Selene whispered, "Where am I?"

"Time to wake up," a dull computer voice said throughout the suite.

Selene's eyes opened wide as she recognized Cecile's voice. Wherever her grandfather had taken her, he'd established the program. Selene shivered. *Grandfather. Captain.*

Shifting to the side of the large bed, she said, "I'm up, Cecile."

"Good morning, Miss Selene. Do you require any assistance?" the computer voice sounded no different from the last time she'd heard it. Captain Tulk had hijacked the program the last time. Was it possible he'd started again the second she was safe in the new quarters? *No,* she thought. That was impossible. The tears he'd shed were real. He was trying to do the right thing. That meant he wouldn't be so bold. He would keep her under surveillance for sure, but not with Cecile. *I have to trust him sometime.* She sighed.

As her feet touched the cold floor, she yelped. Bentley immediately jumped to his feet on the bed and followed her to the floor, barking with excitement. Bentley was far different from Spike.

Unlike the metallic creature, Bentley nuzzled Selene as an emotional response, not one programmed by one of her uncles. His eyes sparkled with a life that Selene had never seen in any other living creature working on or passing through the station.

Selene loved that energy. It set her on fire as she played and danced through the room like a fairy, then as her favourite dragon hunter. She wondered if her laughter was loud enough to echo through the station like a siren. *I bet even Sasha will smile at Bentley.*

"Mr. Grumpy Pants in medical would even smile," she said. "Because you're super cute." The thought of the old medical tech made her giggle, which made Bentley rush across the room and jump on her leg.

For several minutes she played with her dog, chasing Bentley until the dog managed to knock her down and pounce on her chest to lick her face. For a puppy that couldn't have existed for more than a week, he was heavy enough that she coughed and had to turn to the side to push him to the floor.

Selene stared at the dog. *Where did you come from?* Her Uncle Sasha had said he'd been on one of the arks. Was it possible that Bentley had been on the ark Jameson had piloted? It made sense, in a way. Jameson had said something about his son. Was it possible the man had had the dog on the ship and Sasha had stolen it?

"No," Selene said aloud. Bentley would be a full adult if he'd been awake on the ark. He must have been in one of the canisters. "Sasha must have awakened you for me." She must have been mistaken when she hefted the dog in the hall. He'd been revived at this weight.

As though she'd answered the computer, Cecile continued with her litany. "Would you rather have porridge or a grilled cheese sandwich?"

Selene paused. Hearing her stomach growl, Bentley barked twice. "When did you eat last?" she asked him. "I can't remember when I did." She looked up at the speaker on the ceiling. "I . . . I think I would like some porridge." She shuddered briefly as images of grilled cheese sandwiches crossed her mind. They left a metallic taste in her mouth, as if she'd been chewing on Spike's feet.

Selene pushed the dog away to look around the room. It was no different from her original quarters, though it had been decorated by a much taller hand. Pictures of Selene and her mother dotted the wall. Most of the pictures of her mother were taken when the woman was much younger. Selene shuffled toward them, staring at her mother. She'd seen some of the ones taken in the woman's earlier years, but this close, Selene realized how honest Captain Tulk had been, how true her grandfather's words had been. "She looks just like me," she whispered.

Though Selene had never seen the planet, she knew by the background that her mother had been on Earth. There were towering trees in most of the pictures, suggesting Robyn had spent her early years in the woods. The lack of technology made Selene wonder how her mother had come to feel so comfortable first designing and then living on the station. Selene had heard that people from the wilds never enjoyed technology. *Some won't even leave Earth.*

Why would she even want to leave such a cool place? Selene could imagine herself racing Bentley through the trees. Dragons would live in the trees and bounce from one to another. They would unfurl giant wings to buffet her as she valiantly saved her people.

Selene let fall the hand that had been tracing a tree in one of the pictures. She could almost feel the rough bark. They weren't like Sasha's trees. These towered so high that their tops weren't even in the picture. "So big," she mused as she turned to walk toward the latrine. A week in the utility halls hadn't left her clean. There had been times when she'd wanted to just run through the showers, but every time she'd stepped from the safety of her fortress outside Ray's office, visions of Jameson's monstrous face chased her back. It had gotten increasingly worse, until the only reason she'd been able to step from the utility hall was to shadow the security officer.

Glancing toward the shower, she said, "Cecile, please lock the door on authorization Savir-alpha-omega." Ray wasn't there to protect her. "Cecile, encrypt the locking sequence with Ro . . . program Robyn-nine."

That wasn't necessary, she knew. Everyone on the ship knew where she was, even if they weren't small enough to have flushed her from her hideaway. Her grandfather had made sure that she was comfortable. Selene thought about the times she'd forced herself to travel for food and the latrine, wondering how many times she should have been caught. How many times had an officer turned his back or stepped through a door? She shook her head and sighed, wiping misty eyes. *They do want me.* They had played her game like perfect puppets. She didn't need any dragons swooping from the heavens to create her world. She'd managed to take complete control of over two hundred officers as they went about their regular duties.

The bruises had all but faded from her face, though dark circles surrounded her eyes. There was no way to force a smile into her eyes as she could with her mouth. She couldn't mean it right now, even if she wanted to. She didn't want to show her teeth anyway—many were cracked. There were lines radiating from her eyes like the ones her grandfather had.

Selene lined her hand up with the mirror to measure herself. *I'm taller,* she thought. Either that, or the top half of the mirror was shrinking. Dropping her hand to trace the bruises, she whispered, "Have I passed your test?" Was she an adult now? Yet another description given to her by Jameson.

The day she'd been promoted to the rank of sub-lieutenant had been the beginning. She'd proven her ability with the equipment first. *I AM awesome with the robots.* After that she would have to go on a mission. She had to go . . . what was it her father had called his first day? "A walkabout." She had to go on a walkabout to learn what kind of person she really was.

Selene looked down at Bentley as he tumbled around, trying to bite his own tail. "I'm not like you. I'm not chasing my own tail, am I?" What kind of person was she? She had lived alone for almost a year, part of that in the utility halls, like a rat. She'd fed and clothed herself even if everyone had done their best to make it easier on her. And now she was the youngest officer.

Selene interrupted her own thoughts to say, "I'm eleven. I spent my eleventh birthday in a coma." A coma that had come from a severe beating at the hands of the pilot, Jameson. Few others could boast that. It wasn't a typical ordeal. Even those who were caught fighting the passengers usually had a reason.

"What would it take to become captain?" she wondered aloud as she searched the bathroom for a hairbrush. She didn't have much hair, but it still required some care. Several minutes later she found where her grandfather kept his toiletries and made herself presentable.

She had to answer the question he'd asked before she'd run from her father's quarters. Strange, she thought, puckering her brows; they weren't her quarters anymore. Not even those she'd created had been hers. "What do you think, Bentley?" Selene asked the puppy as he looked up from his play. "Should I call him Captain or Grandfather?" The puppy barked twice and returned to his tail-chasing, and she let her eyes wander around the room, until the door chime sounded. Bentley barked and rushed to sit at her feet and stare at the door, alternating growls with barks.

Selene bent to pet the dog, joking, "Did Sasha program you like that?" Of course he couldn't, but it didn't matter. It gave her another boost to know that Bentley was keeping her safe. Maybe one day he would grow as tall as she was. *Try and attack me then,* she thought as she straightened.

"Come in." Nothing happened. "Oh—Cecile, release door lock, authorization Selene-9F5."

As though he were the guest, Captain Tulk pushed the hatch open and entered with a bow. His face was radiant and his eyes were bright, as if he'd managed to get some sleep. There were no dark circles around his eyes as he locked gazes with her. "Hello Selene," he said.

"Hello Cap . . . Grandfather," Selene replied. She motioned for him to take a seat.

Her grandfather's couch wasn't as comfortable as her own and Selene had to pull one of the pillows down to sit without wincing. As she did, Bentley tried several times to jump up to sit beside her. When he failed for the fifth time, Selene bent to lift him onto the higher ledge.

"Growing he may be, but not enough yet," Captain Tulk said with a small smile. Maybe she wasn't crazy, if Captain Tulk was saying the dog had grown.

Nodding, Selene said, "Soon he'll be as big as me."

"Bigger," Captain Tulk said, laughing as Bentley looked up at them as though aware that they were talking about him.

Selene leaned forward to stare at her grandfather. "Captain, I have an answer for you. I do want to come back now."

He lifted an eyebrow. "Are you sure, Selene?"

Matching his earlier smile, Selene winked before saying, "My name is Sub-lieutenant Sotana. I would like to come back from my leave of absence. Must I go to the infirmary for clearance?"

Captain Tulk shook his head. "When you are ready to see the doctor, you can. For now, when would you like to—"

Jumping down to the floor, Selene said, "Right now Granf—Captain."

"Perhaps you should find some more appropriate attire then, mister," Captain Tulk said as he stood and crossed his arms.

It didn't take Selene any longer to clothe herself appropriately than to find the dresser pushed back into the corner. She was ready within minutes, Bentley at her side as she joined Captain Tulk in the main room. "Where will I be stationed?" she asked.

Captain Tulk scratched his chin before replying. "I think the best place for now is in the Lab. We had a ship dock about three hours ago, so we won't be able to hide Bentley anywhere else."

Looking down at the energetic puppy, Selene asked, "Can I take him with me?"

"Of course you can, hon. I can't have him messing in here, can I? He's your responsibility."

Captain Tulk had changed. As he spoke, Selene wondered if he was the same person. His voice and mannerisms were no longer gruff or abrupt, but patient and casual, and his wide smile made her feel welcome. *You actually love me,* she thought as he stood holding his arms out for a hug. He was like a caterpillar—a crotchety old man dispensing only stern lectures during her entire youth that had gone into his cocoon to emerge a butterfly.

Selene didn't mind. It had been too long since anyone had offered her that warm embrace. In an embrace, she could hear her own heartbeat as well as her grandfather's. She could feel the strong, unyielding circle of his arms wrapped around her, keeping the monsters at bay.

Stepping back, Selene looked toward her new puppy. "Cap—Grandfather, I'm not sure I will be able to carry him long. He already seems bigger than he was last night."

Chuckling, Captain Tulk said, "Oh I don't think he's grown that fast, but perhaps for today I will carry him."

He grunted and his face contorted as he hefted the dog. "Perhaps I was wrong. Perhaps I should make sure nothing is missing in the suite."

"He's been with me, Grandfather," Selene said as she reached up to pet the dog. Bentley squirmed.

"Come on, boy," Captain Tulk said as he turned to leave the room. He had to duck as he stepped through the hatch.

Selene's first step from the room took an eternity. Her foot hovered over the kneeknocker until she sighed and released her white-knuckled grasp on the door frame. When she managed to open her eyes, she was in the hall watching her grandfather disappear around the corner, en route to the Lab.

She gasped and turned back to the room, tugging at the neck of her shirt. *Can't breathe. Maybe I should just stay. I don't need to work today.*

Selene had her foot halfway back through the door when Bentley barked. She looked down the hall in the direction of the sound and saw that Captain Tulk had returned. He stood waiting in the hallway, his head bowed.

I can do this, Selene thought. She let out her pent breath and called out, "Cecile, lock door, authorization Savir-alpha-omega." As the door clanged shut, Selene took off down the hall toward her grandfather. She caught up to him as he turned to leave again.

The trip was short, but Selene couldn't calm her nerves. She wrung her hands together, wondering, *What will they think? Will they say anything? Do I look okay?* When they reached the door to the Lab, she leaned against the wall beside it with a sigh, as though it was keeping her from entering. She grimaced, trying and failing to quell her anxiety.

How long it had been? She couldn't remember. But being there brought back all the terrible images—Jameson's fist cuffing her face, her stomach. Her body shook as if she was feeling every strike again, until her grandfather's firm grasp on her shoulder brought her back to the present. She blinked, trying to focus on her grandfather's face.

"It's okay, Selene," he said gently. "We're all here for you."

Selene took a deep breath, let it out. "I'm ready . . . Captain."

"Selene, I am going to support you in any decision you make," he offered as he knelt to lower Bentley to the floor. He remained there, arms around the puppy, eyes on her face.

Selene smiled at her grandfather, holding her puppy. This was a new look for the man she'd only known to bark orders and look down at her. He seemed far happier now. His voice was softer and his smile wider. It was as if something had been lifted from his shoulders. He seemed taller, his chest broader.

Selene wished that her parents had been able to see this captain. Her impression of the man had initially been established by her father, but learning that Savir and Captain Tulk had been at odds cast doubt on the accuracy of that image. *Maybe you were wrong, Father.* In fact, it was possible that Captain Tulk bore little resemblance to the man she thought him to be. He could have always been the happy man who knelt in front of her, and *she* had been the dark soul with the preconceptions.

She walked over and wrapped her arms around him. "I'm sorry, Grandfather," she murmured. He returned the hug with one arm, content to wait until Selene pulled away before standing again. His eyes had misted over and he looked quickly away.

Selene left him shifting from one foot to the other and turned to the hatch door. She laid one hand on the latch and took a deep breath, then another. It took several seconds to calm her breathing before she pushed through the hatch into the Lab.

Before she could even set one foot into the room, the sound of clapping reached her. Two dozen officers stood staring at her, applauding. They stopped as her grandfather followed her through, but resumed when he nodded his approval. *You're clapping for me*, Selene thought. *You're happy to see me, proud of me.* None of them had been able to show their approval since she'd gone missing. *Half of you probably thought I was dead. What am I thinking?* They must have known everything. Her grandfather was the captain. He would have told them so they wouldn't be waiting for her, fretting. They did love her, as he'd said. A smile crept onto her face and she managed to lock gazes with a few of the officers. Selene strode forward with her chest puffed out. Bentley raced around her feet, caught up in the officers' glee. He barked several times and she knelt beside him to calm him.

As the applause faded, her Uncle Dallas approached, nodding over her head to Captain Tulk. "We've built a pen for Bentley so you don't have to worry about him," Dallas said.

Selene looked past the large man to the steel cage the officers had built for Bentley. It was almost as tall as she was, but given how big she imagined her dog would get, Selene was happy with its size. *It's perfect.*

Smiling as Selene glanced from the cage to her puppy, Captain Tulk said, "I think it'll be better for him to do his business in the pen than in the hall. I'm sure you don't want to have to go through the halls after your shift to find his gifts."

Selene thought about cleaning up after the dog and frowned. She didn't want to smell like her Uncle Callum did after leaving the Fuel Room. *Yuck.* Nodding, she said, "I think we can do without that." The gathered officers laughed, and Selene smiled and relaxed, looking from face to face. *They aren't looking away.*

She stood and let Dallas take Bentley to the cage as the crowd dispersed, cringing at the puppy's high-pitched yelps for several seconds until Dallas set the dog on the floor. As Bentley's paws hit the steel, the sound stopped. Dallas grinned at her. "There's a noise dampening unit in the cage. You won't have to worry about that anymore."

Selene felt her chest tighten as the dog roamed around his cage. She knew that Dallas had meant that the officers wouldn't have to endure the noise, but that didn't change how she felt. *I can't hear him. What if he needs me?* Selene bit the corner of her lip.

"Hey kiddo, I've got something for you," Benson called out, beckoning her toward him.

She paused for a few seconds, her gaze lingering on the cage, before turning and following Benson to a short officer wearing the orange jumper of a mechanic. Selene was able to look the man in the eye without craning her neck. She couldn't see his lips, though; a bushy moustache ran the length of his mouth and curled down at either end toward his chin. The man wiped his greasy hands on his suit before straightening to salute. He waited without moving until Benson spoke.

"Hey, Sub-lieutenant," her uncle began. She could see his quick assessment of her fading bruises, but she let it pass. She couldn't cringe every time someone looked at her. She had to be strong, like her parents. Captain Tulk had told her a story about when her mother had a black eye for a week on Earth. Every time she'd gone to school, a new teacher asked her if her parents had hurt her. The truth was mundane and embarrassing, however, as Robyn had brought it on herself by starting a fight with a boy two years her junior. It had taken ten years for her to gain the courage to tell anyone.

Giving the man a faint smile, Selene said to Benson, "Hello, Uncle Benson—uh, Lieutenant Benson . . . Hey, wait; if Benson is your last name, what's your first name?"

Benson smiled and looked away. After a few seconds he took a breath to answer, but remained silent. Finally he shook his head and said, "This is Able Seaman Tony. I've assigned him to get you up to speed on the things you'll need to know. He's one of the best teachers we have."

Licking her lips, Selene said, "School?"

"Sorry, kiddo. We aren't all about playing with the robots down here," Benson explained as he looked around the Lab. The officers had all returned to their own projects, though Selene caught many of them giving her quick glances.

Taking a deep breath, Selene asked, "What do I have to learn about?"

"We'll start with the basics, sir . . . er ma'am," Able Seaman Tony said without looking down. His voice was deep, reminding Selene of the robots in her daydreams. "Once you know the basics, we'll figure out what field you'll be specializing in and focus on that."

"Well, what fields are there?" Selene asked before looking around the bay.

Seaman Tony saluted Benson as the officer left, then turned to Selene. "We have Communications, Internal Systems, Command,

Logistics, Medical, Agricultural, and a whole lot more that I can't even pronounce."

"How will I choose?" Selene asked as the man led her into a small bay on one side of the larger room. It was filled with chairs with flat tables attached to them, which flipped down to lock a person in. An expansive screen covered the wall at the far end. *I wonder how much Dallas had to scrounge to build that,* she thought as she stared at the flimsy screen.

"You'll end up in a field that you like," the able seaman said. "For instance, my primary field is Internal Systems. I'm not too smart about things like star constellations and radiation levels, but I can turn a mean wrench."

Why would a wrench be mean? Selene shook her head as she envisioned a large army of wrenches marching down the main hall, their teeth gnashing together. If the man was good at turning mean wrenches then he must be fast and strong.

Selene bit her lower lip, waiting for several seconds until the man nodded for her to ask her question. "So could I do something in computer programming? I'm good at it."

Shrugging, Tony said, "Sure. So you've done it before? Can I see it?"

Selene nodded. "Of course."

Sliding through the rows of desks, she made her way to a computer terminal and touched the screen. The screen flickered for a second before prompting her for her request. Clearing her throat, she said, "Computer, access personal data tablet for Cecile program."

Within seconds, the coding for Cecile's program was displayed on the screen for Able Seaman Tony to read through. It didn't take him long to step back. Nodding, he said, "I'm not really a programmer, but I can see what she does. Maybe you could expand her to do other things like open doors and stuff."

Selene's mouth fell open, then she frowned. *How can you not love her?* Cecile could already open and lock doors. She could grab information from the data core faster than Selene could. Sighing, she pressed the button to shut down the screen, then crossed her arms. *Cecile is supposed to do so much more. I wish she could.* Cecile was supposed to be able to do everything that Selene wanted. Started by her father, the program was rudimentary. Selene had used it to learn about the station. But the able seaman was correct; the program was the whim of a child. It was nothing more than a basic door opener, even if it woke Selene in the morning. It couldn't even protect itself from being hijacked by Captain Tulk's people.

Selene shuddered as an elevated voice broke her reverie. Frowning, she shifted so she could see who was shouting. Benson stood with his feet planted, his gaze locked forward, his finger thrust toward a junior officer who wore an orange jumper identical to that of her teacher. "What the hell did you think you were doing?" her Uncle Benson bellowed. The seaman's eyes were downcast.

The words he used didn't surprise Selene, who had heard all of her uncles swear, but Benson's tone made her shiver. The junior officer shifted, refusing to meet Benson's glare.

"That stunt could have killed someone," Benson growled. He stood close enough to spray the man's face with spit as he yelled. "If I could I'd send you on the next shuttle out of here, but I can't afford to. Go work with Sasha on the Farm. No, I don't give a good goddamn that you're allergic to wheat. *You screwed up*, so suck it up before I shove my boot down your throat so far, you taste my knee. Got it?"

Selene shook her head as she looked back to A.S. Tony and raised her eyebrow.

He nodded. "Poco left a valve open for an hour the other day. It was very messy. He probably did it again, so . . . Well, you get the picture."

She looked back to Poco, and her stomach lurched. His whole body trembled. His hands were balled into fists as he accepted the verbal diatribe. Though he still refused to meet Benson's gaze, he didn't search out any other eyes for reassurance. For their part, the rest of the officers in the room were trying their best not to look at Benson as he shouted.

Selene had never heard her Uncle Benson even lift his voice. He didn't even look the same, with his face so red and his hand pointing like a dagger at Poco's chest. His narrowed eyes were locked on the other officer, as if he was afraid to look away or the man would disappear.

"Why . . . why is he yelling like that?" Selene asked as she stepped around her guide.

As she passed him, the able seaman reached out to grab her wrist. Like a slingshot, Selene stepped back, her arms windmilling. Then she closed her eyes, willing calm. *He's not Jameson. He's not him. He just wanted to get my attention.* Selene took a deep breath and swiped at a drop of sweat running down her temple. She turned to Tony with a tentative smile, shaking her head. "It's okay. I just . . . it's okay."

"You can't go out there . . . ma'am," Tony said. "He may be your uncle, but when you're on duty, that goes out the window. You're an officer . . . an inferior officer. Don't think your—"

"But he's—" Selene began, but the man shook his head.

Creasing his brows as he stared into the main room, Tony said, "Ma'am, I don't want to step out of line, but if there's one thing I can teach you today, it's that you have to let things like that happen. Lieutenant Benson is a good officer. He knows when to encourage or reprimand."

"And yell?" Selene countered.

"Yes, and yell. If you go out there and try to do anything, all you'll do is undermine his authority. That's not something we can have here. We can't afford to have leadership issues. There aren't enough leaders to go around."

"But he can't just—" Selene began, but the junior officer cut her short.

"He can. He has to," Tony said. His eyes were wide as he stared at Selene. "Every officer is different, ma'am. If you want to lead differently that's your right, but I can tell you without a doubt that you have to be forceful or no officer will ever follow your lead."

Selene shook her head, intimating that she was going to leave the room, but the able seaman jumped up from his position. "Ma'am, please. If you don't agree with me, at least wait until the lieutenant is on his own before you talk to him."

Talk to him? Selene was going to do some yelling of her own. *You can't talk to people like that.* In all of her walking through the utility halls, Selene had never heard an officer belittle another so much. *You can't get away with this.* Her father would never have done that. Savir's voice had always been soft.

Selene shook her head. She'd learned more about her family in the last week than she'd ever wanted to know. Captain Tulk, a hard man who accepted no excuses and expected perfection, had morphed into her grandfather. He was the reason she'd been allowed to remain on the station. *He's nothing like I thought.* Now, her Uncle Benson had become an officer, something she'd never thought about. *I won't be like that,* she thought.

She turned back to the able seaman, whose forehead was slick with sweat. "I will wait. I will watch and I will learn." *I will learn what not to do.*

Nodding, Tony said, "Thank you. I apologize for my behaviour. It was conduct unbecoming and I will submit to any discipline you feel is necessary."

"Wouldn't that be the same as what I . . ." Her shoulders drooped. "You put me in a bad position." Brows furrowed, lips puckered, she stared at the officer. *I can't discipline you for that.* He'd spoken to her in the same way he'd pleaded her not to do with Benson. But then, there were no officers looking to her for support and guidance. *Not yet.*

Selene waved the man away. He nodded in acceptance, then stepped back into the smaller room. He waited with his arms at his sides for Selene to join him.

When she did, she asked, "Where do we begin?"

Smiling, he replied, "Maybe we should start with what we are. What do you know about the station?"

"Oh, that's easy," Selene said, matching his wide smile. "My mom built the place and Dad took care of it for seven years." She waved her arms to indicate the entire station as she spoke. "So the station is a way station where ships fuel up on their way to the planet . . ."

It took her several hours to explain everything she knew about the station. She clapped her hands together when Tony nodded. She giggled when his eyes grew wide at her explanations. *You don't even know some of it, do you?* Though short, his perspective was that of an officer. He didn't have access to the utility halls.

When she was finished, Tony stood rubbing his head. After a brief pause, he glanced into the main hall before saying, "I think I know how we'll start, but not until tomorrow."

"I'm okay. We can continue now," Selene offered. She liked showing the able seaman what she knew. It felt good to see the realization in his eyes that there were things he could learn. She enjoyed every sign he gave that he'd learned something. He never turned away to look into the main hall or folded his arms and frowned to signal his refusal to listen. Selene chastised herself for comparing him to Jameson. He was worthy of the praise her Uncle Benson had given him.

Clearing his throat, the able seaman said, "I'm not worried about us, ma'am. I think Bentley would like to get out and stretch his legs."

Selene snapped her head toward her puppy. *Oh, crap.* In her excitement to show the able seaman what she knew, she'd almost forgotten her dog. *What kind of mother am I?* She hung her head and swallowed the lump in her throat.

Selene jumped down from her desk and dashed out of the room. Before she'd gone three paces, she skidded to a halt and returned to the classroom, and the able seaman. "Same time tomorrow, Able Seaman?"

"Yes, ma'am," the man replied with a rigid salute.

Selene let her arm fall and rushed out to the main hall, where one of the taller officers had already retrieved Bentley from his cage. *I'm sorry,* she thought as the dog squirmed in the man's grasp, eager to jump into her arms. Unprepared for his weight, Selene staggered back, then steadied herself. By this time, the dog was licking her face. Giggling, she pushed him away, but he only jumped again, scratching her arm. *Ouch.* Pushing the dog to the floor, she turned to salute the officers in the room before she left, noticing that most were still looking in her direction.

Chapter 8

By her fourth session, Selene realized how little she knew about the station. For every nuance or detail she had to tell Tony, he had a dozen for her. He was a fair instructor. Even when he corrected her, he didn't make her feel stupid. He didn't look down his nose or roll his eyes when she got something wrong, which happened more often than she thought possible.

Ever since she'd been able to crawl, Selene had moved through the halls of the station. She knew things that the able seaman raised an eyebrow about. He hadn't known that Callum liked to tell fairy tales, or that Sasha talked to himself in French. His eyes had gone wide when Selene explained to him how the coding for the primary computer system was flawed. She savored that moment more than when she'd showed him Cecile's coding. The able seaman had been chewing on some gum when she'd first said the code was simple to hack. He'd swallowed the gum and had to force his mouth shut when she was finished.

There were other times, however, when Selene realized she had much to learn. A lot of it was data and seemed irrelevant to her. *Why would it matter that the fuel lines can pump a million gallons in fourteen hours?* Selene was only interested when the able seaman explained that the fuel was pumped during the dark side pass. Selene had had a eureka moment then, as her father would have called it. She'd slapped her forehead and said, "That's why we don't stop the dark side pass."

After that conversation, Selene sat down in her desk and initiated a new one by looking at the able seaman and saying, "There were originally 1,314 officers on the station."

Able Seaman Tony smiled before replying, "There were ten, originally. The commissioned officers were the first to arrive, with your mother. They established the protocols for the computers, then the first shuttle to pass through the station left half her payload. Since then twenty-five officers have been sent away, eleven hundred killed, three hundred recruited, and one officer born."

"Hey, that's me," Selene said. She stole a glance toward Bentley. Though she hadn't been able to hear the dog whining, she knew by the way he jumped up and pawed at the top of the cage that he was eager to see her. *Later,* she thought. She'd just gone to him. He had to learn that she wouldn't always come. *It won't teach him any manners.*

Before she could return her attention to the officer, A.S. Tony asked, "Do you remember how many geo stations Lieutenant Callum has on the planet?"

Closing her eyes to help focus her mind, Selene said, "Seven."

Tony nodded. "Correct. Though at one time there were three times as many, now there are seven stations around the planet. Each station pumps fuel to the main line, which is then fed to the interim platform orbiting below the station."

"Don't they ever break, Tony? Um, sorry . . . Able Seaman Tony," Selene amended.

The able seaman's eyes strayed across the room. "Sure they break, though not often. We have a couple shuttles to go down to the planet. Callum goes down every couple months to check on everything."

Selene cocked her head to the side. "Has he ever been stuck down there?"

Tony shook his head. "Oh, no. We haven't lost a shuttle for nine years. Not since—" The man's eyes bulged and he looked away, unwilling to meet her gaze. As the silence grew, he shifted his feet. His face turned redder than the suit he wore.

Selene stared at him. "Not since when?"

The able seaman cleared his throat, then shook his head. "Oh, not since we lost a shuttle on the planet nine years ago. It was unfortunate."

A shuttle they lost years ago. "Able Seaman Tony, was it an accident?"

The man relaxed a little. "Oh, of course. No one could have foretold that it could happen."

Selene's face fell as she made a leap of logic. "No one could have foretold, but someone could have been blamed."

"Oh no, Savi—" The man fell silent and closed his eyes.

Selene blinked the tears from her eyes as she stared at the officer. *Nine years ago?* There was no doubt what had happened nine years earlier. She wasn't going to fool the man into answering more of her questions, however. The hair on his neck was standing straight up and he refused to meet her gaze. *You won't even answer if I order you, will you?* she thought.

The truth Selene had been seeking for years had just been dangled in her face like a carrot, but as soon as he let the name slip, he pirouetted and rushed from the room. Turning back at the door, he said, "My apologies, ma'am. I just remembered that I have an active shift. We'll have to return to your studies tomorrow."

In a flash, the prospect of closure was dashed against an asteroid. *Why didn't he just tell me? Why just leave? Stupid able seaman.* Selene went home from the fourth session and cried herself to sleep.

When she woke an hour or so later, Selene spent ten minutes crying into her hands as Bentley nuzzled her legs. "H-h-he almost told me," she sobbed to the dog. Balling her fists, she punched the bed. "I don't want to go anymore. I hate him. He wouldn't tell me," she said through her hiccups. Then she caught her breath when the hatch opened in the main room. *Grandfather.* She ground her teeth. She couldn't afford to let him hear her crying.

Selene wiped the tears away and drew a deep breath, motioning Bentley closer. She wasn't sure how he'd managed to jump up the first time, but ever since, he'd made it his goal to do laps around the room, including crossing the bed and jumping down again. More often than not, he tripped over his large paws when he jumped down and ended up splayed across the floor or bunched against the wall.

Now she wrapped her arms around the dog, closed her eyes, and held her breath as her grandfather approached. As the footsteps came closer, her heart pounded louder in her ears. *What if it isn't him?* She shivered.

The footsteps paused at her door. There was a silent second until her door swung closed. She sighed. She couldn't stop going to her sessions. Her grandfather wouldn't be impressed. He was still Captain Tulk and a promise to him couldn't be broken. Fair or not, however, Selene didn't want to listen to the able seaman. Not until he answered her true question and explained what had happened to her mother.

Selene woke early the next morning. Bentley stirred as she moved and quickly returned to running his laps, only stopping to run to the corner. Selene found the mess as she pulled her feet off the bed. "Crap."

After cleaning up the mess, Selene moved into the latrine. *At least you only go in the corner.* When she was finished, she padded back into her room, stumbling in surprise when Cecile asked, "Will you be going to the Farm today?"

Selene rolled her eyes and shook her head. "Only if you open the doors." *That's all anyone thinks you're good for.* That was what the able seaman said—opening doors. Then, "Recording conversations wouldn't be any harder than opening doors," she mused. "Cecile, display your code on my tablet, please."

It didn't take her long to make the adjustments to Cecile's programming. The most difficult issue was storage space for the data. She knew most of it would be useless so she would end up deleting it, but in the interim she needed storage. *Maybe you can delete the crap,* she thought. She could use her own clearance to request the storage, but then she'd have to declare her reasoning. Savir's code was never questioned, though—or rather, had never been questioned before. She wasn't certain whether it was because they didn't know she knew it or because they'd overlooked her earlier transgressions. Either way, it was still active.

It was possible that when she'd ordered Cecile to cut her connection to the mainframe, the officer masquerading on the other end had become aware of the situation and revoked that code. If that were the case, then she would have to use her own. "Hmmm." She sat down at her grandfather's computer and said, "Menu." Her hands trembled for a second as the possibility of being caught crossed her mind. *What can I say? 'Oh yeah, I didn't feel like listening to my teacher anymore because I hate him. I hate him because he won't answer my questions about how my mom died.'* That wouldn't work. Clearing her throat, she said, "I'm sorry, I just needed the data storage for recording conversations." She snorted. "That would go over like a bag of hammers on Sunday."

Selene stood and moved back from the terminal. She couldn't just ask. She could imagine her grandfather calling it a frivolous use of bandwidth and forbidding her from implementing her plan. She had to do it herself and make sure nothing went wrong. That meant changing Cecile's coding more than just making a request.

Selene brushed the computer terminal to call up the programming screen and set to work, first building a program that would access the mainframe. She had to access the system and partition her data so no one could retrieve it but her. To accomplish that, the program also had to access the audio equipment.

With every new line of code, Selene's smile grew wider. She was the greatest computer engineer. She was going to save her alien shuttle by reprogramming it into a different language. She had to save her crew before they flew into the corona of the red giant.

After several attempts at writing the section of code that would allow her to siphon off the key information, Selene sat back. "This has to work. It needs to choose what words are good. I can't have a list." After some thought, Selene sat up straight. "That's it! I can use the language profile to let her determine what's important. Yeah, then compare it to the conversation topic."

As she wiped the back of her hand against her forehead, her stomach growled. She cocked her head at Bentley, lying on a large pillow pushed against the wall. "I'll leave him, I think." At least he wasn't whining.

Selene then called up Cecile's primary code. "Hmm . . . You'll have to access it anywhere so you'll need the access code embedded into the program. Well, that or add code to be able to hack the mainframe. Nope, that'll take forever."

It was several hours later when the chimes at the door broke her concentration. *What? Oh, crap.* The screen was flashing to indicate messages waiting and Bentley was whining at the door. "Damn it. I should have walked him earlier. That was stupid," she whispered as she jumped down from the seat and walked to Bentley's side, covering her nose as the smell of urine invaded her nostrils. *Oh God, that's gross.* She sighed and felt her face warm.

Selene hugged the puppy. "I'm sorry, Bentley. I promise to do a better job. I'll leave the door to the bathroom open next time. I go there. You should too."

She stood, opened the door, and found a tray of food waiting for her on the threshold. After no one appeared after a moment's wait, she leaned out to collect the tray. *They can't be too far away,* she thought. How else could they collect the dishes, unless they were standing at the ready? The corners of her lips curled as she imagined a growing pile of trays by the door. "I don't think the—Grandfather would like a tower of trays."

She returned to the suite and led Bentley to the shower. "You can poop here, Bentley. Poop here." She dragged him back into shower three times before he sat. He stared at her for a minute, then whined again. Pointing to the shower stall, Selene said, "Poop. Aw, hell." She stepped out of the latrine, closing the door behind her, and turned to the room and, covering her nose with her hand, found the pillow the dog had soiled. Holding her breath, she picked it up by one corner and took into the latrine.

She pushed the pillow toward the dog, imagining herself a master dog trainer. She'd taken courses when she got Spike, and he wasn't even a real dog. With Bentley, she was going to be perfect. She had to make him stop peeing on everything. *Or Grandfather will have both our heads.* Selene made the dog smell the pillow before dropping it into the shower and stepping from the room. As she closed the door behind her, Bentley started howling. Selene lifted her hands to cover her ears. *I'm sorry, Bentley. It's for your own good.*

After eating, Selene retrieved her dog and set off for the Lab. She saluted Able Seaman Tony as she entered, and waited for him to lead her to the classroom. When he had, he turned rigidly to stare at her. She knew he was sizing her up, determining whether she was going to continue pressing him for more information. *Just tell me. It'll be easier for you. But you've likely been ordered not to.* She sighed. *Was it Benson, or my grandfather?*

"What would you like me to learn today?" she asked. *You won't answer my questions, will you? I'll have to whittle away at you.* Tony was no dragon to hack at with a large weapon; she would have to strike fast, tearing at his resolve or slicing free what she could without his knowledge, and Cecile would take care of the rest. She wouldn't even have to listen to the answers. The program would record the information and compress it into an answer she could accept.

"Let's start with the different types of ships that dock," Able Seaman Tony replied as he pulled a small tablet from the desk he'd been using the day before. He passed the tablet to Selene.

He'd given her a lecture in her first session about the need to follow the established decorum. It didn't take her long to learn that decorum meant the enlisted officers' ingrained duty to answer any question a superior officer asked. But she couldn't order him to answer. *You've probably been ordered to lie to me, haven't you?* She'd have to intersperse her questions throughout their conversation before he realized what she was doing and refused to answer. Able Seaman Tony was smart. *Why else would they have him teach me?* It would be like dragging information from her father.

Selene wasn't sure how long it took. She learned that she had to pose her questions couched in some obscure thought. If the able seaman understood the reasoning, he would frown or shake his head and refuse to answer. He was quick to excuse himself from her presence if she pressed for an answer. Even her uncles came to his rescue, relieving him when his face turned red and he looked around the room, unwilling to meet her gaze. If Selene wasn't so determined to get her answers, she would have laughed at him for dancing around the classroom.

That night and on following nights, Selene delved into the recordings that Cecile had accumulated and pieced together the story. Most days she had to be careful to ensure that her grandfather didn't become aware of her questioning. *He'd kill me if he knew.* She was forced to borrow a small communications device like the one her Uncle Dallas wore. *They won't mind. I'll just take it back.*

On the day that she discovered the last vital piece of information, Selene wasn't even trying. Cecile's new recording device made it so easy to recall anything that Selene relied on it to record everything. One question after another she asked, until the able seaman was forced to excuse himself and bring back water to drink.

"Where is Orphan Station?" he asked.

Selene knew most of the answer, but the added flair that Cecile offered was enough to impress the man. "Orphan Station orbits the third planet of Alpha Centauri B, the second of two stars in the Alpha Centauri star system."

Able Seaman Tony nodded, the corners of his mouth twitching upward before relaxing. After a few seconds he asked, "What is the dark side?"

"During the station's orbit, we are exposed to the primary star's powerful radiation for two weeks out of eight," Selene replied as one of Benson's massive robots walked by Bentley's cage out in the Lab, drawing her eye.

Selene was surprised to hear Cecile's voice chirp in her ear, "That is partially correct." She held up her hand, smiling and nodding to the able seaman. "That's partially correct," she said, then parroted what the computer told her. "The radiation doesn't happen every cycle, however, because of the solar flare activity of AC prime. We cannot always determine which cycle will cause the phenomenon."

Selene wasn't sure whether he was more impressed with her ability to say the last word or her knowing it at all. He knew that she had access to further details whenever she wanted to, so it must have been the former. Regardless, she could see by his wide smile that he was impressed.

The computer continued in her ear. Narrowing her eyes, Selene said, "Two weeks is also just an approximation. The flares last for twenty-four to seventy-two hours, but they could happen at any time during the two weeks."

Clapping his hands together, the able seaman said, "That is impressive, Selene. You've learned more than I even thought possible. You're coming up with more gems than I give you. If you keep it up, I'll be learning from you."

Selene smiled at the man, feeling her chest swell at the encouragement. *I'll show you how good I am.* "Does the radiation penetrate the planet's atmosphere?" she asked.

"Sure it does," Tony replied. "We may experience the dark side for only two weeks, but the planet is constantly being bombarded with particles."

"So the pumping stations must be built with the same material that the second section of the Orphan is, then," Selene prompted. It made sense to her. What else would keep the pumps safe if someone was down there for repairs?

Nodding, Tony replied, "That's actually how we found out about the radiation. The first solar flares didn't start until about ten years ago. Hmmm, how do I explain this . . . Alright . . . Back on Earth they found out a long time ago that there is a cycle to the magnetic activity of the sun. Every eleven years the flares get stronger and reach out farther from the sun. Well, no one thought to run the calculations on the stars in this system. When we first got here there was no activity, but a decade or so later, a team down on the planet was hit by one of the solar flares." Frowning, he lowered his head.

Ten years? Her father had always said there was no such thing as a coincidence. If two events happened at the same time in the same place, then they were connected.

Her mother had died on the planet. She'd insisted that she be present on all major repair ventures because she'd designed the geo platform. Something happened when Robyn and a small group of engineers had gone down on a routine repair run. The group had been forced to stay on the planet for longer than scheduled. Savir blamed Captain Tulk for the event. He thought that Robyn should have returned rather than dallying, doing something for Captain Tulk.

"So where were they when it hit? How would they ever know the station was insulated from the radiation?" As soon as the words were out of her mouth, Selene realized her mistake, and what the response would be.

Able Seaman Tony closed his eyes, lips pursed, and saluted. Then, making a show of looking at his wristwatch, he said, "I must take my leave, ma'am. My shift starts in an hour and I need to eat."

It didn't matter. Someone had survived that storm, even though her mother had died from radiation exposure.

Lips trembling, she patted her front pocket. *Empty!* She moved her hand to her back pocket, then to the pouch strapped at her waist. Nothing. She caught her breath and checked her pockets again, tears welling in her eyes. Finally she stopped searching and dropped to the floor to pull off her shoe. She turned it upside down and a small blue package dropped out. Discarding the shoe, she snatched up the package, pried it open, then pushed two green pills into her mouth. Only then did she relax, releasing her pent breath. The pills were the only thing that kept someone safe. Her mother may not have known back then, but her father had. If her father had been on the planet, her mother would be alive.

Selene sighed and wiped the tears from her face. *Stupid seaman.* She crossed her arms. She didn't want to know any more. She didn't want to learn any more. Everything she learned gave her more information about her mother; information she didn't want anymore.

Her mother had died in the same way her father had—radiation. The radiation storm must have hit them while they were outside the station and only when they reached the shelter of the station itself did they figure out the terrible mistake. Then again, they could have gone to the shuttle or the substation. If the substation had given them even a little respite, then that would have been the correct decision.

Selene jumped down from her perch and went to collect Bentley from his pen. "Leading Seaman Davidson, can you help me with Bentley?" she asked an officer standing nearby.

"Sure, I can do—" The rest was lost to silence as the officer bent over the audio dampening unit.

As soon as Bentley was set on the floor, he sniffed at her legs, sensing her roiling emotions. He knew something was wrong. He could tell that she was struggling with the knowledge that her mother had died in absolute agony, like her father.

"That's why Grandfather wouldn't tell me," Selene whispered to herself as she led Bentley from the Lab. "I hate radiation. It takes everything. I wish it didn't exist. Godda—" Selene stopped. She wasn't a child anymore. She had to stop speaking like one. She couldn't let the other officers notice her. She had to be calm. "Come on, Bentley."

She marched from the Lab, her steps measured, meeting the eyes of the officers as she left. Out in the halls, she wandered, always keeping the sounds of activity within earshot. Whenever the hall emptied, she chose a path that would take her closer to officers occupied in their work. Ten steps left—*no*, nine steps left. *I'm taller. I'll have to recount all of my routes.* She sighed. She didn't want to make the same mistake in person that she had with the robot on the day of her initiation.

Seven hundred and sixty-five steps later, Selene arrived at the Fuel Room. She reached up for a gas mask, then muttered, "Shoot," and frowned down at Bentley. "There's no mask big enough for you. I don't want to leave you here, but I need to speak to Uncle Callum."

Shifting from one foot to the other, she surveyed the hall. Though some officers passed, no one came close to the Fuel Room. They wouldn't even approach to pet Bentley as he chased his own tail. The stench chased everyone away. *It is foul,* she thought as she covered her nose, then pulled on her gas mask.

"What am I going to do with you?" she asked the dog through her mask. No one could enter the Fuel Room without a mask and she couldn't leave the dog. He'd learned to mess in the shower stall or in his cage, but leaving him in the hall, even for a minute, wouldn't work; as soon as she was out of his sight, he would pee all over the floor. The only good thing then would be the overpowering smell of the fuel covering the odour. "Fine, I'll—"

Selene fell silent as the door swung open to allow an officer covered in grease to exit. As he passed, the man looked down at her and smiled. There was a second of hesitation before he snapped his heels together and saluted.

Hiding a smile, she glanced at the man's name tag. "I need your help, Seaman Jones."

The officer nodded. "Yes, ma'am. What can I do for you?" He glanced at Bentley and sighed.

The officer was the first man outside of the Lab that she'd come into contact with in her capacity as an officer. The man stood at rigid attention. His face didn't even twitch as he locked his gaze on her, waiting for her to speak. In that instant, Able Seaman Tony's words challenged her: *"Command isn't a right. It's earned, and the respect you garner has to be earned. Don't ever demand when all you need to do is ask."*

The words were in stark contrast to her Uncle Benson's behaviour. He'd spent ten minutes screaming at Seaman Poco. *Where was the respect in that?* Selene sighed. She knew better than to be so naive. Benson wasn't yelling at Poco because he was angry. Poco's transgression could have killed everyone on the station. He'd been told on more than one occasion. Benson was yelling as a last-ditch effort, and Poco had been sent to scrape the ground in the Farm because he couldn't be trusted with anything else. She may not have agreed with Benson's method, but the need was still the same.

With that in mind, she couldn't order Seaman Jones to watch Bentley. The dog was her responsibility, not his. "Seaman Jones, can you get Lieutenant Callum?"

The man's face relaxed. Nodding, he said, "I think he's just inside. I'll go get him."

As the man left, Selene called Bentley closer. When he approached, she draped herself over his back and began to pet his head. "Why are we here, Bentley? I told myself it didn't matter."

Seaman Jones didn't take long to find her uncle; he stepped out into the hall, reported his success, saluted, and moved off to his own duties. A few seconds later, her uncle joined her.

"Hello Sub-lieutenant," Callum said. He stood straight in an environmental suit, though he had removed his helmet. Selene could see the indicator light on the battery pack, indicating limited life.

"Hi, Uncle—er, Lieutenant Callum," Selene said as Bentley jumped up, trying to lick her face.

"It's okay, dear. You can call me whatever you want," Callum replied with a smile.

"Um, okay." Selene stepped forward. Her voice trembled as she asked, "Uncle Callum, I was in my lesson with Able Seaman Tony, but he had to leave. He was teaching me about the fuel system, but never finished. I thought it would be best just to ask you."

"I'm sorry dear, can we do it later?" He wiped a bead of sweat from his forehead.

Selene trembled as she glanced around the hall. She licked her lips before saying, "It won't take long."

"Oh, sure dear, but you'll have to be quick. I have to get back." Callum turned back to the hatch and pulled it shut, motioning for Selene to continue.

"We were talking about the shielding on the station and then he had to leave. I wanted to know whether the fuel needed to be shielded. I mean, I know it is shielded, but is that because of the fuel, or you working down here?"

"Oh," Callum said. He glanced away for a second. When he looked back, he cleared his throat. His cheeks twitched as he said, "This section is shielded for us, not the fuel. I wish I could get some metal from one of the planets, but the ships don't come back this way."

"Oh, okay. Oh, one more question—do you need all the pumping stations anymore? Grandfather said you didn't have as many ships anymore. So do you need the pumping stations?"

Shaking his head, Callum said, "Naw. We didn't even need that many when we gutted them years ago. I just didn't want to tax the system. It makes it easier on us now."

"So we have a lot stockpiled?" Selene pressed.

"Sure. I've been stockpiling it on the moons so we don't have to go down as much in case the pumps give out. We have enough to go at this rate for another five years, and everything points to a reduction in traffic, not an increase."

Selene glanced away and lowered her voice to ask, "One last question, Uncle. When . . . when my mother died in the pumping station, did . . . did she—"

The man sighed and locked his gaze on her. "Hold on, dear. Your mother died with honour. I'm glad Captain Tulk finally found fit to tell you how she died. I hated the way it happened."

"I—I . . ." Selene tried to speak, but fell silent.

Her uncle continued. "The pumping stations can't really house people, hon. When you're on the planet you can't just walk around like you are now. You have to wear these suits. When the team was waylaid, there were only enough resources for one person."

Eyes wide, Selene asked, "Someone lived?"

"Of course someone did. Wait, you didn't know that?" His eyes narrowed. "You have too many questions for someone who's been told. Who let out the secret?"

"It doesn't matter," Selene forced through her dry mouth.

Frowning, Callum said, "Loyal, if nothing else. You can thank both parents for that. Listen Selene, I never liked the way they kept the secret from you. You should have been told everything."

"Can you tell me?" Selene managed to ask. Bentley began to bark. Selene ignored him.

"It should be the captain, hon. I . . . I—"

"Please?" Selene blinked, and felt tears streaking down her cheeks.

Callum glanced toward the Fuel Room as if ready to bolt. After several seconds, he said, "Don't be angry when you go to the captain, Selene. He deserves more."

Selene nodded. "I promise."

Callum closed suddenly moist eyes as he said, "Your mother was supposed to be the one in the cubby hole. We all agreed that it would be her, but she had a different idea. I told her that she had to be the one. She had a child. She was the thread that kept the station together. She knew everything." He paused and looked down to fidget with the controls on his suit. When he spoke again, his tears flowed unabated. "She knew everything except what tolerances the material could handle. She couldn't test the fuel or run the refinery."

Selene stood staring at the man as she mouthed the words, "But you could."

Callum nodded. His breath caught, and he swallowed. "Y-y-yes, child," he said. "It was me. She sacrificed herself to keep me safe. I tried . . . I—"

"Why didn't you—" Selene fell silent as she realized the man was shaking. He'd done nothing. He'd been ordered to do nothing. Captain Tulk had made sure he would never tell. Her grandfather; her father, too. Everyone knew and refused to explain. *Goddamn you. I hate you.*

She knew her grandfather had gone to Able Seaman Tony's school of command and that was why her father had hated him. Her grandfather would have agreed with Robyn. He would have told Savir that he'd ordered Callum's survival so Savir would never question why Robyn would sacrifice herself and their future for him.

Momma . . .

Everything would be different if Robyn had lived and not Callum. Yes, her mother would be alive, but then they might all be dead. Her father would tell himself that they could have survived, could have come up with the solution. And if he knew the truth, then he would have given excuses for her sacrifice, but it still would have eaten at him, just as at one time it would have eaten at Selene. *Sacrifice. She's gone because of you, but you're the most important person here.* She stared at her uncle. He was the reason the station existed.

Selene retreated from Callum, her mouth hanging open. She was no politician, able to weave words into speeches. She had nothing to say. She walked backward until she hit the wall, refusing to release his gaze. As her back connected with the wall, she rocked forward until she could steady herself on Bentley's shoulder. Collecting her balance, she rushed off, her mind racing faster than her feet.

Chapter 9

"Sub-lieutenant Sotana to the Lab."

Startled by the page, Selene put her foot down out of time, and tumbled with a yelp to the floor.

Bentley sat down on his haunches several paces ahead, looking back as though waiting for her to join him. "Come on," he seemed to be saying. He was motionless and quiet, as if he knew the importance of remaining calm.

Selene motioned the dog toward her, saying, "Come here, Bentley." The dog jumped to his feet and ambled back to lick her face, oblivious to her agitation. He was as tall as she was, on her knees. "You are so big," she said, hugging the dog. "How old are you? You've grown *so* much."

Selene closed her eyes, doing her best to ignore the two subsequent summons from the intercom. *I don't want to go back there now.* She wanted nothing to do with the Lab. Her grandfather was there. He would have more excuses. *I have to think.*

She knew it was the right decision to send Callum back to the station. *He was the only one qualified, wasn't he?* But then, couldn't one of his officers do the same thing? Seaman Jones worked in the Fuel Room. Couldn't he learn to keep the fuel flowing? What did that do, anyway? But then, it wasn't about the fuel, was it?

Her mother had saved Callum for his knowledge of metals so he, in turn, could clad the station in the radiation-blocking metal from the pumping stations. She'd saved Callum so he could save Selene, because she couldn't do it. She hadn't abandoned Selene, she'd saved her. She'd loved her. *Maybe she's still down on the planet.* Her mother could have survived. She could be waiting down there for a rescue ship.

Tears flowed as Selene thought of her mother. She had spent her entire life idolizing Robyn, with Savir teaching her how special the woman was, how extraordinary. That didn't change the fact that Selene had questioned why she was gone. As a child, she'd hounded Savir with questions—why was she gone, why couldn't Selene see her? As the years passed, the questions faded.

The sense of abandonment didn't affect Selene until Savir joined her mother. There was no reason for her father to die. He'd chosen to apportion his share of the radiation pills to Selene. He'd chosen to step outside the shield during the dark side. He'd chosen to take so long, to leave Selene. And in the end, he'd chosen to keep Selene at arm's length when he died.

Shaking her head, Selene said, "No. He didn't choose like that. You didn't do that, did you, Father?"

He'd chosen to extend her life. At her age, Selene wouldn't have lived long enough, even with exposure limited by the shielding metal, to wait for the radiation pills to arrive. He had chosen to save her. Then he had chosen to leave the shielding to guide two injured officers behind the shield so their exposure was not prolonged. And in the end, he made the choice that kept her from seeing the terrible cost of his earlier choices.

Selene sighed and stood to march down to the Lab. The pages would stop soon, but then two very large officers would run through the halls calling her name. They wouldn't make the same mistake again.

Selene shrugged, thinking, *At least they're trying.* It might be a little overbearing, but at least they were trying to keep her safe. Obviously the reaction was more immediate because at least one ship was docked at the station, but that didn't change their intentions.

When she reached the Lab, Selene bent to push Bentley through the hatch. He didn't need much help anymore and, given his size, she wasn't much help. He was getting too heavy for her to carry.

The Lab was full of bustling officers rushing in every direction, far more than usual for one typical shift. Selene could see most of her uncles were present, though she couldn't see her grandfather. Benson stood on the far side of the Lab doling out orders to a group of his engineers, while Dallas spoke in a hushed tone to the computer techs and system operators in the operations room beyond. Even her tiny Uncle Hourev was in the room, though Selene could only hear the man's rumbling voice, not see him. She'd never seen this many officers in one room. During their light side rotations there was enough room on the station that she could explore for hours and never see a soul, and most spent the dark side in their quarters or the games room.

Selene supposed that in the first years of the station, this was a typical shift. With over thirteen hundred officers, they would have been tripping over each other. *Then again*, Selene thought, *they likely would have been spread through those sections of the station that have been closed off for years. And from what Uncle Callum said, they weren't tied to this room for years until the solar activity increased.* "They probably didn't know about it for a while," she murmured.

"What was that, hon?" Her Uncle Sasha was at her side. Beads of sweat rolled down his face and his eyes were as wide as if he'd just witnessed Death himself walking through the halls. He didn't wait for an answer. Lifting a trembling hand, he guided Selene toward the classroom. Once there, he glanced back toward the bustle before telling her, "You . . . you 'ave to stay in ze Lab for a while."

"Why, Uncle Sasha? I've been here all day," she said. He didn't make her angry anymore. Not since he'd given her Bentley.

"There's been a terrible—" Sasha fell silent as a violent spasm rocked the station. The desks in the room shifted sideways. Her uncle's strong arm sweep Selene into an embrace.

Selene peeked over the man's shoulder. Although prepared for the onslaught, the officers in the main hall were scrambling back to their feet. Equipment had been thrown all around like a giant whirlwind had torn through the Lab.

"Hold on," Sasha said before swearing in his native language.

As he spoke, Selene felt the floor give way again. *What's happening? Are we falling toward the planet?* She drew quick, shallow breaths as her uncle's arm tightened across her chest.

"Alright, people," Benson called over the din of voices. "Here's the deal. I want Alpha team securing the bay. Get what you can out of there. Beta, make sure those people get evacuated from the ship. I don't want any heroics. Get in and get out. Omega, make sure the other ships are secure. We can't have any chain explosion or we'll all be up in smoke. Davis? Where the hell is Davis? Someone get me that medic—or just tell him he'll be receiving injured in about ten minutes."

Selene stared at the officers shifting around each other before jogging from the room. *They're wearing oxygen tanks.* They were going to a low O$_2$ area. *A ship?*

"Selene?" Benson called as he stepped away from his officers.

Selene moved toward him, Sasha at her heels. She saluted, then shifted back on her heels to await Benson's instructions.

"Get into your cubicle, Selene," her uncle said. There was no smile on his face. He wasn't even looking in her direction. "I need eyes and ears in the fifth hangar bay. We'll turn on the bot when you get settled." He was already moving, finishing the last sentence from five paces away.

Selene froze at the prospect of sitting in that seat again. She hadn't practised. Kneading her hands, she looked toward the cubicle. *Please, no. How can you ask me that?* Sitting in that chair had started it all. If she hadn't been in the chair, she wouldn't have broken the robot. She wouldn't have run from the room. Jameson wouldn't have found her or killed Spike.

"Go, Selene." The harsh tone shook Selene from her reverie. Benson stared at her, the blood throbbing in the veins at his temples. He frowned and pointed at the cubicle. "Move, Sub-lieutenant."

Selene stood blinking. Her vision blurred as tears formed. She wiped her eyes, and saw her Uncle Benson in front of her. He leaned forward, towering over her, and his nostrils flared as he spoke. "Selene, I don't have time for excuses or fear. Those people need our help and I can't have any mistakes. I need you to do it because I know you can. Please don't—"

The rest of his words were lost to the cacophony of another explosion. Though Selene managed to keep her footing, officers around the room were thrown to the floor. She glanced to Bentley's cage, saw him already pacing, agitated, around its perimeter. *I have to help. You'll be okay, boy.*

No one else could run the robots as well as she could. She was the only person who could save the ship. *But what ship am I saving?*

Selene took a deep breath, nodded to her uncle, and stepped toward the cubicle. Her heart was pounding so hard, she couldn't hear the officers around her as they offered their encouragement. The door loomed, looking as ominous in her imagination as a dragon ready to breathe fire. With every step, Selene's breathing quickened. *Stupid robots.* She shivered as she crossed the threshold into the belly of the beast. She had been swallowed whole by her mythical dragon, and everything was going dark. Was that the creaking of chains? No, just the seat shifting toward her.

"Can I help you in, Sub-lieutenant? Sub-lieutenant?"

Selene looked up and blinked several times, unable to focus on the officer. *Who the hell are you?* She knew the man, but something was different. He'd grown a beard. *Oh, you*—the officer who'd helped her into the seat the first time. The flesh around his eyes looked bruised, as if he hadn't slept in a week, and his hair was in disarray.

Selene pulled herself into the seat and waited for the officer to strap her down. *I'm doing the right thing. I have to do this.* She closed her eyes, and the tension melted from shoulders. She hated the machine, not because it had led to the worst . . . the second-worst . . . the third-worst day in her life, she told herself, but because it didn't fit right. The seat made her skin itch, and when she tried to scratch her shoulder, she couldn't reach past the steel framework of her chair.

The officer stepped back after placing and attaching the last few pieces of equipment. "I'll be on the other line, Sub-lieutenant," he said. "I'm not sure I'll have the answers, but don't hesitate to ask any questions."

Selene nodded, then let the visor fall down over her face. She waited for the darkness to coalesce into an image of the fifth hangar bay. That was the last bay meant for medium-sized vessels. *It isn't a big room.* The image flickered.

"What's happened?" Selene asked. She could hear the tramp of boots as a group of officers passed by the cubicle.

"There was an explosion on one of the incoming ships and they couldn't slow down. We've tried to contain the damage, but we won't know the whole story until we can get the crew off the ship." The voice came calm and measured, as if this was no more than a training exercise.

Selene covered her mouth, realizing too late what that would do to the robot. Her chair rocked back and forth as the robotic arm connected with what approximated a face. Sighing, she let the arm drop. *I have to do this right. One step at a time.* She'd learned her lesson once already.

She had to take her steps slowly. She had to measure them. *I have to know how long my step is.* Selene stared at the floor as she took a step forward. *Four feet.* The robot was similar to the one she'd used before, but she was closer to the floor. *Shorter.* She seemed to go farther with each step, however. She couldn't think about that, though; screams filtered through her radio. "Where do I go?"

"You're going to go down the hall to the left from the bay," her guide reported.

As requested, Selene lifted her legs to move the machine forward. By the time she'd taken her tenth step, she had the robot walking ponderously down the hall.

Wisps of haze wafted across her field of vision. *What the hell is that?* Smoke—she'd walked into a plume of smoke. She looked down; red-orange flames licked at her feet and raced along the hulls of several of the docked ships.

Pushing debris from her path, Selene crept closer to the last ship. Flames billowed from its underside, at the point where it had careened into the station. It was large, but not like one of the arks. "An Ottawa class," she whispered to herself, recognizing the design.

"Yes," the guiding officer replied, as though she had queried him. "There are two thousand people on the ship."

Two thousand? Are they still alive? Selene stopped as flames boiled around her like liquid. This wasn't a game any longer. Benson had yelled at her because this was real. He trusted her to make it possible for the firefighters to enter the room. *Two thousand. I have to save them.*

Shifting her robot's gaze around the bay, Selene asked, "Can we turn on the vents to evacuate the smoke?"

"The ship hit really hard," her guide replied. "We're having difficulty doing anything. You may even have to open the bay doors so they don't have to cut through them."

Selene took a deep breath and walked her robot toward the bow of the ship. She swallowed the bile that rose in her throat when she saw the ship's nose, crumpled as if a great hand had crushed it like it was an overcooked pea. Cracks ran the length of the ship on both sides, and the windows had been blown inward. Fire spewed from several ports. Molten steel and plastic dripped to form large pools on the floor of the bay. "Can . . . can you see this?" Selene asked after swallowing again.

"Okay, Sub-lieutenant, I need you to see if you can engage the ship's door mechanism. The people are ready to disembark, but we need to make sure they can get through without being burned."

It took several minutes for Selene to navigate through the debris to the dented and battered door. "Son of a—" *How the hell can I open that?* There was no way to shift the door aside.

After several silent seconds, a voice said, "The station first, Sub-lieutenant. The oxygen levels are depressed in the bay. The fire might go out then, but they won't have anything to breathe in the meantime."

Selene reversed the robot until she could turn and push the robot through debris field to the double doors leading to the hall. Though blackened by fire, they'd remained unmarked by the debris lying before them. But no lights blinked at the terminal beside them.

Selene grabbed the handle on the sliding door and pulled to test the seal. Finding it responsive, she said, "I'm ready."

"Hold for a second, Se—Sub-lieutenant," Uncle Benson said in her ear. "We're having difficulty closing the main doors."

Selene thought for a second before asking, "Can I close the door?"

"I doubt it, kiddo," Benson replied. "That ship did a number on the door. I'm not even sure if one of the doors is attached anymore. Can you swivel you cameras to look beyond the ship?"

Selene turned her head, focusing the cameras on the doors. The billowing smoke obscured her vision for several seconds, until it wisped apart long enough to make what lay beyond visible.

Benson sighed. "That's not going to work. Those doors aren't going to close. We have people working on getting around to the doors from the fourth bay, but they aren't going to be there fast enough. We have to evacuate the people without losing them to lack of oxygen. Any suggestions?" Selene imagined the man rubbing his palms against his eyes.

"Can we tie them together?" Selene asked. That way they wouldn't fly off, even if the vacuum of space pulled at them. A thought that made Selene shiver.

"Sure, if you have a two-mile-long cord," someone replied from the operations deck.

Stupid, she berated herself. *I should have known better.* She looked around the bay, seeking ideas.

"You don't need to tie them all together at once," someone else offered. "The Sub-lieutenant could ferry them to the doors."

There was silence for a moment before Benson said, "Selene, clear a path, and don't waste any time at it. The stuff is junk anyway."

Selene plotted her path to the ship. Shrugging to lift her robot's arms, she shifted them back and forth to clear a direct path. Sparks flew as she hammered at the debris, tossing it aside. When she was finished, the pounding in her ears abated and she could hear soft screams coming from the ship. She gasped. *They're alive.*

"It's okay, Selene. We hear them too. They'll be okay until we can get you started," Benson whispered.

Flames still flickered along the ship as if performing a tantalizing dance. Wisps floated into the air, then pulled back as if drawn by force. Most of the smoke was being sucked toward the rear of the bay, where the large doors stood askew.

Selene wiped the sweat beading on her forehead, whispering, "Damn, it's hot." She knew it couldn't be true, but the seat itself felt warmer. Her imagination showed the flames licking at her legs and arms as though she were ablaze. Was it possible for her mind to play such a cruel trick that she was burned through her imagination? "Damn it, that's hot."

The radio emitted static for several seconds, but muffled voices filtered through the cubicle wall. *What's your problem? What are you angry at now? Is it me?* Selene thought as she recognized her Uncle Benson's voice. He did say that he didn't want to hear her whining. He'd already warned her. *Maybe he's going to take over.*

As her thoughts wandered, Selene felt the warmth fade from her seat. *Oh, thank God.* She could conquer her imagination. *I can do it.*

Benson's voice came soft in her ear. "Alright Selene, the passengers have ropes; all you have to do is grab them and get them over to the hatch. Can you do that?"

Selene nodded, then waited for Benson to respond. After a few seconds, she rolled her eyes and said, "Yes sir."

"Good. Now take a test run. You'll be doing it a lot, so get used to the feel."

Selene practised the manoeuvre twice, placing her foot then running toward the door. On the second trip, she looked at the growing flames with a sudden flash of panic. She was going to burn. *These people will die.* The flames had engulfed the top of the ship; rivulets of fire flowed around her feet. *How can they survive this?* The passengers would have to hold their breath as they passed through a wall of flame. Could anyone hold their breath longer than fifteen seconds? It would be longer if they had no air lock on their ship.

"Okay, Selene, everything is in place. Get to the ship door and start moving those people. I'm going to get the other bot ready—"

Selene snapped her head up at the mention of a second robot. *Why am I doing this alone?* It would go faster if there was a second robot. They could pass the passengers from one robot to another without moving. On her return trip, however, Selene understood why it wouldn't work. *There's no room.* A second robot present wouldn't leave her any room to move if she had to, and she couldn't waste any time when the doors of the ship opened.

As if on cue, the door opened when Selene arrived. She could hear the screams and sobbed supplications emanating from the opening, some calling for help, others calling for a quick death. *How can I save them all? Why am I doing this? Oh God, I can't do this.*

"Don't think about it, Selene," the calm voice said in her ear. "Just start running and don't stop."

Did I say that out loud? Selene thought as she glanced around. Then she reached out and collected a rope, having to wrap it around her hands twice so it wouldn't slip through. She took the thirteen steps she practised to the door, slammed to a stop, and swung her arms forward to release the latch on the door. Several officers lunged through and grabbed the rope. Selene stepped aside to let them pull the passengers through. *Oh my God,* she thought. The first two passengers clearly had broken legs while the others had various other injuries. *Were they that way when we started? I . . . I don't think so. Did I do it?*

As soon as the thought crossed her mind, Benson said, "That's not going to work. They weren't prepared enough."

Selene lifted her hand to her earpiece and whispered, "Cecile. Access and replay footage from the cargo robot in docking bay five on this system."

There was no audible recognition from the computer, but the screen on the visor flickered to show the robot dragging the passengers. As soon as they entered the oxygen-depressed bay, the passengers began to struggle. The first two were standing in the beginning, but with the lack of oxygen, they locked their feet and toppled to the floor. The last two tumbled from the ship and were dragged the distance, flames licking at their clothing. Selene's stomach lurched. *It WAS me.* "They . . . they can't . . . "

"Alright, people. Come up with something, quick. Those people are going to suffocate."

Selene heard the officers speaking in the distance, careful to converse away from the microphone. Most called for more discipline in the passengers, but the passengers' haunted looks were enough to tell Selene it wouldn't work. No amount of discipline was going to solve spacewalking without a suit. "At least they'd be floating in space," she whispered to herself.

"Sorry, what was that, Sub-lieutenant?"

They had to get their feet off the ground, but carrying them wasn't an option. She didn't have enough arms to heft them all. She couldn't even carry half as many people as she'd pulled on the ropes. "Um, is it possible to get them off the ground?"

"No," one officer began. "We have to—"

"Why can't we? All we have to do is cut the gravity in that section," another officer cut in.

"That section includes the hall where our officers are stationed. They won't be able to move either," Benson said. His voice was strained and his breathing was laboured; he must still be trying to set up the equipment for the other bot.

"Who cares? All we have to do is get the people out of the bay. The sub-lieutenant could rocket them from the bay faster than we could pull them. She wouldn't have to move if her aim was accurate. We'll just tie ourselves off." It must have been one of the officers waiting outside the bay who spoke.

"Okay Selene, this is what you have to do," Benson said after a moment. His breathing had stabilized. "Stackhouse will turn on the magnetic locks for your feet. All you have to do is keep hold of the ropes. And Selene, do it fast or they'll be sucked toward the bay doors."

Selene shivered as she took a deep breath. *Spaced.* She held her breath for several seconds, until her lungs began to burn and stars danced across her vision. She could understand if the passengers were afraid of being sucked into space. She wouldn't want her blood to boil and her insides to be sucked out through her nose and ears. It was the only fate worse than dying of radiation poisoning.

When the rope was passed to her a second time, Selene launched the passengers toward the far wall. They floated for less time than it took her to run the distance, until the officers wearing oxygen masks caught and pulled them in. She tensed, waiting for the last passenger to cross the threshold. *Please make it,* she thought, then realized that the lack of gravity made the manoeuvre easy. She glanced back to the ship. *Is there any gravity in there at all?* They seemed comfortable flying through the air. *At least something is working right,* she thought as the robot Selene operated responded sluggishly. It had taken a beating. *It's as if it's as tired as I am.* The floor around her was slick with oil as hydraulic lines burst from the heat. The smoking oil also clouded her vision.

Selene lost count at around the fiftieth group, even that count being questionable, given the increasing number of slack bodies that were tied to the ropes. Though the strength of her robot moved the limp forms as though they were weightless, she wasn't sure whether they were conscious or not. They could have been tied up for hours and then died. It was even possible that their lifeless bodies had been tied up out of respect for the dead.

"Selene, we've lost contact with the ship," Benson said in her ear.

With her own robot barely operating, Selene had to wonder where the second robot had gone. If nothing else, they could replace her robot with a fresh one to speed up the process. *Maybe he couldn't get it past the fires. Who knows,* Selene thought.

Selene bent down to one knee so she could look into the ship. There were no more ropes. "I don't see anyone."

"It's okay, kiddo. I'm surprised you can see anything," Benson said.

As he spoke, Selene felt a firm grasp on her shoulder. *What the hell is that?* She cringed away, pulling her visor off. *Oh.* She scowled at the technician until he stepped away. *Thank you,* she thought, pulling the remaining straps off and dropping them to the floor. She coughed several times, then stood, rubbing her legs. She nodded to the technician that he should lead the way from the cubicle.

Selene emerged to hear her uncle asking someone, "How is it going down there, Jacobs?"

"So far so good, sir, but the hall is so full of smoke that we can't see everyone. The last few ropes ignited as the sub-lieutenant tossed them, so we lost a couple of the passengers. We've managed to collect all but ten; they're too far away. We can see them, but without any gravity it's going to be impossible to get them. Can we . . . ?"

Benson lowered his head. "I'm sorry, Jacobs. The gravity isn't just a switch. We won't have gravity there for a couple days. Is—"

Another explosion rocked the station. Selene didn't have to ask to know the remaining fuel in the ship had ignited. It wouldn't take long for the flames to engulf the other ships. She also knew that those drifting passengers would be dead soon, if they weren't already.

Benson gripped the edge of his desk so hard, his knuckles had turned white. "Jacobs, are you there?"

There was static for several seconds before the officer replied, "Sorry, sir. I . . . We have to evacuate. There're maybe eight or ten people at the far end of the hall, but that explosion just ruptured a large hydraulic pipe between us and them. It's gonna blow."

Pounding the table with both fists, Benson shouted, "Get out! Don't—" He fell silent as they heard the screams of the stranded passengers.

Selene knew those halls were dangerous; she'd been playing in them for years. But now it was no imaginary dragon setting fire to the entire section. There was nothing the officers could do if those pipes were spewing burning oil down between them. They couldn't get around to another hall. The only way to the bay was through the utility halls, but no one was small enough to navigate them. "Uh, Lieutenant Benson, can you show me where exactly they are?"

The technician working at the terminal beside Benson turned and looked up at her, shaking his head. "I can't, Sub-lieutenant. All I can say is that they're down the corridor, just outside the bay door."

The tears streaming down her face did little to make Selene look like an officer. She knew that if she stepped up to say she could save the passengers, she would be disregarded. There was a limit to their belief in her. At best they would pat her on the head and tell her to run along—and that was assuming they were gracious because of what she'd just done. They would think her foolish enough to still want to try, and get herself killed in the process.

Staring at her uncle for several seconds, she asked, "Uncle Benson, can I go lie down?"

"Sure, kiddo. You've done a great job," he replied, then he began pacing. He didn't look her way or notice her wave at Bentley as she rushed from the Lab.

Chapter 10

Selene burst through the Lab door and careened down the hall, falling twice, once when she bounced off of an officer rushing in the opposite direction. Not all of those she passed were the station's officers. Those who weren't tried to stop her, but she ignored them and rushed on. Most wouldn't understand how a child could have so much energy. The children coming off the ships were lethargic, having just awakened from the deep sleep of cryostasis. They'd think she should be in the Medical Bays or the Mess, not rushing through the halls shouting for everyone to clear a path. *Screw 'em.* It didn't matter what they thought. She had more important things to worry about. She had to save those passengers.

She had less than ten minutes to get from one side of the station to the darkest section, and most of that would be by moving through the utility halls. Perhaps those onlookers would think her a ghost of one of the children that had died on the ship she'd just evacuated. *Let 'em. Maybe they'll be scared. Move, goddamnit!*

There was no need to search out the darkened section. As she crossed the threshold, Selene realized her mistake. "Oh, crap." She should have realized the flickering emergency lights were a harbinger of danger. Instead, she was thrown into the air as she stepped into the section without gravity.

"Hey kid, what are you doing? You should be down with the others," a man wearing a full environmental suit said as he approached, pulling himself along on the pipes as he floated, weightless. When he reached Selene, his eyes widened. "Oh, I'm sorry, Sub-lieutenant," he said, "but you really shouldn't be here. This section has—"

Shaking her head, Selene cut him off. "I don't have time to talk, Seaman. Help me back out." Not waiting for his response, she pushed off the officer to land on the edge of the powered section. As soon as she touched down, Selene rushed back to the closest accessway to the utility halls. Time was running short. If the passengers had any oxygen, the flames were going to steal it.

Throwing open the access panel, she climbed into a hall so constricted, it felt like a tomb. The ceiling felt closer and the floor farther away as she clambered down its length. She could almost touch both sides with her outstretched arms. As she travelled, Selene tried to envision the station layout in her mind. "I should have brought my tablet," she muttered, shaking her head. She was on the eighth spoke, the least used section on the station. That didn't matter, however; her mother had designed them symmetrically.

"Fourteen," Selene said as she took off down the hall. She counted her steps as she ran: ". . . eleven, twelve, thirteen." Her count came to an abrupt halt as her head connected with a low-hanging bulkhead. She fell to the floor and rolled, groaning, for several seconds as stars floated across her vision.

When she opened her eyes, the pain lancing through her forehead made her stomach lurch. She threw up. Stars sparkled in the darkness, as if she were in the dead of space. *Did the station blow?* An explosion could have split the hall in half, pulling her into the void. Her last action might be watching as her insides were sucked out of her. *I can't hold my breath long enough. They'd never find me.*

She wriggled around to locate the station and recognized the hard floor underneath her. *I haven't gone anywhere.* She wasn't going to die from having her insides yanked through her mouth. Still, she felt a chill that made her tremble, though it washed the tension away. She smiled as the pain surged back into her forehead. "Well, I feel it, so I must be alive." Selene brushed her hand across her forehead; it came away slick with blood. *It hurts. Oh God, that hurts.* Her vision blurred as she pushed up to her knees, then winced and fell forward. Gritting her teeth in determination, Selene crawled up the wall and set off at a ragged trot, seeing everything in double vision.

At the end of the next hall, not far from where she'd injured herself, she came to the dead section. Now she was able to swim along this narrower hall like the officer she'd encountered in the main hall, quickly reaching the entrance to the fifth bay. There she paused and pressed the button on the radio in her ear. Taking a deep breath, she said, "Cecile, can you contact the Lab?"

The radio crackled for a few seconds before Benson said, "Selene? Selene? Where in the nine hells are you?"

I can't deal with your crap now, Uncle, Selene thought. She was having enough trouble keeping herself from puking. "I am down in—"

Benson didn't let her finish. "What in the nine hells are you doing, Sub-lieutenant?" he shouted. "I just had an officer tell me he passed you down on—no, I don't care. Turn your ass around and get back here. *Move*, goddamn you, before I come down there and drag you back. Are you listening to me Selene?" Benson sputtered. She imagined him dripping with sweat, his eyes spinning like tops as he glared at the officers around him.

Selene sighed. "Yes, Lieutenant, I am. I can hear you perfectly."

"Good. Now, Sub-lieutenant Sotana, *get your ass back here. Now!*" Benson said through gritted teeth. Selene was sure she heard one of his teeth crack.

Shaking her head as if the man could see her, Selene said, "I can save them."

"No, Selene, you can't. They're already dead. And in about thirty seconds they're going to spread out over the entire deck. *Get back here*." His voice was hoarse.

"I can save them. All I have to do is open the door and reach out. I—"

"Listen to me, Selene. The fire is spreading through everything. If you open that door, we're through. The flames will enter that hall and climb through the wiring. Please, don't."

Selene knew that her uncle was only trying to keep her safe. Opening the door would fan the flames until they evacuated the air on the deck. She wouldn't be in any more danger than she was right now. *You're just making it up.* Snorting, she wondered how her uncle was going to react when he saw the gash on her head. *Grandfather is going to kill me.*

"You are not a hero . . . "

The words alone were enough to raise Selene's ire. Benson was right. She was no hero. What she planned wasn't heroism. She was going to save these people because they deserved it, and those officers weren't capable. But even if Benson wanted to talk semantics, perhaps he should talk to her parents.

"Everyone seems determined to keep the fact secret that both my parents died doing the right thing," she replied. "You may consider their actions heroic, but I don't. I resent them for dying. I resent them for their choices. And I resent myself for understanding why they did it. I am not sacrificing my life. I am doing the right thing. If you stood in this hall with me, with those passengers on the other side of the wall, I know you'd do it too. So please, don't lecture me on heroics."

It was the first time that Selene had admitted to herself, let alone anyone else, that her parents weren't just around the corner. In the beginning, being "gone" meant living on one of the planets. She'd been shielded from the worst by her father at first, then by her grandfather and uncles. Her parents were gone—dead—never to return.

Selene balled her fists. *I guaran-goddamn-tee that you wouldn't be here, though. You'd send one of your lackeys. Stupid, stupid, stupid.*

"I am not lecturing you on heroics, Selene. I am lecturing you on following orders," Benson said, so quietly that Selene wondered if he'd even said it. "Return to the Lab so we can save the—"

The rest of his speech was lost to the vacuum as Selene reached around to hammer the latch for the door. With a loud clang, the door swung outward to reveal the flames beyond. The air rushed around her, the heat almost unbearable. She yelped as her skin sizzled. *Bloody hell, that's hot!*

The smoke had dissipated a degree as it was sucked into the hangar bay. It wafted over a dozen bodies strewn about the bay. Although some shifted, most were still. Some of the bodies were charred, their clothing hanging in tatters. The rope was in ruins. *What the hell?* she thought as she realized there was gravity in small sections of the bay. *Did they reset it somehow?*

Selene blinked as her breathing accelerated. *So light-headed. Need oxygen.* Eyes wide, she reached back into hall and groped across the floor until her hand closed on a small tank of oxygen. She pulled it toward her, staring at the words *For Dragon Hunting* written in white paint on both sides before pulling the mask over her face. She cranked the clasp to release the gas, sighed deeply, and stepped into the bay.

The soles of her shoes sizzled as they touched the searing-hot grating. Ignoring the heat rising through her shoes, she pulled the closest bodies into the utility hall, moving easily in the lighter gravity, leaving them in a pile just inside the door. There was just enough gravity to keep them grounded.

By the time she began pulling the last woman toward the hatch, Selene was only managing to move her a few inches at a time. The farther from the hatch she travelled, the heavier the gravity seemed to get. Her oxygen tank pulled at the straps around her shoulders. *They must have done something with the gravity.* Everything was so hot.

"You have to move, Selene. We have to evacuate the air in less than a minute. Please hurry. We . . . we can't wait for you." Benson's voice had changed; now he pleaded with her to complete her task.

Her breathing was shallow as she tugged again at the woman. A glance down confirmed that the woman was still alive, but not for long. The woman's face was blistered and her hair had been singed to within an inch of her scalp. Another inch . . .

The heels of her shoes burned through. With a scream, Selene fell to her knees, then struggled to stand, her eyes stinging with tears. The pain in her forehead was nothing compared to the boiling skin on her feet.

Another inch. *Goddamn you woman, lose some weight.* Her feet felt as if she were walking on sharp spikes, and her pants were stuck to her knees like they were glued. She tried another tug, and screamed again.

"Give me her hand," a stern voice said beside her. One of the passengers held out his burned hands to take hold of her charge. She nodded, passed the woman's arms to him, then moved to lift her legs over the bulkhead.

"Close the door," someone called out.

"No," Selene replied, shaking her head. The flames had breached the utility halls and were licking at their heels. If they closed the hall on this end now, the flames would spread to the rest of the station.

Selene hiccupped for a second before saying, "We . . . we have to leave."

Though they were isolated in the utility hall, the passengers weren't faring well. Half of them wouldn't be able to walk on their own and two weren't moving at all. Their dull eyes stared at her as though mocking her inability to work fast enough. *I wish I had the strength of a robot. Then you'd all see.*

"Air—I need air," one of the passengers gasped, pulling at Selene's legs.

Selene nodded and took a deep breath before removing her oxygen mask. She knelt, blinking her tears away, and placed it over his face. "Breathe normally," she whispered. She held it in place for five seconds, then pulled the mask back and moved to the next prone form. As she pulled the mask away she helped each person to stand and pushed them away from the docking bay entrance.

"Move, Selene, *move!*" Benson shouted.

Selene's clothing ruffled and she felt the air being sucked out behind her. She shuffled forward, but her legs buckled, her knees unable to support her weight anymore. It didn't matter—there was no more gravity. Selene was able to pull herself forward. She bent to pull at one of the still forms, but a steady hand appeared on her shoulder and she was pushed away toward the hall. *Dead,* the gesture told her.

As they came to the bend in the hall, the last woman Selene had dragged from the deck turned to her and asked, "Wh-who are you? Are you an angel?" The woman wasn't dressed like most of the passengers, but in a black uniform.

Selene glanced at the others in sudden realization. "You're all from the crew," she whispered.

"Keep moving, Seaman," the man who'd helped Selene earlier said. "Keep your head down as you go through here."

You must have your own radio, Selene thought as he took control of the situation. He was the ranking officer, accustomed to giving orders. He would keep them moving.

Though the flames didn't move as quickly as Selene and the ship's officers, the air was warming up. When they reached the section with gravity, the officers were forced to crawl. A dozen medical officers waited as they emerged into the light. Without asking, each team of two bent to drag one of the ship's officers to a stretcher. They trotted off without worrying about the others, their attention focused on their patients. *They must be from the ships,* Selene thought, staring at the medical officers. Every ship with cryotubes had to have a dozen or more doctors ready to help the passengers when they woke. They were the first to wake and the first to go through the thaw.

The last officer was dragged away, leaving her grandfather and two of her uncles staring from Selene to the officers disappearing through the halls. When they looked back down at her, their faces were flushed deep red, and her grandfather stood with his arms crossed; he looked like he was holding his breath.

Captain Tulk opened his mouth several times as if about to speak, then simply knelt and hugged her. He tried to stand twice before returning to his knees for another embrace. When he did at last stand, he turned away, his cheeks glistening. His hand came up to swipe at his face before he looked back, nodded to Callum and Benson, then marched off, his hands balled into fists. Not once had he met Selene's gaze. Her heart skipped as he left. *Where are you going, Grandfather? Why won't you speak to me?*

As he turned the corner, another medical officer arrived. The man saluted then stood at attention until acknowledged before kneeling beside Selene to tend her injuries. He looked up twice, about to speak, each time lowering his gaze. *Don't speak,* Selene thought, shaking her head. Wincing as the man pressed gauze to her face, Selene said, "What's going on?"

Silence met her question as the man focused on stanching the flow of blood. He retrieved a needle and thread from his kit and wordlessly sewed up the gash on her forehead.

There's no pain, Selene thought. The technician must have laced the gauze with medication. How else could the pain disappear? It had been real.

She reached out to steady herself as her vision blurred, then glanced up as Dallas said, "You are dismissed, Lieutenants." Selene shuddered. *Where did you come from?*

Like her grandfather, Benson refused to look at Selene before marching away. His face had turned dark red, and sweat ran down his temples. He was shaking. *What's wrong with you?* Selene thought. Callum was gone in the other direction before Selene could even look at him. Something was happening between her uncles that they weren't telling her.

Both had vanished when a pair of MPs from Ray's office arrived. She caught her breath. *Police? What the hell is this?* Perhaps they'd found the person who'd caused the crash. If that was the case, the MPs would have to detain the person. *That's it,* she thought, nodding.

"Sub-lieutenant Sotana," Dallas said as he turned to Selene. Still unable to stand on her blistered feet, Selene looked up at him. His frown had deepened and his cheeks trembled, but his eyes looked through her. Not waiting for the medical officer to finish, he said, "Sub-lieutenant Sotana, do you have anything to say to the charge of disobeying a direct order?"

"Well, Uncle Dallas—" Selene began, but the man cut her short with a wave of his hand.

"Listen to me, Selene, this is no joking matter. Did you or did you not disregard Benson's direct order?" Dallas's eyes were puffy; he looked like he was about to burst into tears.

"Well, I . . ." Selene fell silent. After several seconds, she said, "I . . . I did ignore his orders and I would do it again, if it meant saving those people."

Unable to meet her eyes, Dallas said, "Sub-lieutenant, you are hereby remanded into police custody until further notice. You are charged with willingly and knowingly disregarding the orders of a superior officer and willfully putting the safety of this station and the souls aboard at risk."

"What are you talking about, Uncle Dallas? I saved those people," Selene said. She turned her head to look at the two MPs. *I saved them.* "I saved them." Her mother had disregarded orders to keep Callum safe. Her father had left the safety of the shield to save those officers. Selene had just done what she knew was right. She hadn't done anything wrong.

"You . . . you don't understand," Dallas said through gritted teeth. "It is my fault this happened. I thought that if we treated you like any other member of the crew, then you would embrace it and become assimilated. But you aren't an adult. You don't understand the things you need to."

"I . . . I don't understand, Uncle Dallas," Selene said. Tears traced down her cheeks and she hiccupped. He didn't have to be formal while he made her feel like dirt. He didn't have to try so hard. *Are you enjoying this?*

"Don't you get it, Selene? You left the door on this side open. The reason you weren't sucked into that vacuum was because it would have sucked us in, too. You should be dead. Benson had to order that. You made him make that choice so he could save the entire crew and then you put him in a position where it wouldn't have even mattered. The only thing that saved you was the heroism of those officers *ordered* out onto the hull of the station to repair the port doors. They are the heroes because they followed orders. You . . . you . . . "

Looking up at his face as he sputtered, Selene said, "I should be dead?" Her shoulders slumped and she looked at the floor. *Dead? Why did you say that? I saved them. I did that.* She'd also left the door open. She'd left a link to the rest of the station. She'd broken the hermetic seal. She'd been the one to cause so much trouble. If they hadn't noticed it or if she hadn't called them at the last second, then the whole station would have been ejected into space. Four thousand souls would have been traded away for her stupidity.

Turning to the MPs, Dallas said, "Take her to her room. The captain will be there soon."

Spasms wracked Selene's body as the two MPs bent to lift her by the elbows. The medic raced to finish wrapping her feet with the gauze before they set off toward her quarters.

Selene ground her teeth, wondering if they would even have waited for the man to finish, if he'd continued at his normal pace. *Probably not.* It didn't surprise her much. Of all the security officers, her Uncle Ray was the only one she had any use for—he'd proven himself. The others were so restrictive that she couldn't understand their actions. They were as much robots as the machine she'd controlled from the Lab.

"I—you're hurting me," she whispered as the two MPs marched down the hall, their footsteps echoing like hammers.

The first released her without stopping. In one fluid motion, the second officer pulled her close to his chest. The first officer dropped his hand to his sidearm and followed them, his gaze dancing in every direction, as though expecting an attack.

"Wh . . . what are you waiting for?" Selene asked him. He didn't answer.

Her grandfather was waiting in her quarters when they arrived. He sat in his chair with his arms crossed. It was odd seeing him sit with his back so straight in a chair designed for relaxation. His face was a terrible mask, his eyes sunken and his cheeks glistening with tears.

"I don't understand, Grandfather. What's happening?" Selene asked as the two MPs deposited her on the couch.

Captain Tulk looked at the two officers and waved his hand, saying, "You may wait outside the door." The MPs nodded in unison and marched to the door.

Selene stared at her grandfather. *Why don't you speak to me?* It was possible that this was all a ploy to scare her. She accepted that she'd made a mistake, but it wasn't a mistake that was insurmountable. There was an officer standing behind her when she'd entered the hall. He couldn't have gone far.

"You've put me in a bad position, Selene," Captain Tulk said as he leaned forward. "What am I going to do with you?"

Selene shook her head. "What do you mean, Grandfather? What . . . I don't understand. Why was Dallas so—"

Swiping his arm through the air like an axe, her grandfather said, "Stop it, Selene. I know you understand what's happened. Though inexperienced, you are smarter than most of the officers on the station."

"But . . . but—"

"No, Selene. Just think it through."

Think it through? Think what through? Her grandfather had hugged her and then Dallas had charged her with disobeying a direct order. He'd told her she could have killed them all and that she should have died. "Does Dallas want me dead?" *Why does it matter?*

Her grandfather narrowed his eyes and rested his elbows on his knees, sighing. "No, Selene, we don't want you to die. That's why we didn't want you there. He was right. Benson can't even think straight because he had to order your death just to save the rest of us. Do you understand what that means?"

Could she understand why he had done it? Of course. The logical explanation would dictate that the greater good outweighed her life. That was why she had done what she had. She couldn't fault the man for his decision. If nothing else, the events of the last few months had taught her the value of that decision. Couldn't he just accept that?

Her grandfather didn't let her finish her thoughts. He pushed himself to his feet and began pacing. "It's not acceptance, Selene. These people love you. You are the reason why they stay here. What else could keep a man sane except knowing they do their work for a reason? You made him choose to destroy that reason."

Selene frowned and shifted on the couch, trying to meet her grandfather's gaze. *Look at me.* What she knew wasn't much. Benson loved her. They all did. The thought made her smile. She had disobeyed the order, something no one was fond of. Benson had been forced to order the door closed, which meant he'd ordered her death. It hadn't worked that way, but it could have. They didn't want her dead, but it could have happened, just the same. "I . . . I think I understand."

"I hope so, Selene," Captain Tulk said with a sigh. "Because I don't know if he'll be able to work again."

Work again? Why would it be such an ordeal? If it came to it, she would have made the decision. Her mother had made the decision to save Callum and her father had done so to save more officers. *Why is it so important?*

Selene's voice didn't tremble as she asked, "Grandfather, who did Father leave the shield to save?"

The man's foot came down with a resounding thud. He pirouetted to stare down at her for several seconds. When he spoke, his voice trembled. "Benson and Dallas."

The air in Selene's lungs turned to dust. She couldn't force herself to breathe. Her mind raced. Benson and Dallas and Callum. The men she'd come to know as her uncles were all the men her parents had sacrificed themselves to save. *They all think they owe me their lives.* "I . . . I didn't know," she said. She hung her head. She was no officer. She was just a child, playing.

"I know, child. I know," Captain Tulk whispered.

Dallas was right. They shouldn't have pretended she was an adult. All that had gained them was heartache. She'd spent the months since her commissioning trying to make life more difficult for them. She couldn't even pretend otherwise. She should have gone back to hunting dragons or playing with dolls. Spike would agree.

Selene's eyes widened and she gasped. *Bentley!* She'd left her companion in the Lab so she could accomplish her goal of destroying her Uncle Benson. She sighed. Of course that wasn't true, but it mattered little. One of her father's many gems of useless knowledge had been the saying, "The road to hell is paved with good intentions. Watch where you lay your pavement."

She stared at the floor, blinking rapidly. "I'm going to hell. I should be dead and going to hell," she whispered.

Captain Tulk's eyes widened and dashed to kneel at her side. "Don't think that, Selene," he said. "Dallas didn't mean it that way. He just wanted you to understand. He just . . . "

She knew Dallas didn't want her dead. She could work through the logic, recognize the difference between should and want. What hurt was that no one had said yet that they wanted her. No one had said thank you. *I did save them.*

As though tuned to her thoughts, Captain Tulk said, "I wish there was a way to show our thanks and have you understand the need for order. Benson had already dealt with the reality that he was condemning those officers. It wasn't an easy decision. If you had accepted the orders, none of this would have happened. You understand that, right?"

Selene looked away, nodding. *At least it is a thank you.* She forced a smile to her lips.

"These men don't have families, Selene. They are learning as they go."

Selene rolled back on the couch. Pulling her feet up to her chest, she laid her head on the pillow. Her eyelids drooped. *I just want it all to go away,* she thought. *I just want everything to go back to what it was before. Before . . . before Jameson.*

Her grandfather paced as she rocked back and forth. He hovered for a few minutes before saying, "I have to check on the passengers, Selene. I will return."

Selene sighed as he left. She didn't want to talk to anyone anymore. Silence was what she needed. *No,* she thought. *I deserve silence. I deserve to be alone. No one should be with me. All I do is cause pain.*

Chapter 11

Selene swatted at the flies buzzing around her head. When one landed she tried to squish it, but she was never fast enough. "Go away," she mumbled as a shadow crossed her vision. Opening her eyes, Selene found Bentley bending low to lick her face. He soaked her face with his saliva before she could turn away.

They wrestled for several minutes, until the door to the suite chimed. Looking up, Selene said, "I don't want to talk."

There was silence until the hatch opened far enough for a tray of food. The officer had placed the food in sealable containers so Bentley wouldn't scoop up the food before Selene had a chance to eat.

"They don't know about my feet," Selene whispered to the dog. As she spoke, she felt a cool breeze on her feet and looked down. Someone had removed the wrappings. She sat up and ran trembling fingers over her feet. They were blistered, but not throbbing, as they had earlier. "The salve," she said, pressing her fingers against the blisters. Glancing to Bentley, she said, "I might be able to walk soon, Bentley. Then we can . . . "

Selene sighed and lay back down. *Can what? I'm locked up in here.* Her grandfather had grounded her. There would be a security officer standing at the door with his arms crossed. He may even have one hand on his weapon. He wouldn't smile at Selene. He wouldn't care if she wanted to walk through the halls.

After an hour, Selene's stomach began to rumble so loudly that she was torn from sleep. Bentley had managed to open the lid on one of the containers and cover the suite floor with its contents. *You must have carried it around for ten minutes.* Her father would have called them loser laps. She turned her eyes to the other food containers. *Twenty paces at most. I can make it.* She could take slow steps.

Selene set her feet on the floor and gripped the arm of the couch to pull herself up. She teetered for a few seconds before sliding her left foot forward. As she followed with her right foot, she was forced to put her full weight on her left. *Pain!* Screaming, she pitched forward onto her knees. As she landed, Bentley rushed to her side, whimpering. *At least you aren't licking my face,* Selene thought as he lay down at her side. She leaned forward and rested her face against her forearms. "Damn feet," she moaned. "Why the hell don't you work with me?" When the throbbing pain eased, she crawled the rest of the way.

The galley had prepared more than one meal. There were a few containers filled with fruit and other small items and two containers with food she couldn't describe. The container that Bentley had dragged through the room had been filled with meat. *Meat supplement,* she amended. Meat was a scarce resource. They wouldn't leave it for Bentley to throw all over the room.

The last container wasn't filled with food, but various medicinal products. *Thank God.* She opened the lid and searched through the bin for a few pain pills, which she swallowed without any liquid to wash them down.

Pulling out another vial, she read, "Liquid callus." She opened the cap and stuck it under her nose. The stench rising from the vial made her gag. It reminded her of how her Uncle Callum's Fuel Room smelled. She contemplated it a moment as her feet throbbed, then dribbled some on her fingers. "Ooh, that tickles," she exclaimed as she dabbed the cool, clear liquid on her foot. By the time she was finished it felt more like a soothing cream, sending alternate sensations of cold and warmth through her feet. Then, before she could wipe her hands, it thickened further and hardened.

She wiggled her foot, eyeing it, then sighed and carefully stood, thinking, *Please work.* She teetered a moment, assessing how it felt. *Like a soft cushion, like I'm floating on gel.* She looked down at her dog. "See, Bentley, it worked! I bet Uncle Sasha made this. He makes some really cool things in the Farm. One time he created a pill that made you think you were full. That was way back when we didn't have much food, though. Now it doesn't much matter."

Humming happily, she stuffed a couple of the tubes into her pocket, then turned to her food and ate, passing several pieces to Bentley. When she was finished, she looked around the room and sighed. "I'm bored, Bentley. What do you want to do?"

Selene wanted to go back to work. She wanted to get back to her courses. With Cecile's help, she was learning faster. She could record everything and then go through the important points in the evening. Just sitting in her quarters was going to drive her crazy, even if she had access to the computers. It was the people she missed.

"I am not a child," she reiterated as she walked toward the couch. *Could a child save all of those people?* Would they have trusted her with the robot? *No.* She emphasized that by shaking her head. "I might not be an adult, but I'm not a child, either. They can go to hell. No, they don't deserve that, do they? They are doing what they have to. I just have to show them that I can do the right thing." She looked down at Bentley as he curled up at her feet. "Come on, Bentley. I need your help."

The dog bounced to his feet, tail wagging, and set off on his haphazard racing through the suite again while Selene changed her clothes. When she was ready, Selene checked the liquid callus on her feet, then eyes her new pair of shoes. "Hmm, I don't think the socks will fit." She slipped them over her bare feet and moved to the door.

Bentley came to her side, and she noticed he stood as tall as her hip. *I bet I could jump on your back and ride you through the corridors. Would you be strong enough to carry me?* She smiled at the vision, stopping when her imagination brought her to the Lab and her Uncle Dallas waving his pudgy finger at her. Sighing, she said, "I am not a child."

Bending low, she pulled the dog close and whispered, "Go to the Lab, Bentley. Go to the Lab." Then she straightened and flung the door wide open. She pushed out the food tray for one of the guards to collect and as he accepted it, she released her hold on the dog. Bentley burst through the door, upsetting the tray, then bounded down the hall, his ears laid back on his head.

"Oh, please," Selene pleaded as he ran off, "can you get Bentley? Gr—Captain Tulk won't like it if he gets lost." The officers stood unmoving until Selene added, "Oh, I don't know what would happen if one of the passengers saw him."

The first security officer started off in pursuit without waiting to see what the second did. Selene knew she had him the second she'd invoked her grandfather's name. The other officer pressed the radio in his ear. Before he could call any backup, Selene grabbed his arm. "You know no one will get here in time. Bentley is so big he'll be to the far side of the station before anyone can help. You have to block him into a hall. Go—please. I don't think I could make it far enough to call him back now."

The man's jaw twitched for several seconds before he nodded and set off after his partner.

Selene's mouth curved into a smile as she watched him leave. She hadn't told a lie. She needed to have Bentley back and she couldn't chase the dog down. There was nothing wrong with taking a stroll until they returned. Head held high, she giggled. *Could a child do that?* "No," she whispered. Her smirk remained as she limped around the corner.

Selene automatically headed toward the Lab. Then she stopped. "What am I doing?" She set off for the Farm. It was the hub of the station; every spoke led to its centre. There were enough utility halls leading to it that she could go anywhere.

Selene felt the liquid callus tearing away from her feet as she shuffled along, and the blisters started burning again; by the time she reached her destination, she was limping. She sagged back against the wall of the utility hall she'd used. "Oh, that hurts," she muttered, reaching into her pocket for a pain tablet. Cracking open the access, she searched the main hall up and down with her eyes as she swallowed the pill. She didn't see anyone, but that wasn't surprising. Most of the crew would be dealing with the passengers. There were more ships present than the one that had crashed, so they would be processing for days.

Selene held her breath and crossed the hall to the Farm entrance. With every step her shoulders straightened, and a smile grew on her face as she sniffed the air. *Is that smell real, or am I just imagining it?*

Selene couldn't remember the last time she'd been in the Farm. *A month?* She stroked her hair. *More.* It had been over a month since she promised herself she wouldn't return. She huffed. "Only a child would follow through with that promise. I am not a child."

Selene imagined herself grabbing the handle, turning it, then strolling in as if she'd never said anything to her Uncle Sasha. She would be accepted like a hero, because Sasha and his people worshipped her. They would appreciate her saving those people from the ship.

"Excuse me, miss, are you supposed to be here?" The voice seemed to come out of nowhere.

Selene froze, looking up at an officer she didn't recognize. *Who are you?* The man was dressed like the officers from the station, but he walked with a wide step, like someone who wasn't familiar with gravity. His movements were sluggish, as if he didn't have the muscle mass to carry himself upright. His eyes were sunken and blisters dotted his skin.

"Oh, I'm sorry," Selene said. *Oh crap. He's a passenger.* She looked around the hall and turned to leave.

"I said, do you know where you are supposed to be?" The man spoke to her as if he thought she couldn't understand English. "Passengers aren't to leave the quarantine."

Selene opened her mouth to tell him off. Isn't that what the passengers usually did? They were ill-tempered and complained at every opportunity and had nothing good to say about the station officers. They didn't speak like that to the officers' faces, but deep within the utility halls, she'd learned their true feelings. *That might have something to do with the sleep,* she thought.

Selene knew, however, that she couldn't draw any attention. She didn't want anyone asking her questions, or worse, asking the crew questions. In either case, her grandfather would find out, and she would be locked up again, ending this vacation for sure. She braced her legs and looked down before saying, "Oh, I must have turned a wrong corner."

Narrowing his eyes at her, the man asked, "What ship are you from, child?"

Crap. Selene held her breath, unable to answer. She'd spent so much time studying with Seaman Tony, she hadn't paid attention to what ships had docked. It wasn't that long ago that she would have chosen to skulk through utility halls instead of working in the Lab. *Then,* she would have known everything about the docked ships, because she would have shadowed their passengers, curious about what they said. *Not this time,* she thought. She hadn't played in the utility halls for so long that she couldn't even remember what it was like. Instead of overhearing snippets of information or learning what it was like to be looking forward to a new home, all she had was the station, her family, and Cecile.

Cecile. Selene sighed and lifted her hand to her ear, as if she were scratching her head. Pressing the small radio in ear, she murmured, "Cecile, the docked ship?"

Still staring at Selene, the man again narrowed his eyes. After a second he shook his head and said, "Is that your name, Cecile? Okay, Cecile, what ship are you from? I will escort you back to your section." As he spoke, he lifted his hand to her shoulder. "We don't want—"

Selene's world slowed to a robot's pace. She could see the man lift his arm to guide her away from the Farm. She could feel the pressure of his hand on her skin. Her breaths came faster and her vision blurred. She could remember the man's face from a second earlier. But now something changed. It was as if two men stood in front of her: this man with a clean-shaven face, and a dirty, sweat-stained, unshaven monster with a sweet, heavy odour and a toothy grin—Jameson.

Don't touch me! Selene stepped back from the man's outstretched hand, sputtering. The man wasn't the drunken pilot that had destroyed her childhood. She knew that he wanted to lead her back to a place where he believed she belonged. What she couldn't see was a path from her shrinking world. But she had to leave. She had to find respite so she could calm her breathing and her racing heart.

As she stepped back, preparing to leave, Cecile said in her ear, "The ships docked at Orphan Station include the *Salient*, the *Blue Turtle*, the *Ottawa Express*—"

Ignoring the rest, Selene said, "I . . . I'm from the *Blue Turtle*. I'm sorry, sir. My father is going to be anxious. Perhaps I should just go now."

Selene ducked under the man's outstretched arm and rushed away as fast as her liquid calluses would allow. She didn't bother to look back, but she felt his gaze chase her around the corner. She shivered as she moved beyond his sight.

Selene came back to herself when she couldn't lift her legs anymore. She looked around, chest heaving, unsure where she was. *I'm on the far side of the Farm,* she realized, watching several station medical officers handling the queue of passengers from one of the ships, working without rest to complete medical exams before the ship was scheduled to depart. No one left without a physical. The last thing Captain Tulk wanted was passengers dying on the last leg of their trip.

Most of the passengers kept their eyes on the floor as they waited. *I wonder if they have to go to the bathroom,* Selene thought of those shuffling their feet. They looked like she did after a long day of work, bouncing from one foot to another. Even the adults danced. *I don't blame you,* Selene thought. The explosions that had rocked the station and buckled the floor earlier would have thrown children and adults alike off their feet, and scared even her father. *I'm surprised the gravity was kept on.*

"Hello," a soft voice said behind Selene.

Selene jumped and turned from her observation of the milling passengers to find a boy staring at her. He looked to be her age, though taller, and with olive-coloured skin. He gazed around with wide-eyed curiosity. *You probably have never seen the inside of a station,* Selene thought as she smiled, feeling sorry for him. The boy's eyes were shadowed and he looked too thin. He reminded her of Bentley, after the dog had run through the shower and shaken his fur into disarray.

Stepping closer, the boy said, "Hello. I . . . I think you saved me da."

"Your da?" Selene asked. She glanced back the way she'd come, checking to see whether the man had followed her. She lifted a hand to rub her shoulder where he'd grabbed her and realized that her arms were trembling. She took a minute to calm herself before looking back to the boy.

He had backed to lean against the wall, and she caught him sighing as she returned her attention to him. *I should leave.* She tensed, preparing to do so, then changed her mind and relaxed back against the wall beside him. Clearing her throat, Selene said, "Your father?"

"Yeah," the boy said with a quick nod. "My da is . . . was . . . captain of the ship."

"Oh, I didn't do anything there," Selene said. She couldn't tell him the truth, couldn't have the boy running all over the station, telling everyone that she was the person who'd saved them. Her grandfather would breathe fire if he found out she was even talking to him.

"Don't worry," the boy said, dropping his voice. "I promise I won't tell. My da made me promise not to even look for you, but I couldn't help it. I wanted to thank you . . . show my appreciation."

Selene narrowed her eyes. His language wasn't that of someone confused after long slumber. He spoke more like her grandfather than one of the officers. He was educated.

"Sorry," the boy said as he noticed Selene's look. "Is there something wrong?"

Shaking her head, Selene said, "Uh, no. I just—it's just that you look like you just woke up. I wasn't expecting . . . well, I just wasn't expecting."

"Oh, uh . . ." Smiling again, he lifted his hand to pat his hair down. "Um . . . don't tell anyone, but I was never asleep on the ship. I was born there."

Selene felt the air leave her lungs. *Born there?* Oh, what a target the boy would have painted on himself if Jameson had seen him! A boy awake on a ship? That would have been too much for that monster to handle.

"Does that make you angry?" the boy asked as he stepped forward.

Holding her hand out to stop him from approaching, Selene said, "No—just a memory." She relaxed the line of her brows. The boy was more observant than some of the adults on the station.

But more than just a memory angered her. Jameson's face haunted her every breath. She saw him in her dreams and even in random strangers. There was nothing she did that could wash the putrid stench from her nose or wipe his dull stare from her mind.

"So . . . um . . . I just wanted to say thank you. I heard how hard you took it in the ear for doing it, and well . . . you know."

A smile flashed across her face before Selene bit her lip. She wanted to beam with joy. *At least someone recognizes that I did a good thing. Someone appreciates me.* She wanted to run through the halls, screaming about the great things that she'd done. Her new friend would run and yell with her. It would be like her adoring fans who always clapped in her imagination when she saved another life from the asteroid mines.

Just as his gratitude raised her hopes, however, his next words dashed them against the rocks of that asteroid mine. "How did you get here? My da heard you were thrown into the brig."

The brig? Her story had already gone through the ranks? Would they be making fun of her now? *"Oh, Selene, the child who can't follow orders."* Would that be how she was greeted when she reported for duty? She sighed and shook her head, turning away so her new friend wouldn't see her glistening tears. *I am not a child.* A child would cry. She couldn't. "I . . . I have to go."

"Wait," the boy said.

Without turning back, Selene said, "What?"

"I . . . It's been so long since I had someone . . . someone my age to talk to. The crew always talks down to me, like I'm a child. It drives me crazy. And there wasn't a child on the ship to revive, though my da wouldn't let it happen anyway. He says it was bad enough when the second crew was awakened."

Are you like me? Selene thought. Was it possible they could be so similar? What were the chances of meeting a boy born on a ship? But then, she realized, she wasn't treated like a child. That was the fundamental problem that Dallas had pointed out. He had said that she was a child and they had to start treating her as such. But then, wouldn't that turn her into the boy standing in front of her? She would be crazy with anger because none of them gave her the time of day. They would pass her in the hall and ignore her when she had something to offer. *Then again, there would have been no Jameson.* Selene shivered.

"I am the person I am," Selene whispered as she turned back to the boy.

"Sorry, I didn't hear your name," the boy said as he pushed out his hand in greeting. "I'm Sam."

Taking a deep breath, Selene said, "Hi Sam. I'm Selene."

Sam inclined his head. "Uh, I'm not really supposed to be away from the quarantine in my section."

Nodding, Selene waved her hand. "Come with me. I know a place where we can talk."

Glancing around, Selene ducked into a side hall and led Sam toward the closest entrance to the utility corridor. There she released the latch and pushed Sam through.

Sam glanced around the hallway, eyes wide. "What is this?"

Cocking her head to the side, Selene quipped, "It's my office." The she explained, "These utility halls criss-cross through the station. I spent my childhood exploring them. Now I hunt dragons here. Well . . . I used to until I got commissioned as an officer. I spend my time working in the Lab now." She shrugged.

The boy raised his eyebrow. "Don't you get to play?"

Selene let out a breath of air. "Of course not," she said. "I am an . . . I'm not a child anymore. I can't afford to play in here when the crew works to keep the station safe."

"But, you're a kid," Sam said as he shook his head.

"*No!*" Selene said, emphasizing the denial by chopping the air with her arm. "I am a member of the crew. They need me."

"But . . . you're a kid. You shouldn't have—"

Selene turned away. "And all you want is for your crew to treat you like an adult? What right do you have to lecture me?"

"No, wait," Sam said. He hung his head when she looked back at him. "I didn't mean to say it that way. I just . . . I just mean, when do you get to be a kid? I don't want to be a part of the crew; I just want to be heard every once in a while. I . . . I don't have anyone to talk to. My da is always at work and my mom . . . my mom . . ." Sam's voice trembled and he looked at the floor, shoulders shaking.

Selene stared. *What else do we have in common? Did you lose your mother too?*

Wiping the tears from his eyes, Sam said, "I . . . I lost my mom a couple years ago. She used to talk to me all the time. Even when she was working."

"I never knew my mother," Selene told him. "Father used to say she sang me to sleep when I was a baby. I haven't heard a song in . . . well, since father died."

"Both?" Sam said, covering his mouth with both hands. "I'm . . . I'm sorry."

Selene looked away for a second. She couldn't understand why she felt so at ease with him. He was a child that wanted to be an adult. His vocabulary was far more advanced than a child's. It was more advanced than hers. Stepping closer, she asked, "How old are you?"

"Oh, I don't know," the boy replied. "There aren't really any years on the ship. If I use Earth's year, then I guess I'm eleven, but if I use our new planet's, I'm nine."

"I just turned eleven." Selene tipped her head back, trying to grasp the concept of different calculations of years. *A year is a year, isn't it? The time it takes for a full rotation of the planet.*

Sam said before she finished her thought, "You're twelve Earth years, then; maybe thirteen."

"Hmmm," Selene said as she continued to think about the prospect. She was eleven, another year closer to adulthood. She didn't need to have it forced on her. It would be something else the crew could use against her.

"I guess it doesn't really matter," Sam said. "Other than for your birthday, I suppose. We use Earth because they have a real calendar. We used to, anyway."

"What do you mean, used to?" Selene asked as she motioned for the boy to follow her down the hall.

"Well, Earth isn't there anymore. Well, I should say that there aren't any people on it anymore. By now if they haven't been evacuated, they aren't going to make it."

Earth, gone? How could there be no people on Earth? She knew people were travelling from the planet to other systems, but there was no way they could all be gone. She imagined an entire planet, silent, its buildings empty. She shivered. "What happened to Earth?" she asked.

Sam shrugged. "Well, I wasn't there then, but Da says that we made a huge mistake, way back when, and didn't clean up the mess. The forests are always on fire and there isn't much left of the resources. Da says that if no one is on the planet for a hundred years or so, it might become habitable again."

Visions of dragons flying through the skies, belching blue and red flames, crossed Selene's mind. But now there were no humans left to hunt those dragons. There were no humans left to rebuild. The silence returned.

"What're you thinking about?" Sam asked.

Shrugging, Selene said, "Dragons."

Her response made the boy raise his eyebrow. "Dragons. See, you can be a kid. You can daydream."

He's right, Selene chastised herself. Daydreaming about hunting dragons was a luxury she couldn't indulge. There would come a day when daydreaming would make her make a mistake, whether by pressing the wrong button or not realizing what she was doing. If she continued to daydream, she would get someone hurt. She was no robot or superhero, able to fly around the station. *I am what I am.*

Sam pursed his lips. "Wait, no, that's not a bad thing."

He acted like Captain Tulk, seemingly able to read her mind—or maybe her emotions were easy to read on her face. Her father had always known, too. He had trained her to read others. The eyes, he said. Watch the eyes. Perhaps it was something everyone was taught.

"My da says that he daydreams too. He says some days, that's all that gets him through. What else could keep him sane after thirty hours of plotting trajectories through plasma storms? He says it's normal."

Normal? How could it be normal to see the scaly hide of a dragon slithering through the dim utility halls when she walked through, or marks of the creature's sharp teeth every time she cut her hand? It was a luxury she had to dismiss.

"I once heard my captain say he got bored until Da built the VR unit on the ship," Sam said. "After that, the captain said he was more relaxed. He was able to work through a lot of issues so he didn't take them out on the crew. When I heard that, I wanted to try the VR, but Da wouldn't let me. He said it wasn't for kids."

"I've used ours," Selene said as they came to a ladder leading down. "Uncle—er, I mean Lieutenant Benson let me use it a couple times. It gave me a headache at first because I couldn't keep the VR world separate from the real world. I kept seeing both."

"Oh," Sam said as he waited for her to climb down the ladder. "That doesn't sound fun."

"It is, actually," Selene said as the boy joined her on the level. "I built my dragon hunting world in the VR. But then I realized I could imagine it better anytime I wanted. That's when I—"

"Cool," Sam interrupted. "I wish I had an imagination like that. I don't even know what a dragon looks like."

Lights came on automatically as she led the boy toward the end of the hall. "Oh, they're large," Selene said. "Some are almost as big as a ship. They have scales bigger than my hand and their eyes are like glass. Some have wings as large as they are long. Once I saw one that had horns five times my height."

"Wow," Sam said.

"Wait." Selene held her hand out to stop him. "Duck your head through here."

The boy looked at the low bulkhead and frowned. She could imagine him splayed out on the floor, as had happened to her when she'd gone to save his father and the rest of the crew. Her forehead began to throb in response to the memory.

Retrieving another pill from her pocket, Selene pushed it into her mouth and hid a grimace. It made her mouth feel like she'd licked Bentley's fur, but she couldn't chance asking anyone for water. They'd ask questions.

"Hey where are we going?" Sam asked as he bent to walk under the beam.

"Oh, we're going to get my dog. I sent Bentley to the Lab earlier, so I'd better get him."

"Your dog?" Sam asked.

"Yep. Grandfa—um . . . Captain Tulk gave him to me for my birthday. He's a German shepherd," Selene explained as she stepped over and opened a hatch.

Within minutes, the pair stood at the bottom of a cylindrical shaft with a ladder attached to one side. Voices echoed down from above. Selene led her new friend up the ladder, pausing on the platform at the top to peer out through the small grate.

"Where are we?" Sam asked as he joined her.

"The Lab," Selene supplied. "This is where I work. Look through, over there. You can see the operations room on the far side, and that tall thing there is the room with the robot control seat."

Placing his hands on the grate, Sam pulled himself closer. "Can I see it?" he asked, eyes on the room beyond.

"Uh, it's not really for civilians," Selene replied. "Maybe you could have your father ask for a tour or something."

Sam shook his head. "I doubt it. I see him at night when he gets back to the barracks. He's spending all day negotiating for one of the other ships so we can get going."

"The other ships? Oh, you mean the shuttles the crew originally came on. That makes sense. We won't need them again I guess, and they'll want you gone soon because the dark side is coming."

She reached into her pocket for a green radiation pill and swallowed it, thinking of the ships in the landing bay. *It makes sense for them to take one of the ships. Their ship isn't salvageable.* Even if the flames were snuffed out after she'd left the robot, the wiring would be ruined. Benson wouldn't have enough in stock to rebuild. *What about us, though? Those ships are for evacuation. Maybe they can take one of the smaller ships in the seventh bay.*

"What's wrong? Is there something wrong with the ship?" Sam asked, giving her a sidelong glance.

"Uh, no," Selene said. "I was just thinking about losing the ship."

"Oh, do you need it?" Sam asked.

Selene sighed and hung her head. "You're right. You need it more." The ships were designed to evacuate the entire crew. Even with those destroyed in the crash, they had enough ships for ten times the crew. "Sam, how many—"

"There were 2,314 when we started and there will be 1,405 when we leave," he blurted, as if it were an accusation.

Selene stared at him. *I saved them. I saved who I could.* She couldn't remember how many people she'd transported with the robot. *Was it that many?* Selene shook her head to clear it of the screaming voices and swallowed the bile in her throat. *How can I be so selfish? I'm worrying about a ship that hasn't been used since it got here before, I was born. They've lost everything. I shouldn't even be dragging Sam with me to find Bentley.* "Sam . . . is . . . is there anything I can do for you?" she asked, blinking tears from her eyes.

Sam shook his head, his smile still wide. The sound of clanging metal drew his eyes back to the grate. "What are they doing?"

Selene leaned forward. "Where?"

Sam pointed across the Lab to activity beside the operations room. "There. With that."

Selene froze, her eyes going wide. The two security officers were crouching to grasp Bentley in their arms. She could tell they were both swearing as they tried to pull him up. After a few seconds she let out the breath she'd been holding and smiled as Bentley fell to the floor, instantly scrambled to his feet, and ran off again. As if he sensed her presence, the dog turned and loped toward the grate, easily outdistancing his would-be captors. "That," Selene said, nearly squealing, "is my dog Bentley."

"Oh." As Bentley rushed forward, the boy shivered and stepped back, forgetting he was on a narrow platform. As his foot fell back on the ladder he screamed, arms flailing, before Selene caught his hand and pulled him close.

Cupping her hand over his mouth, Selene watched wide-eyed as the large dog stuck his nose against the grating and woofed. *Please go away, Bentley. Please go away. Not here.* She shuddered as Bentley's human shadows approached, their footfalls echoing on the floor grating. "Oh bugger," she whispered as one officer swooped in low and the other lunged out to block the dog's path forward.

The first officer crashed into the grate with a heavy clang, breaking it away from its moorings. Selene bit her tongue to stem a brewing scream. Sweat broke out on her temple as the man tried to pull himself free of the steel wreckage. She could feel his breath on her face as he said, "Damn it, this dog is irritating. The lieutenant could have held on a little harder."

"Ha! He probably let him go on purpose for what you said about the kid," the other officer shot back, his hand darting for Bentley's collar.

"Well, it's the truth. Why doesn't anyone get it? She would be happier just going to one of the colonies and living her life on a planet. She could take the damned dog with her, so we wouldn't be playing babysitter."

"And that's why the lieutenant let the dog go, you idiot. You ever wonder why they keep her around? She's smarter than the two of us put together and she'll be around long after you're dead from radiation poisoning. Got it?"

"Who cares if she lives longer if she'll be living alone? I'd rather be on a planet with people who—"

"Who what? Cared? Loved her? You don't know what you're talking about. I've never seen anyone love someone like the officers love her. And where would she go? She knows the station. What would it mean to be plopped down on a strange planet?"

They both scrambled to their feet and wrestled the dog into their arms. The first security officer continued the argument as they turned to leave. "Plopped down? Who doesn't know what he's talking about now? Millions of people have been plopped down since we got here. She'll likely be set up with a happy family with a gushing mom and dad, and won't have a care in the world. She won't have to worry about gravity or fires sucking the air away into the vacuum. Like I said, I'd take the planet over this place anyday. Come on; the old man will tear us a new one if he finds out we left Selene for over an hour."

Sam stared her, his mouth hanging open. Selene was so lost in her thoughts, she didn't care if he saw the tears in her eyes. "I . . . I have to get back to my quarters," she mumbled. "Come on, I'll take you back to the main hall."

The conversation between the two security officers played across her mind like a video screen. *The kid? Gushing mom and dad? My mom and dad are gone, you damn screw-off.* She could read the words on their mouths before the sound reached her ears. *Leave? How many feel the same? Would you all be happier if I left?*

Selene climbed down the ladder and didn't wait for Sam to join her as she stomped along the utility hall. *Stupid officers. Goddamn you.* After several minutes she stopped. Sam ran into her back. "Crap."

Sam stared at her for several seconds before she managed to say, "I . . . I'm not sure I have enough time to take you back to your section."

"Oh," Sam said, glancing around at the low ceiling with wide eyes.

"Wait." Selene held up her hand, then slipped her earpiece into her palm. "Take this. When you have it in your ear, say, 'Cecile, lead me to,' then say where you want to go."

Sam accepted the unit, placed it in his ear, and cleared his throat. "Cecile, lead me to the section seven barracks."

Though she couldn't hear the computer's reply, Selene knew her program would perform perfectly. It wasn't coded to her voice and she had no false assumptions that Cecile was a real person. The computer wouldn't snub a new voice. Selene took a deep breath, waved to the boy, and set off—then stopped and turned back. "Wait. Make sure you close the door to the utility corridor. Promise me."

Sam nodded. "I promise."

Selene made her face a mask as she said, "I swear to all that's holy that if you don't, I will find you."

Sam shivered, then wordlessly moved off, following Cecile's directions.

Selene knew she should follow the boy to ensure the hatch was closed. Leaving a hatch open had put her in solitary confinement. Having a hatch hanging open when they crossed over to the dark side would be a disaster. People could be hurt.

Selene watched the boy turn off down a side passage, holding his hand to his ear as if he thought her communication unit would fall out. She waved to him one last time before heading for her quarters.

She was conscious of the silence as she walked. Whether it was because she didn't have Cecile at her call or because Sam was be gone, she didn't know. It had been fun to speak to someone her age. She'd even enjoyed teaching him about different things. Though he looked at her with sad eyes, they weren't filled with pity. She felt warm with him, as if enriched by his company. *I like him . . . liked him.* She wouldn't be seeing him again. If someday the station was closed down and everyone was sent to the planet, Selene wouldn't recognize him if she happened to meet him. He would just be another of the passengers that had come through the Orphan.

When Selene arrived at the door to the main hall, she lifted her foot and kicked it open. *Go ahead. Punish me. Send me to the planet. Stupid officers.* She didn't care if she was caught now.

Back in her own quarters, she kicked her shoes across the room and fell onto the couch as if it offered a loving embrace, tears rolling down her face. When she was able to take a breath, she rubbed her throbbing feet.

"Stupid feet. Stupid seaman," she said as she rolled up to a sitting position and reached into her pocket for the vial of liquid callus. The cool sensation spreading through her skin as she applied the tincture was enough to relax her tense shoulders.

The door to the suite swung inward without notification as she finished her ministrations. There was no sound as Bentley was deposited inside, tail wagging. The door swung shut before the dog could turn to bark at his captors.

Chapter 12

Selene wasn't sure whether hours or days passed before she saw her grandfather again. When he entered, the man looked haggard. His face was pale and shiny with sweat. *Your clothes look too big,* Selene thought. Captain Tulk she knew wouldn't be so careless. Captain Tulk she knew would have yelled at an officer for looking like he'd rolled from bed; everyone was expected to have perfect creases, perfect pleats. There was never an excuse.

Selene stared for a few more seconds before her breath caught in her throat. She patted her pockets for a few seconds before she found the pill she sought. Careful not to let him see her—she couldn't let him see fear in her eyes—Selene slipped the pill into her mouth and swallowed. *Stupid radiation.*

They weren't on the dark side pass so it couldn't have been accidental exposure, the cause of death for her parents, but that didn't exclude every kind or cause. Seaman Tony had taught her of several types of radiation that could kill a person, and some that were used to help people. He even said people let off a type of radiation themselves. It was small, but detectable. At the time, the conversation had given Selene a nightmare about being the source of the radiation that had killed her father. It had taken two hours of research to understand it couldn't happen that way.

All that didn't change the fact that her grandfather stood leaning against the wall, his palms digging into his eyes as if they were burning. It didn't change the fear that she was going to be orphaned again. *What do I do now? Who will watch me?* Who would take her in? Would she be known as the cursed girl? *"Don't take her in or you'll be dying of radiation poisoning in a week."*

No one would want her then. Even her uncles, the lieutenants, would be eager to send her on her merry way to one of the colonies. She could imagine their wide grins. They wouldn't have to worry about her leaving a door open in the utility halls when danger approached. They wouldn't have to clean up after her dog. And there would never be a need to cook grilled cheese sandwiches, though the prospect still sent spasms of pain through her stomach and she hadn't even requested them since her walkabout.

Selene rubbed her own eyes before saying, "Hello, Grandfather."

He sighed. "Hello, Selene. How are you feeling this morning?"

Selene was lying on the couch. She shifted to a sitting position so she could inspect her feet. She poked the blisters several times to determine whether they were as sore as they had been when she'd returned to her quarters. "I think they feel better."

Her grandfather smiled. "That's good. And how is Bentley? I heard he had an escapade earlier."

Selene froze and stared at her grandfather. *Do you know what happened? Are you testing me?* The man could read minds, even if he was sick. There was one course of action that she could take. Bentley jumped down from the couch as she shifted in her seat and said, "Grandfather, I have something to tell you." She watched the dog pad away. "I sent Bentley away so I could slip out of our quarters. I . . . I was so angry that all I could think about was getting back at you. I'm . . . sorry." She hung her head.

Her grandfather smiled gently. "Thank you for telling me. Now, if you were me, what would you say?"

"Well," Selene began, "I would say that I should be punished."

Shaking his head, her grandfather said, "Punishment isn't the word I would choose, Selene. Yes, you did something wrong, but I've realized that I did too. No—" he held up a hand when she drew breath to speak "—hold on and let me finish. I am not going to rehash what Dallas said. I just want to start over again. I want you to be a child for a time. Let's start with that. Okay?"

A demotion, or a rebirth? Selene wondered, thinking at first that it was more punishment, but then thoughts began to roll around in her head. A fresh start was more than anyone could ask for. That was what all the colonists were looking for. She could wash away her mistakes and live as she had before . . . before Jameson.

"Can I grow my hair long again?" she asked, looking up to her grandfather. Short hair was for boys. It made more sense for a girl to have long hair. *Mother had long hair.*

He nodded. "If you want."

Taking a deep breath, Selene said, "But what about the Lab? Does that mean I can't go and help anymore?"

He held out his hands. "Let's start small, okay? We'll talk about that later. I don't see anyone showing up with supplies, so we'll have a while."

After a brief silence, Selene jumped down to the floor and walked over to her grandfather. Closing her eyes, her mouth stretched in a wide smile, she wrapped her arms around him in a warm embrace. She could feel him return the hug and hold it for several seconds before she pulled away.

She moved back to the couch with a bounce in her step, jumping onto the cushions and twisting back around to watch Bentley run through the suite. She felt as free as the dog racing around the two humans. *Free*, she thought.

The prospect of freedom would mean more to others. She would be a kid for Sam and a kid for that security officer. *Stupid seaman.*

As she had hours earlier, Selene thought about the greatest things she'd been able to do since the terrible day when she was assaulted by Jameson. She'd run the robot with her Uncle Benson for hours the first day, helping to fuel and salvage some of the electronics. It had given her so much joy to be a part of the team. And that led to Benson asking her to do it again to save the people from Sam's ship. She wanted to do that again. She wanted to run the robot and save people. She wanted to be part of the team. *I want to be wanted.*

Selene glanced at her grandfather, the man whom, until recently she'd known only as Captain Tulk. He'd always been strict with her, dispensing discipline whenever she did something he didn't approve of and rarely offering congratulations. Selene had to admit that there were times when he'd given praise. When her father Savir had been alive, Captain Tulk had showered her with approval for all of her achievements. He'd been the first to tell her how her computer program Cecile could someday run the station. He was wrong, but that didn't change the fact that he was showing her his appreciation. There were other times; he'd been the first to clap when she was showing off the new tricks that Spike could perform. At the time Selene had figured it was Captain Tulk's right to clap first. She didn't know the truth then.

Her grandfather smiled at her, his eyes gleaming. One corner of his lip quirked up, as if he were smug, possessing a great secret that he couldn't tell anyone. Selene imagined that was how she looked when she found a new corridor to explore or coded a new command for Cecile to make life easier. *You're happy. You want me to be a child.*

Selene opened her mouth to speak, then closed it. Her furrowed brows relaxed and her fists uncurled. *Maybe I should be a kid. I can play dragon hunter and house. I wonder if you'll play house,* she thought as she matched his smile.

"Sir, there is a child here to speak with Selene." The words broke Selene's concentration and she looked at the security officer hanging through the doorway. Selene recognized the officer who had suggested that she would be happier on the planet. He saluted Captain Tulk, glancing at Selene. *I wish you could go to the planet,* Selene thought. At least there, he would be where he couldn't bother her.

As soon as the man spoke, the smile fell from Captain Tulk's face. He licked his lips as he walked toward the door, purposely standing between Selene and any newcomer.

It can only be Sam, Selene thought. The boy was supposed to be on his way to the colony. She was never supposed to see him again. She smiled. *But isn't he supposed to be on the ship, rather than wandering the station?* Selene scratched her chin. *I'm sure no one else saw,* she thought, casting back in her memory to her meeting with Sam. She lifted her hand to wipe her forehead. *No one saw. I'm sure of it.*

Selene took a few short steps forward, saying, "Grandfather. I didn't . . . He won't tell. I promise. His father was one of the officers."

153

Captain Tulk waved her away. "I know. I was just hoping he wouldn't be so brazen. Show him in, Seaman."

The security officer nodded and stepped to the side, allowing Sam entrance.

Sam's eyes looked sunken and dark as he came around the officer to look at Captain Tulk. He glanced at Selene before saying, "Sir, I'm sorry to come, but my da said I had to bring this back."

"Pardon, son? What do you have there?" Captain Tulk stepped forward with his hand outstretched.

Sam stared at the floor, tapping his toe as if getting ready to run from the room. He looked up once, his face flushed red. Selene shifted closer to hear. "My . . . my da thought I stole it. He was going to ground me, but I told him you'd prove that I didn't steal it."

"And why would I say that?" Captain Tulk asked as he planted his hands on his hips.

"You wouldn't," Selene began. The room was somehow brighter as she spoke, as if a spotlight were shining on her face. Sam had promised not to tell, but if he had been backed into a corner, what choice did he have? *He's just doing what I would.* Selene sighed and said, "He has my radio connection to Cecile. He didn't steal it."

Selene's grandfather, now wearing the mantle of captain, turned around to stare down at her, his eyes penetrating her mind to read every secret she'd ever had. He cleared his throat, the low, guttural cough sounding like a monster from her nightmares. "And how will that make a difference, Selene? You know how important it is that people don't learn about you, and now both this boy and his father know, not to mention anyone who could have overheard them. How am I supposed to deal with this?"

Selene opened her mouth to respond, but Sam was faster. Stepping forward with her radio, he lifted his other hand to tug Captain Tulk's pants for attention. "Sir, I promise no one else knows. My father and I weren't near the rest of them. I know how to keep a secret. He doesn't—"

"Sam is like me, Grandfather. He was born on the ship. He knows what it's like to be different." The words were out of her mouth before Selene realized what she'd said. As she finished, she rocked back on her heels, crossing her arms. *It's true. He knows.*

Brows furrowed, Captain Tulk stared at her for several seconds before looking at Sam and nodding. "Where is your father, Sam? Does he know where you are?"

The boy mirrored his nod. "He's helping load supplies into the new ship."

Captain Tulk licked his lips before saying, "Okay, that's fine." He turned back to Selene. "Go with him and prove him right to his father. As soon as their ship leaves, we are packing it in for the dark side. I want you back here as soon as possible. Is that understood?"

"Yes, Grandfather." She stared at him, wondering, *Is this the captain speaking or my grandfather?* He was sending her to speak to Sam's father. It made no sense to send her if it meant being caught. The travellers could send word to other ships coming to the station, and that would mean no end of trouble for her grandfather.

Captain Tulk bent low to meet her gaze. "You understand how important it is that you remain a secret, right Selene?"

"Yes, Grandfather," she repeated. She sat down and pulled her liquid callus from her pocket to apply a new layer to her feet. She shivered, then sighed as first cool, then warmth coursed through her soles. Retrieving her shoes from beside the couch, she slipped them on darting from the room.

The halls were empty, the passengers from the other ships gone, on their way to the colonies. It took ten minutes for Selene and her friend to pass through the utility halls in search of his father. *You can never be too cautious,* Selene thought, focused on the last words her grandfather had told her.

They found Sam's father speaking in hushed tones to several officers as they loaded several boxes onto a cart. Though most of the officers were station crew, there were a few Selene didn't recognize, wearing bandages on their exposed skin. *I may not know them, but they'll recognize me from the hallway,* she thought. Turning to Sam, she asked, "I can't go out there. Can you have your father come here?"

He nodded and walked forward, while Selene ducked back into the darkest corner of the hall leading toward the landing bay. She glanced back to the utility hall they had emerged from, and nodded. *It will be safer back inside. Seven . . . no, six paces,* she thought as she took a step. She cringed as more officers entered the hall, laden with supplies from the Farm.

Sam didn't wait for his father to finish speaking before grabbing his pant leg for attention. He cupped his hands over the man's ear and whispered something before looking back toward Selene. His father followed his son's gaze, peering into the darker corridor.

Selene sank farther back into the darkness as the officers marching from the Farm passed her. *Grandfather will kill me if I get caught,* she thought. She had to prove herself to Captain Tulk. There would be no chance of returning to the Lab if she couldn't do something as simple as keeping herself secret. *I have to trust Sam.* He and his father had kept her secret so far.

Selene froze and gasped, her eyes going wide as Bentley skittered around the corner, barking. *Oh crap.* "Oh no, no, no," she whispered to herself as she shot a quick glance back to Sam and his father. She couldn't let anyone see the dog. She had to protect Bentley because even if they left without asking questions, they might take the dog. *I have to keep him secret, too.* There was no way to keep anything secret if Bentley tore through the gathering. Those officers would question Captain Tulk. He would keep her secret, but Selene hadn't seen him with Bentley enough to know whether he would sacrifice the dog for her.

Reaching out, Selene snagged Bentley by his collar and took the six steps to the utility hall entry. Her hands shook so badly, they slipped off the latch twice as she tried to open the door. She swung it open slowly, making sure it didn't clang back against the wall, and stepped through, pulling Bentley in behind her. Then she dropped to her knees, wrapped her arms around the dog, and clamped her hand around his muzzle.

"*Please*, Bentley, you have to be quiet," she whispered into the dog's ear.

Then she pulled back. "How did you get out?" she asked. Selene narrowed her eyes. *Why are you out?* Bentley couldn't leave her quarters without someone opening the door. *Grandfather was holding your collar when we left.* Bentley couldn't have escaped unless someone deliberately let him go. Captain Tulk wouldn't have waited in the room. He would have other things to do. That would have left the two security officers. The security officer who had announced Sam must have done it. He must have let the dog go. *That bastard. But why? Why would he do that?*

"Selene?" Sam whispered from outside the door.

Selene stood, letting go of her dog's collar but holding her hands on his nose a second before pushing the door open a crack. She slipped through and stared a warning at the dog. "Now, stay quiet."

Sam stood with his father just outside the door, Sam trying to look beyond Selene into the utility hall. He and his father shared the same crooked smile, the same way of standing.

"Hello Selene. My name is Lieutenant Anthony Perkins," Sam's father said. The blisters on his face weren't as angry as some Selene had seen, though they were still puckered. "Sam says you want to say something to me."

Selene nodded. "Yes. I wanted to let you know that Sam was telling the truth. He didn't steal my radio. I gave it to him."

The smile faded from the man's face as he stared down at Selene. Finally he nodded and said, "Okay, Selene. I accept your explanation. Sam, run along now."

Sam stepped forward to hug Selene, and she stiffened as he hugged her. Her body shook within his embrace, and she fought the urge to run. The only person she had let touch her since Jameson had hit her was Captain Tulk, and that only when she'd learned he was her grandfather. *But you aren't like Jameson*, she thought. Sam wasn't trying to hurt her. He'd proven his friendship. Selene lifted her arms and hugged the boy back, holding tight. *You like me.* Her lips curled into a smile.

They parted, and Selene wiped her eyes as she watched Sam disappear around the corner. *I will not cry,* she thought.

Anthony knelt beside Selene. He licked his lips before saying, "You didn't have to say anything, Selene. I thank you. Sam thanks you."

"You're welcome," Selene said. She turned to leave, but stopped and looked up to the man. "Sir. There's something else. It's not really my position to say, but I don't think he will. He . . . Sam wishes you would treat him like an adult."

The smile returned to the man's face. "You know, Selene, I wish I could. But there's a reason I've treated him the way I have. I'd gotten so caught up with doing everything, I didn't give him enough attention. But soon that will change."

"Change?" Selene asked. What could change to make him spend more time with Sam? They would have to work just as hard when they reached the planet. *But then, I suppose Sam could work at your side.*

"Yes . . . change," Anthony was saying. "Our destination isn't the second planet orbiting Alpha Centauri. We are heading for the primary planet."

Who cares? Selene shook her head. "What does that have to do with it?"

"Oh, you wouldn't get that news from the planets back here, would you? We receive regular updates. There's very little need for us on the planet. The colonists have been developing the planet for so long that their children are old enough now to do our jobs. My people have been replaced before I could even get them there."

"Oh," Selene said. She had learned a lot about the planets from her time with Able Seaman Tony. She knew there were two colonies, one established some time after the other. The crew of the Orphan could never learn more, however, because the radiation field broke up any radio signals.

On a planet already colonized, Sam would find himself in the same position as Selene. The closest he'd be able to get to doing real work would be in his dreams. She sighed. *Sam will get bored. I'd get bored—well, I'd get bored after I explored the planet for awhile.* At least Sam could learn something new. The rest of the passengers would have nothing. They were trained to build a civilization that was already built.

Selene chewed on her lip for a moment before suggesting, "Why . . . why don't you stay here?"

Anthony laughed. He didn't stop for several seconds. Selene stood with her mouth open. *What's so funny?* she thought. *I wasn't joking.*

Seeing her scowl, Anthony fell silent. Taking a deep breath, he said, "Oh, how I wish I could, my dear, but that is not in the works for me. My destiny is to transport my people to the planet—unless, of course, you know another Met tech who could chart the course."

Selene sighed. "No." She looked at the floor. "I just thought that if everyone wasn't needed . . ."

Anthony also sighed. "How I wish I could. I can't stay, however. Perhaps we will see each other again someday. Until then, you have my thanks and my thoughts." He bent over to be at her level and waved, then straightened and set off toward his new ship.

Selene watched him walk off, then gusted out a sigh and turned to flip the latch on the utility entrance. Before she could open the door, Bentley jumped up to push it open, and it slammed against her chest. *Ouch!* He took off down the hall as though he knew where she intended to go. *Damn it.* She glanced around before hissing, "Come back here!"

Selene ran down the hall after her dog, then skidded to a halt when she saw an officer standing in front of the dog; she didn't want him to notice her. She watched the man speaking to Bentley, noting that his hand was balled into a fist. She didn't recognize the man, though she felt she should. *He must have been on the ship,* she thought as she slipped back around the corner. *Come on, Bentley. Get out of there.*

She knelt and peeked around the corner and said loudly, hoping her voice would carry to the dog, "*Bentley.*"

Bentley was too far from her to hear, however, and his focus was on the human as the man grabbed his collar. He barked and tried to pull away, but the man's grasp was as irresistible as a robot's. "Shut up, you mutt," the man growled, shaking the dog's collar.

Don't do that! Selene leapt to her feet and stepped around the corner, then hesitated and retreated. She did this several times, opening her mouth to call out to the man. She slapped her balled her fist against her thigh in frustration. *Let him alone!* She could only watch, trembling, until the man lifted his hand to cuff Bentley. She stepped forward, shouting, "Stop that."

The man straightened and looked at her. "What are you doing, girl?"

When Selene approached, Bentley pulled back against his captor. He bared his teeth and growled at the man. The sound from her amiable companion was louder than Selene expected, and alien to her ears. It sent a shiver through her body.

"Get out of here, kid. Go back to your quarantine section." The man pointed an authoritative finger toward the hall behind her.

Like hell, Selene thought. She took a deep breath and mustered her best impression of her Uncle Benson. "Let the dog go."

With his attention split between Selene and her dog, the man didn't notice the dog shift. As though he could turn inside his skin, Bentley yanked back on the collar and twisted far enough to latch onto the man's wrist. He bit down hard, and blood spewed across the floor.

Yelping in pain, the man released the dog's collar to defend himself from further attack. As before, he wasn't fast enough; Bentley bit the man's arm and leg twice more before rushing off to stand in front of Selene, his teeth bared, his head low, growling deep in his chest.

"Are . . . are you okay?" Selene asked the man, but it was too late. Blood pouring from his arm unabated, he rolled and thrashed on the floor, screaming.

He lifted his head long enough to growl, "Get away from me, you rotten—"

"Shut your ugly gob, Lieutenant. What the hell have you done to yourself?" a woman asked. She was beyond Selene's line of sight.

"That damned dog just bit me. I don't even know what the hell they have it on the station for," the man said as he tried to stem the bleeding with his slick hand.

The woman came around the corner. "I don't even care how or why, Lieutenant," she said. "Get yourself down to the infirmary. We leave in less than an hour, and you'd better be ready." She turned away from him and walked toward Selene.

Paralyzed, Selene watched the woman approach. All that crossed her mind was, *Damn.* She was shaking so hard she couldn't keep a grasp on Bentley, who was huddled against her chest.

"Who are—" The woman stopped and stared wide-eyed at Selene. "I know you. I've seen you before. You . . . do . . . exist. What is your name, child?" She took two steps closer, her arms out, as though she were going to grab Selene's shoulders. She paused as Bentley growled.

Selene flexed her arms to pull away from Bentley. She had to escape, had to run and hide before the woman caught her. If she remained any longer, she would be forced to explain her presence. She would have failed Captain Tulk. *You stay there and I will disappear,* she thought at the woman. *Just think you were seeing things. Maybe think I'm the ghost.* It didn't work.

"I . . . I'm from one of the ships. My name is Robyn Sotana," Selene said at last.

The woman's brows lifted. She stared at Selene and her dog before clearing her throat to say, "Robyn Sotana, eh? And which planet did she come from?"

Do you believe me? Can I get away with it? Selene stared at the woman, her jaw clenched. "Are you stupid? I said I was from a ship. I came from Earth twenty-five years ago. Where else could I have come from?"

"You don't have to get snarky with me, child," the woman said as she stepped closer. She kept her gaze fixed on Bentley, as if ready to defend herself from the dog's sharp teeth by will alone.

"How else would you have me respond? I've been asleep for twenty-five years," Selene said. She licked her lips before adding, "I'm sorry, but I have to go." Whirling, Selene walked away, leaving Bentley blocking the woman's path.

Selene waited until she made it around the corner before breaking into a run. All she could manage to think of was placing one foot in front of the other as she raced through the halls. *Goddamn it. I screwed up. Damn it.* She didn't notice if anyone else saw her as she put distance between her and the woman.

Selene's steps faltered as she approached her quarters. With every second step, she turned her head to search the hall for Bentley. *Come on, boy. Come home.* The dull thrum in her ears subsided as she turned the last corner to her quarters—and immediately skidded to a stop. The two security officers again stood before her door.

"What were you thinking, leaving the door open for that long? Were you trying to get us flogged?" one of them said.

"No, but listen, man, I heard some talk; a guy from that crashed ship says they could take her," the other officer said.

"When would you have enough time to talk to anyone that the subject would just come up, without bringing up the topic yourself?" the first officer snapped. Frowning, he shook his head and paced away.

"So what, if I took the initiative? You *know* I'm right on this, Jay. She can't—"

"Can't what?" the other officer interjected. His cheeks twitched as he spoke. Shaking his head, he said, "I'm going to go look for him."

Selene didn't wait for the rest of the man's statement; she took off again, her face hot, her breathing laboured. *I can't go home. Maybe in there,* she thought, spying the entrance to the closest utility hall. No one would be able to catch her and send her to the planet if she was in the utility halls. The station was going into the dark soon, so the ship would have to leave. At least then she would be safe. They could start over.

Selene made her way through the station. She didn't bother to call for the lights as she moved into the deeper sections of the utility halls. Everything was a blur anyway. She counted her steps aloud as she moved. "Seven, turn . . . one, two, three, four, five steps . . . ladder."

"What the hell are you doing with a child on board, Captain?"

Her stomach lurching, Selene stopped and looked around. *Where am I?* She moved to peer through one of the grates and found herself overlooking Captain Tulk's office.

Her shoulders slumped. She'd failed. Everything she'd tried to prevent was about to happen. She was going to be taken from her grandfather and uncles. There was no dragon's back she could jump on to carry her aloft, safe from the woman.

"What are you talking about?" Selene's grandfather asked. He sat in his chair, eyes intent on the computer screen on his desk. He'd changed into a new uniform. The woman Selene had encountered in the hall stood with her arms crossed in the open doorway behind him.

"I asked you how you could keep a child on the station. Did you not know? Did one of your officers kidnap her from one of the ships?"

Captain Tulk looked up from his computer and turned his chair to face the woman. Now Selene couldn't see his face, but his voice was rough, as if he was trying his best not to scream. "What are you implying?"

"I saw a child today," the woman said. She stared at Selene's grandfather with narrowed eyes.

"Congratulations," Captain Tulk replied. He glanced at his screen and added, "I can find you seventy-nine more, if you want."

"She wasn't from any ship," the woman said. Her trembling voice carried through the grate as if she was speaking within the utility hall itself.

Captain Tulk leaned forward. "That would be difficult. Perhaps you saw a ghost. I've heard there was one on the station." He waved his hand to encompass the station.

"Shut up and listen to me," the woman said, nearly screeching through clenched teeth. "There is a child on this station and she didn't come from any of the ships docked here. She was here before any of our ships arrived."

"That's new," Captain Tulk said with a shake of his head.

"Cut the crap, Captain. She said her name was Robyn Sotana. It didn't take long to look it up. Your daughter died years ago. A passenger wouldn't happen to have the same name."

Stepping around his desk, Captain Tulk said, "I have better things to do, Captain Tyner. Please get to your point."

"Let her go, Captain. I don't even care what you've told her to keep her here. Let her have a real life on—"

He slammed his hand onto the desk with a resounding bang, startling the woman. "You want the truth, woman? That child is Robyn's daughter. She has been here for her entire life. We are her family. She has a *real life* here."

The woman dropped her voice. "Captain, I understand. You're the child's grandfather. But this is no life for a child. Just look at her scars. Let her go."

"That *child* is more than you or I will ever be, Captain. She is the reason you are alive. Do you understand that? You would be dead twice over if she weren't *here*. Not a passenger or crewmember would be alive. She is a valued member of our crew, filling a very—*very*—important role." His face had gone several shades redder.

Selene's shoulders relaxed. *Very important.* She pulled back and sighed, a smile on her face. She didn't have enough energy to listen to any more of their conversation. All that she cared about was that her grandfather applauded her actions. He wasn't angry that she hadn't followed Benson's orders. *You're proud.*

Selene left Captain Tulk's office and the conversation behind her. The woman's voice was lost in the other sounds in the utility halls as Selene marched on. *Where can I go?* she wondered. The security officers were still guarding her quarters, but she still needed to be in the inner section. *I can't go outside of the ring.* They would be going into the dark side pass and that would leave few places to hide, beyond the halls where Jameson had found her. The Farm, though viable, would still have a few officers from the ship present. *I can't go there. SHE might be there. I have to go to the Lab.*

Selene' mind was more focused on the conversation in the captain's office than on her destination. Hearing voices passing by out in the main hall, so she took the ladder to the lower utility level and travelled through the lesser-used sections. She found herself ducking and crawling more often than she remembered, but soon she reached the hatch leading to the inner section.

As she opened the hatch, Selene gasped. A bandaged officer stood staring at her for a second before grasping her firmly around her chest. Her chest felt constricted as he tightened his grip, closing her airway so she couldn't scream. A hand was placed over her mouth for good measure.

No, no, no! Let me go! she screamed in her mind, struggling against her captor's grip, visions of another Jameson flashing against the backdrop of the silent utility halls. *Let go of me!* Her body shuddered violently.

Selene jerked her head to the side, freeing her mouth long enough to bite her attacker's hand. Salty blood oozed into her mouth as another officer came through the hatch to fill her vision. She kicked out, connecting with his chest, and he groaned. There was nothing she could do to prevent the man from lifting a syringe to her arm and injecting her with a dark liquid. "Goddamn you," she hissed. "What the hell do you think you're doing? Do you honestly think you know . . . what'ssss good for me, yooo . . . piece . . . of . . . dog . . . crap?"

Chapter 13

Selene woke to silent darkness. "Hello?" There was no answer.

She lifted her hands as high as she could, and her fingers brushed against a cool, hard surface. *Where am I?* She kicked out, finding no end to the black tomb. When she lowered her foot, however, it settled gently on soft padding.

What could be so hard on the sides yet soft as a bed within? *There's nothing on the station like that.* She shifted, and caught her breath. *I'm belted in. It must be a bed.* Lifting her arm, she relaxed it and it didn't immediately drop. *There's no gravity.*

Again she reached out, exploring her tomb with her hands. It curved above her head like a coffin, and was clearly built for someone much larger. There was a headset lying on the cushions above her head. "I'm in a sleep chamber," Selene said aloud. *There aren't any on the station so that means I'm on the—goddamn it, they've taken me to the ship!*

Selene shifted to press the release latch hidden at the edge of the lid. It lifted in three steps, like a fan folding, to reveal a large, open bay lined with rows of similar pods. Belted in, Selene couldn't sit up to see over the edge of her pod, but there was enough light from above to illuminate her pod and show her the catches on the harness holding her that, released, would give her freedom. *I have to get off this ship. I have to get back to the station before the ship leaves.*

The harness was like those in the robot control room. *I can do this.* She pulled hard to release the first catch. *Did it!* she thought as she floated from the pod, imagining she was Selene Sotana, expert

166

astronaut. She could do two flips in the air under limited gravity; navigating the sleeper bay would be simple. *I have to find the airlock. It must be starboard. That's where Mom would put it. It's where I would put it.* Everything important was to starboard.

Selene didn't care if it wasn't the female captain who had actually performed the abduction; it was her order that sent those officers scurrying into the depths of the station. *They must have followed me right after I left my quarters.* The thought brought images of the security officer to mind. *He led them to me.* If they followed her, Selene mused, then the woman's conversation with grandfather was a distraction. She'd been wasting time, giving her officers the time they needed to find Selene. *I bit one of them,* she recalled as she floated through the air. *At least I will be able to figure out who that is.*

As she came to the wall, Selene kicked off and somersaulted end over end, levelling out to fly toward the far side of the bay. She connected with another wall, bending her legs to prevent herself from ricocheting backward and grabbing for the edge of a catwalk above her. She pulled herself up onto it and crouched to look around.

Several officers were moving through the ranks of pods, pausing to work on some. *Medics.* They were too far away to notice her. Though they weren't putting the passengers back into the long sleep, they were locking them down. *It must just be temporary or I wouldn't have woken up.*

She turned and focused on the hatch behind her, using the catwalk to pull herself over to it. Zero gravity wasn't an ideal environment for opening a hatch, she realized. *I should be better at calculating for this. I have to get better if I'm going to get off this boat,* she admonished herself. Selene's muscles bunched as she pulled on the latch. She stopped and held onto it for several seconds as she tried to calm her trembling body. She tried again. *Open, damn you. Just open or I'll take a flamethrower to you. Open up.*

The handle shifted, and Selene scrambled through the opening before she tumbled backward, hooking the edge with her foot first, then pulling herself through into the airlock.

Seconds later, she stepped into the gravity beyond the airlock, and froze. A dozen officers stood ten feet from her, their heads bent close as they spoke. Oblivious to her entrance, they continued with what was a heated conversation.

"What was that about, bringing a child onto the ship minutes before we depart? Who the hell is she?"

"What are you talking about?" Selene recognized the speaker as Sam's father, Anthony.

"Captain Tyner brought a girl aboard and stuffed her into one of the pods," an old man replied gruffly, eyes on the female captain. She stood with her arms crossed.

Turning to Captain Tyner, Anthony asked, "What did you do that for?"

"You are out of line, Commander. Do not question my authority," she snapped.

"Authority? You are captain by attrition, just as I am commander. Don't presume to think that I respect your authority now any more than I did when you crashed us into that station."

"You know full-well that I didn't want to do that. It wasn't my—"

"Your fault? You better damn-well believe that it was your fault. It was your decision to come out of the shipping lane too fast, after I told you not to," Anthony retorted, his face growing red.

"I made a choice, Commander," Captain Tyner said. "And if you're so damned concerned about qualifications, why don't you take a look at the officers on the station? The only original officer there is the captain, and perhaps a few of the command staff. The rest are vagabonds and drifters. The man responsible for fuel refining never finished high school, let alone university. Yeah, that's right. We're flying with fuel that we have no proof was correctly refined. And don't get me started about the terrorist they have running the Farm."

Selene shook her head as she stared. *What the hell does that mean? It's not true*, she thought. Callum was a genius with the fuel. Her mother had believed it so much that she'd sacrificed herself for him. He was the only man smart enough to process the fuel.

"Hey, what are you on about now?" the gruff old man asked.

Captain Tyner sighed. "Didn't you recognize the man? Sasha Leblanc was exiled from Earth—"

"He was acquitted," someone else said. Most of them looked at one another, shaking their heads. The old man threw his hands in the air and turned away.

"Who cares?" Captain Tyner said. "I asked around. He may have been acquitted, but he's still playing with genes. That dog everyone kept hearing is real and it grew to almost full size in a tenth of the time it should have. Think about it. What do you think he could have done to this girl?"

Selene knew the woman was talking about Bentley. *But why would Uncle Sasha play with a pair of jeans? He hates them.*

"This is ridiculous," Anthony said as he turned to leave.

Before he could get far, his captain called out, "Stop him."

Two of the officers followed him and dropped their hands onto his shoulders. He stopped, sighed, and pulled hard against their grip before his eyes widened and a half-smile twisted his mouth. "So, what's your plan, Captain?" he said.

"You are going to go to your cabin and plot our trajectory and I am going to go speak to the station. As soon as we hear from the station, we'll leave."

"It's that simple?" Anthony asked, spreading his arms wide.

"Yes, it is," Captain Tyner replied.

"And what is your backup plan when they realize you've been lying about being captain and that you've abducted the girl?"

The man made a good distraction, but Selene couldn't see how she could take advantage. She was pleased to learn they were still docked, and their departure was not imminent. *At least I have a chance to get off.* All she had to do was reach the ship's airlock, and she could slip out unnoticed. *I'll get back to Bentley, and Grandfather. But I have to find the hatch.*

She ducked back into the shadows to think. For all of her playing, Selene had never been on this ship. If she guessed wrong, she could lose her chance. Travelling down the wrong hall could carry her *away* from the hatch. She would be stuck on the ship while it shot off into space. *No Grandfather or Bentley or—Cecile.*

Selene lifted her hand to her ear to press the button that would summon her computerized friend. *Damn, Sam still has it. But where is he?* She turned back to the bay of sleeping pods, then sighed. *I couldn't even find him if I tried.* She glanced back to the gathered officers, and Anthony. *Maybe he's still out here. They didn't make him go to sleep before.*

As she peered at the officers, something shiny fell to the floor behind Anthony, tinkling faintly as it struck the grating. *Is that—yes!* Her radio nestled in one of the ribs of the floor grating. *So close,* she thought, frowning. *Only a few feet. How do I get it?* She took a cautious step closer. *I can do it. No one is looking.* Another step. *Just one more,* she thought as the ship's captain began her diatribe again.

"We shouldn't need a backup plan. Everything will go as we want it."

"You're kidding, right? You think everything will be perfect? Over there is a group of grown men who—"

Raising her voice, Captain Tyner cut him off. "It won't matter. I've made arrangements with some of the station's crew."

"Oh, what a tangled web we weave," Anthony drawled. Only Selene knew why he shifted his footing—he was blocking the radio from Captain Tyner's view.

Selene's heartbeat throbbed in her ears so hard that she couldn't hear the conversation as she knelt to grab the radio. She inched back into the shadows, slipping the earpiece back into her ear. *I made it. I MADE IT!* She tapped the button with a trembling finger and whispered, "Cecile?"

The radio emitted static for several seconds until the computer replied, "Hello, Selene."

Selene's shoulders relaxed and she smiled. *I can get off. I can do it.* "Cecile, contact my grandfather. Tell everyone that I have been taken to the ship. Tell them that I am healthy, but I want to come home."

"Yes, Selene," the computer said.

As one, the crowd of officers turned to leave. The ship's captain had doled out her orders and she was approaching Anthony. She glanced at the two men holding his arms before addressing him. "Will you plot our course or should I have you relieved?"

Selene saw him glance into the shadows where Selene hid. "I will not."

Selene knew that he was trying to stall for her, but it wouldn't matter if they just locked him up and put someone in his place. *Unless you're the only one who can do it.* He'd said it had to be him. Perhaps he was the only one. If that were true, it would take them hours to figure out the right course. If it weren't true, they had someone available to chart their course. *I have to do something to buy time.*

"You will do as I tell you or—"

"Or what, Meghan? There isn't anyone who can do my job— here, or down there in those pods," Anthony said, squaring his shoulders. "You can't just fly away, even if you know where you're going." *Her first name?* Selene thought. Referring to the captain by her first name was punishable by lashing.

"Of course we can," Captain Tyner said. "And that's what we're going to do. There isn't anything in this star system to stop us from just leaving."

There wasn't when you left Earth, Selene thought. Those on the station had learned the hard way how wrong they were. Her mother had been the first casualty of the radiation from the second star. No one was ever told about it until they were leaving the Orphan, because it added as much as a week to their trip—a week while the passengers dried out from the cryosleep. That meant a week with very irritated, very cold people. Inducing a natural sleep in the pods wasn't cryosleep. They would soon hear the wailing that wouldn't stop for days. It was possible that they would have landed before the symptoms faded. *And likely not then,* Selene thought. The choice the captain proposed was flying through the radiation cloud. *You wouldn't.*

Selene shivered and stuck her hand into her pocket to retrieve a radiation pill. There was no guarantee that they weren't being blasted by radiation already. She stared at the captain, thinking, *You could take us right into the path of the radiation and not know it. You have to be stopped.*

It wasn't about just getting off the ship anymore. This captain was endangering the passengers. Her current plan would get them killed. *I have to do something. I have to stop her.*

Selene took a step forward and said loudly, "There is something in the system that you don't know about."

Captain Tyner whirled to glare down at Selene for several seconds before her face softened. She took a deep breath before saying, "You should return to your pod, hon. It's safer there."

Selene stared at the woman for several seconds. *Hon?* She arched a brow. *You dumb, dizzy witch. How stupid do you think I am?* She refrained from even using a *b* instead in "witch." Even on the ship, her grandfather would know. He would teleport over to scold her if he could. He wasn't there, though. Instead the woman who had orchestrated Selene's kidnapping was, acting as if Selene had awakened from a bad dream, and she planned to pat her on the head and send her back to bed. *You must be oblivious to your own stupidity.* Aloud, Selene said, "You must think I'm stupid. You kidnap me and now just expect me to act like one of your passengers. Well, I'm not, so stop acting like it. What I am is a member of the station's crew, and I have information that you need, Meghan."

"Child, I don't know what they did to you on that station, but you are not a member of her crew. You need to be a child instead of worrying—"

"*Stop it!*" Selene screamed. "Didn't you hear my grandfather when you stormed into his office? Of course you didn't. You were there to waste time while your cronies found me and dragged me back here."

"Listen, child. You don't know—"

"Cut the crap, lady," Selene interjected. She was Lieutenant Benson dressing down one of his officers. "We don't have time for it. You have to let me go or they aren't going to grant you a flight path."

Captain Tyner sighed and drawled, "And why would I need a flight path?"

"Because this star system has a radiation field that the planet enters periodically, and we're about to enter it." When she finished, Selene stuck her hand in her pocket to finger the few pills she had left.

The officers still present went silent as the words left her lips. Every officer gaped at her as though she'd commanded them to walk through fire again. Captain Tyner shook her head in disbelief. Anthony smiled and nodded.

Selene looked away from him, wondering if the man thought her words a ruse. *Do you know the truth? Did Grandfather give you the course?* If he knew and was refusing, then he also knew what she was doing.

Selene split her attention between Anthony and Captain Tyner. He was the better person, having already shown more logic and compassion for Selene and the officers alike. Captain Tyner, on the other hand, had shown nothing but disdain for her people. Anthony had even said she wasn't qualified. *Why follow her, then?* Selene wondered, then sighed. Her grandfather would expect it. So would Dallas. *Qualified or not, she is the captain of the ship.*

"So you think you can lie your way off this ship?" Captain Tyner asked. "You know I'm doing this for your own good."

"No," Selene said as she met the woman's gaze. "Ask them. They already know that I'm here. They have nothing to hide."

The ship's captain frowned. Her lips twitched and she shook her head. She watched Selene approach, looking like Sasha when Selene got caught playing in the fields—her eyes bugging out of her head as if she could shoot lasers from them.

Selene opened her mouth to speak, then paused as static echoed in her ear. She shuddered when the voice that greeted her wasn't Cecile's. Instead, her Uncle Dallas asked, "Selene, can you speak?"

Nodding, she said, "Yes."

"Good. Now listen to me. We're working on a way to get you out, but unless they start talking, it won't matter. You know we only have a short window—"

Selene didn't hear the rest of what her uncle was saying. A violent explosion rocked the ship, sending everyone to their knees. Within seconds the gravity let go, throwing them all into the air.

Staring at the ship's captain, Selene said, "What have you done? Oh God, that was your backup plan. What did you do?"

"We decoupled." The matter-of-fact answer slipped from the ship's captain's lips as if she spoke of a normal process.

"Decoupling is never that violent," Selene said. She tapped the radio in her ear.

After several silent seconds in which the ship rocked, Dallas's voice returned, higher pitched and the words uttered faster. "Selene. I'm sorry. We—there's nothing we can do." He paused as if catching his breath.

There was a small beep and then her grandfather's voice filled her ear. Without offering any salutations, he asked, "Can you see Sam's father, Selene?"

Selene's voice cracked as she said, "Y-y-yes."

"Good. Now Selene, I can't have you ignoring these orders. I want you to submit to the man's command. Don't even look at the captain when you say it. Just turn to him and say it. Go, *now!*"

Selene knew what the order meant. Something had gone wrong outside in the landing bay and now the station's crew realized there was no way to get her. They were giving up. Her tears flowed unabated. *It's done.*

"Listen, Selene. I know you think we are giving up on you, but don't. Your safety is my first priority. It always has been. I just can't have you trying to escape that ship right now—and trust me, I know that you are capable of it." As Selene drew breath to respond, her grandfather added, "Please, Selene. Trust Sam's father. He is a worthy man. He will keep you safe."

Tears streaked down her face as Selene managed to whisper, "I'm scared, Grandfather. I don't want to leave you."

She could almost see the smile on his face as the man replied, "Don't worry, my dear. We'll see each other again. Now go, quickly. We have to go to the inner section now. Be safe."

Selene winced as she realized she was grinding her teeth. Her grandfather wasn't asking her to do anything she didn't expect him to, but that didn't make it easier. They weren't going to save her and now they asked her not to save herself. *The docking bay exploded.* The only reason they couldn't get to her was if there was no bay.

Selene swallowed hard. She knew they loved her, but leaving meant she would never return. *How can you see me again? And what about Bentley? Maybe you can come and get me on the planet.*

Selene looked at the officers. They stared at her, most noticing that she had a radio in her ear. *At least I don't have to submit to you,* she thought as she looked to the ship's captain. Then she turned to Anthony. "Sir," she said in a loud voice, "I have been ordered to submit to your command. Please accept my commission."

There was a collective intake of air as every officer saw who she was speaking to. They stared at each other for a few moments, then they began to shift, taking sides. When they were finished, over half of the officers stood at Anthony's side, looking across at the ship's captain.

Anthony nodded to himself and looked at Selene. "I accept your offer, Selene. And I believe so does the crew."

Captain Tyner shook her head before saying, "I think not, Commander. You are being escorted away. I will have you put into a sleep pod if I must."

"No, Captain. If I've learned nothing else from spending the last few weeks under your command, I've learned that I don't like it. You have repeatedly placed the crew and our passengers in danger, and now you kidnap a child—and yes, I do call it kidnapping. It pains me to enact this duty, but I hereby call out Captain Tyner. Seamen, please take her into custody."

Throughout his speech, the officers on both sides began to nod. A few sighed before pushing off and floating over to Anthony's side of the room. One by one they shifted, until the only officers floating at Captain Tyner's side were those gripping her shoulders.

Floating through the crowd, Anthony said, "Selene, I promise to—"

Like her Uncle Dallas's words not minutes before, the rest of what the man said was lost in the resounding crash of a violent explosion at the ship's stern. His head snapped up and he motioned the officers to their stations. Glancing in her direction, he said, "Come with me, Selene."

Selene stared at the man. The lesson her grandfather had been teaching her for months teetered on its edge. By accepting Anthony as her commander, she'd emboldened the man enough to disregard his own commander. *By doing the right thing, I have made you do wrong,* she thought as she shivered. *No, that's not right. I follow Captain Tulk, my grandfather. He is my commander.*

Selene pulled herself into the bridge after Anthony. Officers sat at their stations, some showing signs of being burned, others clear of injury. The new captain glided to the side of a man sitting at a dark computer screen and said, "What's happening, Jake?"

"Oh, hello, Commander. I was trying to contact the captain—"

Glancing back to Selene, Anthony said, "Don't worry about the captain. Just tell me what's going on."

The man fell silent for several seconds, refusing to meet the new captain's eyes. Then he sighed and said, "Captain Tyner wanted me to decouple from the ship early, but the fuel line was still attached."

Selene could hear her heart beating in her ears as Anthony said, "Do we have a camera view of the bay?"

The officer shook his head. "I . . . I don't need it. There's a fire in the bay."

"Will pulling away let the fire burn out in the vacuum?" Anthony asked.

"It—"

Floating closer, Selene interrupted the man. "It won't. It could have if the fuel hadn't been flowing, but that will keep burning until . . . until . . ." She hiccupped.

Turning to her, Anthony asked, "What can we do? Can't they just shut off the fuel?"

Selene shook her head. "No. They're locking themselves away from the radiation."

Anthony mumbled something under his breath, then licked his lips. "Jake, get me someone from that station. Selene, can we detect the radiation?"

Selene felt the sting of tears as she shook her head. It wouldn't matter whether she was right or wrong if that fire consumed the fuel supplies. The fire would burn through the valves in the line. It would take less than ten minutes for the fuel to explode and the station would be no more. "Captain. The only thing they could do is use one of the robots, but—" *The robots.* "Which bay are we in?"

He shook his head. "I— oh, three. We're in bay three."

"Bay three," Selene repeated. She began tapping her leg as she tried to remember the placement of Benson's robots. Failing in her recollection, she lifted her hand to her ear. "Cecile."

There was static for a few seconds before the computer replied, "Yes, Selene."

"Is there a robot in landing bay three?"

"No."

Selene fell back as if she'd been shot. No one could enter the bay without one of the mechanical men. And they couldn't transport the robots through the station fast enough. *Not through the station,* she thought, and asked, "Where is the closest robot?" If there was one near enough, the robot might be strong enough to open the bay door.

"The closest robot is in the first bay," the computer answered.

"No," Selene groaned, drawing the eyes of several officers. She looked at Anthony. "There isn't one close enough. We can't take it through."

"Can't they just—"

"There's nothing," Selene interrupted. "They can't just take the robot and plop it down in another bay like that. There isn't any way."

"It's okay, Selene," Anthony said gently before turning to ask, "Can you get anyone, Jack?"

Jack shook his head. "No, sir. I can't get a link to the officers. I don't even know how the kid got anything."

As quick as a whip, Selene said, "My name is Sub-lieutenant Sotana."

The man rocked back in his seat and winced. "I'm sorry, ma'am." Lifting his hand to his ear, he said, "Wait, I have the station, but the connection is sketchy." He waved his other arm in the air to ask for silence, and listened a moment. "Sir, they've got people in the bay. They have respirators, but they won't last long. There's no way they can get back to the inner section."

The blood drained from Selene's face as she listened to the man. *Someone caught? Why would there be someone there, unless they had been trying to get to the ship?* She stared at the communications officer. *They were coming to get me.*

Gritting her teeth, she looked around at the bridge crew, the co-conspirators with the previous captain in her gambit to claim Selene for their own. And now they'd killed her family—at the very least, the officers stuck in the bay, possibly the rest of the crew. They wouldn't even have a chance to reach the rest of the shuttles for escape.

"I don't see the problem," an officer said from behind her. "All you have to do is move one of the robots that we saw in the other bay."

Selene took a deep breath, planning to scream at the woman. As she opened her mouth, she paused. O*ut. We can go out.* They could eject the robot from the first bay and somehow push it along outside the station toward the third bay. It wasn't going to be as easy as a dragon swooping in, but there was a slight chance. *There has to be,* she thought, *or I'll be the only one left.*

"B-Benson," Selene stuttered. "Lieutenant Benson is the only officer able to run the VR machine."

Anthony looked at her. "What do you mean, Selene? What can they do?"

"There's a robot in the first bay. My Uncle Benson could find a way to get it down to the third one. He could stop the fire. He could do it."

"Sir, the station says they can't control the robot because Lieutenant Benson is one of the officers caught in the bay."

Selene's body went numb. Her stomach lurched and she threw up over the communications console. Had there been any gravity, she would have fallen to the floor. Instead, she floated away from Anthony, oblivious to the rest of their conversation.

"Selene," Anthony said, shaking her shoulder.

Selene shook her head before looking at the hand, then lashed out to strike him. "Get away from me. *Don't touch me!*"

He dropped his hand. "Can you hear me, Selene? The station says you can operate the robot. Is that true?"

Selene paused, struggling to recognize Sam's father, then to understand his words. *Who? What? Operate the robot? How can I operate a robot from the ship? The robot is on the station. But then again, so is Cecile.* Selene opened her mouth and said, "Yes . . . yes, Captain." The words rolling off her tongue felt wrong. She shivered. *There's only one Captain.*

"What do you need?" he asked.

Selene blinked away her tears and saw that he was conversing now with Seaman Jack. His words were garbled, as if he were speaking through water.

Her own words sounded like they weren't hers. They were slow and deliberate. "I would need a VR unit and the control program, but it doesn't matter . . ." For all that she cared for her family, Selene knew the ship had to leave. Her grandfather, the real captain, had been right about that. The star's radiation would be reaching for them like a monster born of her worst nightmares. She had to respect her grandfather enough to follow his last orders. *I owe you that.* At least that way the ship, her crew, and its passengers would survive.

"*Sub-lieutenant Sotana!*"

The words broke Selene from her reverie. Looking up, she said, "Yes, Captain."

"Get over yourself and move. Get down to the engine room. *Go, go, go.* I'm right behind you," he bellowed, so loud she could feel it in her chest. He grabbed the front of her shirt and yanked her forward. She hurtled toward the hatch, grunting as she crashed hard against the doorframe. "Go back to the hall where we were talking and turn left. At the end of that hall you'll find the primary engine room."

Selene's heart raced as she swam toward the engine room. *Can we save them and get away at the same time?* It all came down to the distance that the radio connection remained active. *It could work.*

When she arrived, Selene glanced around the room. It was as large as the sleeping pod bay, with a vaulted ceiling that she could just glimpse. A dozen pipes ran the length of the walls, connecting large cylindrical tubes the size of ten men to a tank at the end of the bay. Wires as thick around as her legs wound through the room in a complex spider web.

Four officers floated around an archaic version of the seat she'd used on the station. Wires ran in every direction, as if they'd yanked the seat from its original position and threw it down on the floor.

"Sir, I didn't know what else to do," an officer said from the corner as he tore the wiring harness from the radio on the wall. "We don't have anyone that knows enough about radios, so I had Davies go down and crack some of the pods. There are a couple . . . passengers that could help."

Sam's father glanced down at Selene before replying, "Good idea." He paused before adding, "Check to see if there are radiologists and engineers."

The man nodded, lifting his hand to the radio in his ear before repeating the order for Davies down in the pod bay. And then he was gone as Selene dismissed his existence and pulled herself to the VR seat. Everything was moving too slow for her. Everyone's words were slurred and nothing moved as fast as she wanted it to. *Too damn slow. Have to hurry to save Benson.*

"It's almost done, if you want to get in," one of the officers said. He had his legs anchored around one of the computer stations as he wired the seat to the floor grating.

Selene jumped into the seat. Anthony pulled himself up beside her. Beads of sweat glittered on his forehead. "I will let you know as soon as we find a passenger to boost the radio signal. In the meantime, work quickly. We'll be moving away from the station soon, to stay out of the path of the radiation."

You did know. You know what path to take. Selene sighed. It could take hours to plot a path like that, even for an experienced Met tech. Her grandfather must have authorized him to get the information. Selene nodded, watching as the officers strapped the various pieces to her arms and legs. When they were finished, Anthony dropped the helmet over Selene's head and darkness prevailed.

Chapter 14

White screen static greeted her when Selene opened her eyes. *Oh, come on,* she thought. She clenched her jaw until the screen flickered to reveal the inside of a cargo hold on the station.

"How did you get—"

The screen didn't wrap around her eyes, so she could see the engine room in her peripheral vision on both sides. It was difficult not to focus on the movement as officers passed her chair. She saw Anthony move to her side. "Don't worry about that, Selene," he said. "Just get the job done."

"Yes, sir." Selene drew a deep breath. *I can do this.*

Though her new chair had been set up similar to the one on the station, everything squeaked as she shifted in the cracked leather seat. She tested the hand controls, squeezing the handles. *It's tighter.* She tried again several times before shifting her legs. Those controls weren't as responsive in her new chair, but she managed to set the robot into a slow, lumbering walk down the main hall toward the bay. After taking a dozen steps, she could appreciate the differences. *Three inches short here and push harder there. Now, go!* As she walked the robot forward, she said, "Cecile."

" . . . Selene." The garbled response came after a slight lag.

"Can you patch me through to Uncle Benson in the third bay? I mean, I want to talk to Lieutenant Benson." Much as she wished otherwise, Selene knew the computer was no human and couldn't understand her casual references. She just hoped she'd programmed enough variations for the computer to connect her.

There was a brief pause before the computer said, "I am sorry, Selene. I cannot reach Lieutenant Benson. I will keep trying."

"Thank you, Cecile," Selene said, disappointment subduing her response.

She guided the robot into the empty landing bay. As she went through her motions, one of the officers asked, "Hey, uh . . . how are you going to get around to the other bay?"

She shifted her head so she could see the man out of the corner of her eye. He was frowning down at Selene with his arms crossed, his attention shifting from her to the hatch leading from the bay as if he was waiting for someone.

"What are you looking at?" Selene asked as she refocused her eyes on the screen.

"Oh, nothing," the man replied, looking to the floor, his face flushing.

Nothing? I am trying to save the station. How is this nothing, you complete moron? Selene shook her head. He refused to look in her direction, though she noticed he was wringing his hands together. And one of those hands—Selene felt her heart stop. She stifled a gasp as the white splash of a bandage crossed her vision. There was a red splotch on it—the wound underneath had bled through the bandage . . . the wound Selene had given the man when she'd bitten him on the Orphan. *Son of a bitch,* she thought, compressing her lips. *You . . . you . . .*

How was it possible she could recognize so many men Anthony couldn't trust? *I have to tell him.* Was Sam's father playing to their tune or oblivious to their actions? *The latter,* she thought. He'd spent so long with them, trust was inherent. They had to trust each other.

Craning her neck to see where the other officers were floating, Selene whispered, "Cecile?"

The response took too long. She knew she had to focus on the robot, but the bugs crawling over her skin wouldn't release her. Hoping the computer was listening, Selene said, "Cecile, backup copy kernel, authorization Sub-lieutenant Sotana to transport ship *Blue Frog*. Execute."

Selene managed to walk her robot to the main doors before the computer replied, "Hello, Selene." She sighed as she recognized the soft voice of the computer, free of static. That wasn't enough, however. Integrating Cecile into the kernel wasn't something the program could do herself. Selene had to choose her words to avoid the need for authorization.

She had the robot grab for the manual unlocking mechanism and release the catch. Selene shuddered as the door swept open, revealing the void of space. Swallowing hard, she stared into the darkness. *I hate space,* she thought as she blinked and balled her fists.

Selene pushed her robot as far as her legs would allow, engaging the magnet so she could rest on the wall. She shook the robot from side to side as she walked toward the outside of the station. There was no sensation of air pushing past, nor did she feel the absolute cold, but the blinking stars gave her vertigo. Her stomach lurched even as she was entranced by the view.

"Is everything okay, Sub-lieutenant?" bite man asked.

Shaking her helmeted head, Selene said, "No. I just—I'm not a fan of being in space." *Or of you standing five feet from me. Screw off and leave me alone.*

The words seemed to loosen the tension in the room as several officers laughed. She wasn't sure why, but the knots in her stomach faded. The cold chills she had been feeling earlier subsided and she was able to focus on the screen.

"Okay, Sub-lieutenant," another officer said at her side. "We can see you now, so we can help guide you."

"Good," Selene said. "Because I think I'm lost."

As the laughter faded, Selene glanced around at the other officers. She counted three, two that had sided with Anthony before the line was drawn in the sand. The third officer stood behind the others, exchanging glances with bite man.

Selene navigated the robot along the exterior of the station, forcing one foot in front of the other. *This isn't so bad,* she thought as she looked at the stars. The most she'd seen of space outside the station before had been in a picture, but it was enough to keep her terrified of being spaced. *I am a robot. I am inside of the engine room,* she reminded herself. Her arms were heavy metal bats and her legs were stiffened, as if she couldn't bend her knees.

"Sub-lieutenant—"

Selene sighed. "Call me Selene."

"Okay, Selene. I can see that the ledge ends in ten feet. The door is still open from our departure. You just have to drop down," the officer said at her side.

Selene followed the man's suggestion and soon stood overlooking the bay. The fires still burned, though Selene could see they had waned near the edges. Several bodies littered the bay floor. Most lay inert, though some showed signs of life as she guided the robot through the door.

"I have to close the door," Selene said as the vacuum pulled at the bodies. There was no reason to assume them dead. Sending them into space was a cruel fate she couldn't impose on anyone.

By the time Selene managed to close the door, what remained of the fuel line had snaked out toward the door. Fuel splattered the floor and instantly ignited. The fire arced across the floor and set the plastic moulding on the walls aflame. The gooey mess pooled on the floor like jelly.

As soon as the door closed, Selene disengaged the magnets on her feet and turned. She counted seven bodies. *Oh God,* she thought as her vision blurred. Three were obviously dead, their bodies scorched black from the fires. Two crawled away as the robot approached, their suits darkened from the smoke wafting through the bay. Selene couldn't see the last two clearly.

"Benson?" Selene asked as she stepped toward the first pair of bodies.

As she waited for a reply that didn't come, bite man said, "Shouldn't you be worrying about the fire?"

"Yes, but my uncle is here. He's—"

"We're here to stop the fires," the man said. His tone said more, however. Selene heard him say, *Stop crying like a child. We're here to do a job.*

Nostrils flaring in anger, she glanced at the man. *I hate you.* He'd spoken the truth, though. She'd been engaged to save the station, not sort through the bodies of the officers hadn't been quick enough to return to the inner section. *I'll check later.* There would have to be time after the fires were put out, and that very act would help to keep the officers safe. *Assuming the radiation hasn't already killed them.*

At the thought of the radiation cutting through the station, Selene automatically pulled back her hand, only to realize she couldn't extract her hand from the controls to retrieve one of her pills from her pocket.

Almost in a whisper, she asked, "How far have we made it from the station?"

"Not far enough, so keep working," bite man replied, his condescending tone implying that she should know more, but didn't. *I hate that.* He spoke to her as if she wasn't an officer and couldn't understand the complicated process of the VR. *Like a child,* she thought.

Selene's robot shuddered as her chair shook—the engines had ignited.

"Hurry," bite man said.

Selene sighed. *Do you want me to save them or just be finished so we can fly away?* Every time the man spoke, Selene's trembling returned and she broke her concentration to look at him, half expecting him to attack her from the shadows. But he was right, she did have to move faster. She did have to stop worrying about the few officers that remained if she was going to save the others. *I'm so sorry, Benson.*

Taking a deep breath, Selene whispered, "Cecile, can you make it so no one can hear our conversation?"

"Yes, Selene," the computer replied.

Selene waited until bite man looked away before asking, "Cecile, what can you access on this ship without needing authorization?"

"Currently, I can access anything without authorization," the computer replied.

Currently? Selene thought. That meant it was possible to lock the program out. "Cecile, can you access anything if you're locked out of everything possible?"

"I have access to—"

Bite man yelled, drowning out the computer, "Selene, can you hear me? Get your hurry on."

She shook her head and glanced around the visor. She couldn't hear the man until he yelled. *Maybe that will work for me.* "Cecile, can you make it so the computer can't hear anyone?"

"Yes, Selene," the computer replied.

"Can you make it so the computer doesn't understand when they type at the terminal, too?"

There was a pregnant pause before the computer replied, "Yes, Selene."

"Cecile, can you do both of those if you are locked out of the system?"

"No, Selene. I can lock out verbal commands, but not those typed in if authorization is given."

That will have to do, Selene thought. When the time came, she could pretend she had power that in truth she didn't. When bite man made his move, she could buy Anthony a little time. *He's going to do something,* she thought as he glanced again toward the hatch. *I can't trust him.*

Selene's robot slowed as back pressure mounted. *It feels like my legs are tied,* she thought as she swung her robot's gaze around.

"The fuel," someone said from behind her.

Selene looked to the fuel line, understanding the officer's horror. Her vision was blurred, not from static, but from the heat generated by the fires. The fuel in the line had been vaporized and now the air itself was burning. Every second step she took, the robot broke through the floor grating.

She sniffed back more tears as she looked around for the fuel shut-off valve. *It was up at the front,* she thought. Every step she took, her line of vision dropped closer to the floor. Smoke billowed from her feet as the rubber coating dripped away from steel hydraulic lines.

Selene pumped her legs as fast as she could, forcing her robot to run. With every footfall more oil sprayed up into the camera, leaving her little visibility. Each step was more difficult than the last, until all forward movement stopped. Her muscles burned and she was drenched in sweat. "Son of—"

"That is enough, Selene," a woman's voice said.

The familiar voice sent shivers down Selene's spine. She glanced around the visor, her fears confirmed as the deposed ship's captain floated into the room, two of her supporters in tow. Anthony was nowhere in sight. *Crap.* Taking a deep breath, she whispered, "Cecile."

"Yes, Selene," the computer replied.

"Make it so the computer can't hear anyone's commands or input anything on the terminals, on my authorization."

"Yes, Selene."

It isn't much, but I don't know what else to do until he gets here. If anyone had the authorization to countermand her program, it was the deposed captain floating through the door. Anthony wouldn't have had the chance to supplant her codes.

All of that wouldn't matter to her family, though. Their only chance was for Selene to force her robot to the fuel valve. She was so close, but for all her machinations, she couldn't move forward. The resistance on her legs was absolute and she couldn't swing her arms far enough to topple the robot.

"You can stop now, Selene," Captain Tyner said. "We are leaving this system now."

Glancing around the visor, Selene said, "That is not Captain Tulk's order."

"Cut the crap, girl," the woman said, scowling. She stood like Benson had the day he'd dressed down the officer in the Lab.

Selene flipped the visor up. "You aren't the captain. You don't have authority."

"You sad child," Captain Tyner said as she floated by bite man. "Anthony won't be coming to your side this time. He has been removed."

"What have you done?" Selene asked, a voice in the back of her mind urging, *We're wasting time.*

"I have done nothing. His crew has realized the error of their decision to support him. He will be detained and you will be removed from this . . . this apparatus. Victor, if you would?"

"Wait," Selene said. "Please don't. I'm almost done. I just . . . I just have to move a little bit farther. Please. *Please!*"

"No, child. It is done. Your family is gone. Now run along. Everything will be okay. I promise."

Selene's heartbeat roared in her ears and she began to shake. She spoke through her clenched teeth, her voice sounding like gravel. "My family is not dead. They are waiting for *me* to save them."

There was a silent second before Captain Tyner lifted her hand to muffle her laughter. "No, Selene. They are gone and now so, too, will we be gone. Now please disengage yourself before I have Victor do it."

Selene stared at the woman for several seconds. She'd changed so much since the first time Selene had seen her. In the hall, Selene had thought the woman was concerned over her safety. Now she was staring daggers at Selene, her lips twitching. *Just let me get to work, you witch.*

A thought crossed her mind. It made perfect sense, why the woman was acting as she was; why the officers had released her. She offered certain freedom, Anthony had offered a chance, on the assumption that Selene finished in time. *They aren't following you because you're right, only because you offer safety.*

Taking a deep breath, Selene said, "But you know the reason why I'm doing this isn't just to save them, right? We've been locked out of the system and the only way we can remedy that is to re-establish the connection to the station. That means I have to stop the fire and we have to re-dock."

"Oh, Selene," Captain Tyner said as she crossed her arms. "I've been warned of your lies. I've even heard them from your own mouth before. I don't believe you."

"Fine," Selene said. "Try the system."

The woman rolled her eyes. "Fine. Computer, acknowledge."

Silence. The other officers fidgeted. Half of them couldn't meet Selene's gaze while the others glowered at the deposed captain.

There'd been a time when Selene thought she could tell a lie well enough to fool the woman, but she was smarter than to fall for a simple ruse. Selene had to make it believable. *This has to work. I will beat you.*

Clearing her throat, the woman said, "Computer, this is Captain Tyner. Acknowledge."

Selene's heart pounded so hard that she couldn't hear the woman order the officers to investigate further. *I have to get back to work*, she thought, watching Captain Tyner gesture at this officer and that. "Don't you get it?" Selene sneered, "The only terminals we can use are on the bridge of the station."

"And you're just telling us now? Or does Anthony know about it and that's why he hasn't been here?" Captain Tyner shook her head. "They wouldn't dare." She huffed. "I told you all that he was lying to you. I am the only one capable of getting us free." Turning her hard stare on Selene, she said, "And how're you going to move your robot? Anyone can see that you're stuck."

"Shut up!" Selene screamed. Her voice was hoarse when she said, "Let me do my job and we'll survive."

Bite man and an officer floating at his side glanced first at Captain Tyner and then to Selene's chair, their eyes wide and cheeks trembling. After several seconds bite man pointed to his terminal and said, "Look."

Selene glanced toward his terminal and saw her robot sway on the screen. At her angle she couldn't determine why, but as she watched, her chair began to stutter as the accelerometers reacted to the robot's movements. She threw her head forward, dropping the visor over her face in time to see a man's gloved hand. *Who—?* Selene thought in dismay. The man would have been fine if he'd remained on the far side of the bay, but this close to the fire, he would be dead within seconds.

Selene searched for the other two officers and saw them trying to approach as well, but their boots had sunk deep into the melting steel grating and they soon fell to writhe on the floor, their suits ablaze. Within seconds, their small oxygen tanks exploded in a burst of colourful flames.

Wiping the sweat from her brow, Selene said, "I can go now."

She pulled her hands up above her head, reaching out to grab the grating. Her first attempt managed to collect liquefied metal. Her second found purchase on an I-beam, allowing her to pull the robot forward. By the time she reached her destination, Selene's arms were trembling. With every movement of her arm, hydraulic oil was spewing from the robot's cylinders. Not only were the cylinders emptying, but the robot was slick with the oil. Nearly every attempt to clamp down on a beam failed, the robot hands slipping off. *It's taking more effort to move it*, she thought. *I have to move faster.*

She heaved as hard as she could, trying to lift her right arm. The back pressure generated by the seat to simulate the robot's inability to cooperate forced her to stop, however. *It has to work. I have to save them.* Tears streamed down her face and her body was wracked with sobs as she said, "I . . . I can't do it. It's too heavy."

"See?" Captain Tyner said as she pointed at Selene. She was like Bentley when he ran around her quarters, unwilling to quit. "Now can we leave?"

Leaning forward, bite man said, "Don't you have any compassion? The girl you had us kidnap is trying her hardest to save her people and all you can think about is destroying her dream."

"I'm thinking about getting us to safety," Captain Tyner replied. Selene could see the veins at her temples throbbing. The woman flung her arm out to point at Selene. "And she sits in the way."

In the visor, Selene could see the growing flames licking at what remained of the robot. She sensed that some of the officers around her were gravitating to her defence, but their sentiments were irrelevant if she failed. *I have to do it differently.*

"Here," bite man said as he floated to her side. He smiled down at her and nodded as he set his feet on the arm of the chair and grabbed the frame around her arm with both hands. "Tell me when."

With a choppy shudder, Selene lifted her arm. Balling her hand, she forced the robot to grasp the valve and then pull. "Push down." Inch by inch, the two of them turned the valve. "Lift." Selene felt the pressure of the straps bite into her flesh as bite man pulled.

"What are you doing?" Captain Tyner asked.

"What you should have done a long time ago, Meghan; helping," bite man said through clenched teeth. Sweat drenched his face and he had to catch his hand as its grip on Selene's arm slipped.

Inch by inch, they worked the machine. Bite man would lift the arm and Selene would work the hand. After a time, there was too little oil left in the robot's hydraulic cylinders for her to tighten her grasp around the valve. She was forced to lock the robot's hand underneath the valve's metal crosspiece.

With the last turn, bite man's foot slipped and he was thrown back into the air. He floated back toward the turbines. He was drenched in sweat, but the smile on his face was real. He'd helped her for her sake, not his own. Selene frowned. *I don't get it. Why are you all so scared of her?*

In the silence that followed, the officers—once glued to the screen showing Selene's progress—began to clap and cheer.

Selene shifted her camera, panning around the station's bay. The fires still burned, but the flow of fuel had been stopped. It couldn't pass through the valve now, but that didn't eliminate the danger. The fire could still set the station ablaze through the plastic mouldings. *I have to stop the fire.*

There was little left of the robot as she turned the head toward the door. Its legs were engulfed in flames and the hydraulic hoses had melted through, spewing oil in every direction. The bodies of the two officers who'd tipped the robot over were nothing but charred masses.

"Have . . . have we done it?" bite man asked.

"No," Selene said. "The fire won't stop on its own. We have to get—"

"Hey. What's that?" Victor called from the far side of the room.

It was difficult to see through the oil splatter on the camera, but she saw movement on the far wall. Selene recognized the last officer she'd seen when she entered the bay. The man turned to stare at the robot for several seconds, then he waved his hands. He saluted before pressing the buttons on his forearm. There was static for a second before Selene heard her Uncle Benson's voice call out, "It's alright, kiddo. You'll be okay." He saluted again and pirouetted before stepping toward the bay doors.

No, no, no. Don't do it! Selene turned her head aside and threw up again, then watched him take another step toward the bay doors. "Please don't. You don't have to. I can do it." Her breath caught as she watched the dark line of space growing between the doors. At first it was only large enough to let debris fly out, but soon the officer himself was torn through. Selene's face contorted, and tears clouded her vision.

There was no sound of metal on metal as the robot was pulled toward the door. Wisps of fire danced around her as she tumbled end over end into the void.

Chapter 15

The stalemate didn't last after the connection to Selene's robot was lost. She knew without looking that the officers would be waiting to see if her prediction came true. They would be wondering if the station would release its hold on the ship so they could move to safety. Selene couldn't keep it from them; she couldn't be caught in that lie. Captain Tyner would continue to attack.

Clearing her throat as quietly as she could, Selene whispered, "Cecile."

"Yes, Selene?" the computer replied.

"Cecile, can you remove the program lock now?"

"Yes, Selene."

Flipping the visor out of her way, Selene said aloud, "We have to leave now."

Before anyone could reply, a loud knock came from the other side of the hatch. After several seconds another bang came through as someone pounded with their fists. Then a voice: "Hey! Let us in."

Selene didn't recognize the voice. *It must be the passengers Davies was sent to get.* She frowned. She hadn't met all the officers from the ship. It could be one of Captain Tyner's people, or one of Anthony's backers. *They could be part of the coup,* she thought, then wondered, *Is it considered a coup if the original captain is trying to take back the ship?*

Turning to bite man, Selene said, "Can you help me get out of this chair?"

"I don't think so," Captain Tyner said as she pulled a pistol from behind her back. Several officers gasped as she pointed the weapon at Selene, then at bite man as he moved to assist her from the seat.

"What are you doing, Meghan?" bite man asked, balling his hands into fists.

"I'm taking control of this situation. Now, leave her there. At least we'll know she can't get in our way."

"You brought a weapon into the engine room?" bite man asked incredulously, his face flushed. He glanced around the room.

When she'd first seen the man in the engine room, Selene had wanted to kill him for his actions, but now as he stood defending her, Selene felt a cool shiver rush through her body. *Thank you.*

"You know I brought it in," Captain Tyner was saying. "Now get to work. Get these engines turning."

"It doesn't work that way," Selene said. "Those people trying to get in are supposed to know about these engines. They're here to help us move."

"And it took them this long to get here?" Captain Tyner retorted.

"I don't know," Selene answered. "All I know is that you can't just turn them on. We don't even know if there was damage when *you* pulled out of the station."

"*Let us in!*" an angry voice bellowed through the door.

"Fine," Captain Tyner said. She motioned Victor toward the hatch with her pistol as she floated back toward the end of the compartment.

Glancing once toward bite man as he moved, Victor said, "Y-y-you don't have to point your gun at us, Meghan. We all want to get out of here."

"You will address me as Captain," she snarled as she set her feet against the wall.

Victor reached the hatch and opened it just as the man on the other side lifted his hand to pound again. The scowl the man wore as he floated through the hatch deepened as he noticed The deposed Captain Tyner with her weapon. He sighed. "That won't help you much in here."

"That's not your problem," Captain Tyner drawled, motioning for him to approach.

"Listen, lady. I remember seeing you before we boarded. I know you wouldn't be here if these people didn't trust you, so why don't you just put the gun down so we can get to work."

"What are you talking about?" she asked.

The man threw his hand in the air to jerk his thumb back toward the bridge. "The captain just asked me to help with the engines so we can get to the planet. I'm not really sure I feel comfortable doing it when you're waving that thing around like a flashlight."

Selene narrowed her eyes at the man. He was well-spoken, almost eloquent with his words. She found it odd that although he continued to wear his scowl, the man was neither scared nor confused by the situation. *How can you take this in stride?* Had they awakened a man already crazed by his long sleep? It was possible. There'd been enough time for the passengers to feel the effects. *I don't want to deal with that now,* Selene thought.

Floating through the room, the man took no notice of Selene's chair. But he managed to place himself between the chair and Captain Tyner's weapon. As he set himself against the chair, Selene realized he was blocking the woman's view. *That's weird. Maybe . . . maybe he isn't a passenger.*

Taking a deep breath, Selene shifted her arm. Moving deliberately, she unlatched first her left arm, then her right. Her skin had been lacerated by the straps, leaving her arms cut and bruised. Selene looked down at her legs. *How do I get those with her finding out?* There was no way she could move fast enough before Captain Tyner emptied her weapon into her chest—or that of her protector. Shuddering at the thought, Selene looked for other options. *Maybe Cecile could do something.*

Behind her, the newcomer was saying, "Alright, so I have to get down to those terminals under you. Are you going to stay there or move away?"

Captain Tyner's response was muffled as the room shook and something groaned deep within the engine compartment. The screech of metal tearing preceded a knocking, as if someone was hammering on the hull.

"Is someone going to look into that?" the man asked with a sigh. "Can I? Come on, people."

Selene glanced back at the man as he chastised the officers. *How are you so confident?* It could have been another side effect of the thawing. Perhaps people became overconfident, fearless, when they thawed out. There was no stutter in his voice, however, and he wasn't shaking, a classic symptom of the thaw. *You're more stable than the rest of them.* The officers within the room were the ones showing signs of the thaw. Selene could hear their chairs rattling. Those close enough to see had bloodshot eyes. *Maybe you just went through the transition sooner,* she thought as she glanced back at the newcomer. Selene sighed. It made no sense that those who should be experiencing the thaw weren't and those who shouldn't were. *Everything isn't as it should be.* Anthony had chosen this man for a reason. *He knows you, doesn't he?* Selene thought. *But from where? Sam would know.*

Clearing her throat, Selene asked, "Where's Sam?"

Glancing down at her, Captain Tyner said, "Why does that matter? We're—"

"Why don't you explain that to her, lady?" the newcomer interrupted.

"Shut your mouth," Captain Tyner blurted. "If you want to check the generators, then go. Go with him, Victor."

"Why me?" Victor asked as he shot the man a glance.

With everyone focused on the man as he complained, Selene reached down and flipped the toggles on the leg straps. She floated up from the seat. Taking a deep breath, she repeated, "Where's Sam?"

"Tie her back—"

"*No!*" Selene shouted. "You will answer me." She scowled at the woman. *Sam has the answers. He knows the truth.*

The officers fell silent, staring wide-eyed at Selene. *They're all so tired,* she thought. Half of the officers couldn't control their tremors and the movements of the others were jerky, and they were unable to focus their gaze on anything for longer than a few seconds. They would look for a time, then their eyes would droop and they'd shake their heads and try to focus. *But now you,* she thought again, looking at the man beside her. He wasn't showing any signs. *You weren't in deep sleep, were you? You're an officer.* If she was right and the newcomer—more fleshed-out than the emaciated officers—

was the true officer, they were all lying for a reason. *Why keep up the ruse now? What are you afraid of?*

Selene pushed off the chair so she would float to the man's side. "Why are you all lying? I can see that you are more of an officer. You're all shaking like you've thawed out, so stop lying to me."

Silence enveloped the room. Even the generators bowed to her will as the knocking stopped. Every eye in the room followed her as she moved to the centre of the group. *I have to prove I'm smarter. I have to get this ship turned around. Maybe we can find Benson in space. He's got time.*

"You all think you're doing the right thing by taking me from the station, but you aren't. You don't even know what you're doing, do you? You run around playing at house, hoping the ship will fly itself. Do you even know what a capacitor is, let alone know how to fix one if it blows? And trust me, there's at least one gone, by the sound coming from the back." She didn't need to lie. There was a dull thrum emanating from the engines. "I suspect that except for you," she looked at the newcomer, "I am the most qualified person to fly this thing. *No*, you will listen to me. Stop thinking you can lie yourself out of this situation, Captain Tyner."

Their stares were getting more furtive as the officers gave up all pretense of hiding their jitters. Most had a white-knuckled grasp on something so they wouldn't float off into the air. The newcomer sitting against Selene's chair, however, looked on with mirth in his eyes. His smile, as her father would describe it, was from ear to ear. "You are very astute girl."

"Shut—" Captain Tyner began, but Selene cut her short.

"Listen, you fool," she said. "We're in a serious spot and you're spending your time worrying about who's in charge when none of you are qualified for the job. Look at you. All you've done since I came aboard was fight. You've already said that was what happened before you crashed into the station. At what point did any of you think you were qualified?"

There was a pregnant pause as the officers hung their heads. Just as she was about to speak again, bite man said, "We aren't."

Captain Tyner waved her gun around and shouted, "Don't, Cole!"

"Can it, Meghan. She's right. If anyone is qualified, it's the Sub-lieutenant. At least she's a commissioned officer."

"Don't make me laugh," Captain Tyner said. "It's a cruel joke the station captain played on her, making her think she was—"

"Think?" Selene blurted, thinking, *Stop changing the subject.* The conversation was running away from her control. No one was acting like an adult. She laughed. By the time she realized the others were staring at her again, she couldn't contain her mirth. The tears streaking down her face no longer stung. She tried to speak. "I . . . I . . . was just thinking how funny it is that you're all acting like children and here I am, a child, trying to get you to act like adults."

Where her screaming and ranting had failed, Selene's insult succeeded. Every head in the room sank as the adults capitulated to her abuse. High on her perch, Captain Tyner lowered her weapon, unwilling to meet Selene's gaze. *I did it,* Selene thought as she let out her breath.

Rubbing the bandage on his hand, Cole said, "Come on, Meghan. She's right. We have to stop fighting and get out of here. She's already proven her ability, so let her continue. Keep your gun if you have to, just let us work."

By the time he'd finished speaking, Captain Tyner had dropped her weapon, struck by a violent shudder. It floated out of her reach. Jumping from his perch like an acrobat, the true officer caught the weapon and locked the safety as though he'd done it a thousand times, then shoved the weapon into his belt. *A real dragon slayer,* Selene thought, and smiled.

"Okay, Selene," Cole said, floating to her side. "What do we need to do?"

"Cecile?" Selene asked aloud.

Looking to Cole as he floated around the chair, Victor asked, "What is she on about? Has she lost her marbles?"

Ignoring the man, Selene repeated, "Cecile?"

"I am here, Selene."

The officers around her shared a glance. *They're afraid.* "Cecile, do you know where the radiation is in the system?"

"Yes, Selene. The information has been downloaded onto the ship's computer."

"Can you show us on the computer terminal in the engine room?" Selene said.

There was a collective sigh of relief as the computer retrieved the information. Most nodded to Selene and mouthed words of thanks to Cecile as they crowded around the terminal.

With Cole's hand on her shoulder, Selene pointed. "We have to take that path there." She stared at the screen for a minute, then her hand slid into her pocket. She fingered the tiny pill several times as she looked around at the officers looking to her. *I can't panic. I have to get to work.* "We must get beyond the radiation before it penetrates the hull."

"It's going to be difficult," a voice said from behind them. Selene turned toward the true officer, floating out from beyond the generators. He wore a frown and his eyes were distant, as if he were lost in thought. He focused as he approached the crowd. "We're down to three generators unless someone knows how to rewire them," he said. "At some point there was a fire back there."

"When we broke free," Victor said. "It wasn't bad, though. The emergency system cut it out really fast. I was down here then."

Selene shook her head, then glanced back at the generators, the mystery of the blown capacitor solved. The officer was correct in his assumptions. Without proper power distribution, they wouldn't be able to fly in any direction. They would fly around in circles forever. They likely hadn't gone more than a couple hundred kilometres from the station itself.

Cocking his head to the side, the officer replied, "Well, at least that's good news. Did any of you think to get the schematics or a manual before you left the station?" Silence. His scowl deepened.

"Wait," Selene said as the man's face turned red. "We have to work together. I can get the schematics with Cecile's help. You all get someone who can work on the engines. Did Davies find more useful passengers? We need to find him. You—what's your name?"

"Lieutenant Rogers," the officer answered. "I think your man Davies is still down with the passengers, going through the list."

"Good," Selene said. Pointing to Victor, she said, "Go find him and get those people back here. And get Sam's father . . . Anthony. Please tell me that he's still alive."

"Of course he is," Captain Tyner said with a huff as she pushed off from the wall. "We just locked him in one of the pods."

"Good, go with Victor and get them back here," Selene ordered.

Selene caught the woman's look as she nodded and floated after Victor. The others hid looks of contempt for the woman as she left, but wouldn't speak as Selene continued to dole out the orders.

"Rogers," Selene said, "what is your occupation?"

"Engineer, but I don't do wiring. That was Ziggy's job."

"And Ziggy is . . . ?" Selene asked.

Shaking his head, Rogers answered shortly, "Not here."

"Who is here, then? How many officers are left from your ship? Anybody?"

"Rogers and Anthony," Cole replied as he pored over the diagrams on the computer screen.

"And—fine, answers later. What do we need, Rogers?"

Looking up from his own terminal, the man said, "From what I can gather, we are actually moving in the right direction, though not fast enough. We need more power to ignite the rest of the engines. To do that, we need to rewire the back generators. That said, I'm not sure this old tub has extra wiring just lying around."

Selene snorted. If there was nothing else she had learned on Orphan Station, it was that every ship did have extra wire lying around. *This, I can do.* "What gauge does it have to be?"

"Heavy," the man replied. "Four—maybe two. Coated—at least half an inch. I'd say about eighteen or nineteen hundred feet."

"Cecile?" Selene called out. "Can you use the ship's speakers to talk?"

Gibberish came through the speakers in the room before the computer answered, "Yes, Selene."

"Good," she said. "Can you read the ship's schematics?"

"Yes, Selene."

"Okay, I want you to read the schematics and catalogue every wire, gauge four and above, that is longer than ten feet."

There was silence for several minutes. Captain Tyner and Victor returned with several passengers, Anthony close behind them. He sported several bruises on his face and nose and a long gash ran the length of his cheek. Though the blood had stopped, he still acted as if he were afraid it could start again with any sudden movement.

Before the newcomers could voice their questions, Cecile said, "There are twenty-seven pieces of electrical wire that fit your criteria."

As the computer spoke, the room erupted in a loud cheer. There were several handshakes and a few audible sighs. Selene shook her head. Trying to speak above the raucous laughter was fruitless. Finally Rogers put his fingers to his mouth and whistled loud enough to kill the revelry.

Selene nodded her thanks and addressed the computer: "Cecile, if we removed all the wiring that is connected to the generators, how much would be left?"

The pause was shorter before the computer said, "There are ten."

"And of those, how many can we remove without compromising any primary systems?"

Before Selene could even look to the screen, the computer said, "Rephrase question."

"What the hell does that mean? Rephrase question?" Victor asked as he threw up his hands. "It's the damn systems that we need to fly and breathe."

"Cecile, do you know what an environmental system is?" Selene countered, eyeing those shrugging or shaking their heads.

"The environmental system is designed to recycle air, water, and—"

"That's right, Cecile. Now in the computer program that operates the ship, can you see other similar subroutines that affect the ship's functions, like environments?"

There was a pause before the computer asked, "Do the sleeping pods count as a ship's system?"

Nodding, Selene said, "Yes, Cecile, they do." *Please be smart enough to answer. Prove Able Seaman Tony wrong.*

"There are three wires meeting your criteria."

"Can you show me on the screen?" Selene prompted as the crowd shifted to see.

The computer screen flickered several times, stopping to display the three wires highlighted on the schematics. One ran the length of the ship from bow to stern. It was labelled *gauge four*, though no reason was given for its use. The other two wires were offshoots from the main line.

"Cecile, what are the three lines for?" Selene asked as she traced the lines with her fingers. If they could use the lines, they wouldn't have to splice them; the main would almost be enough on it is own.

"The wire is for secondary backup for liftoff sequences of the captain's capsule at the bow of the ship."

"The what?" someone asked from the back of the crowd.

"There is an emergency capsule in the bow," Rogers explained, eyes fixed on at the screen.

"Someone find me some hacksaws and screwdrivers," Selene said as she turned back to the growing crowd. More passengers had come through the hatch. It wasn't an army of rat dogs, but Selene had no choice. "How many of you have worked with electrical wiring before?"

Half a dozen hands rose. Selene scanned their faces. They looked as haggard as those pretending to be officers. Most were showing signs of thawing jitters, leaning against others for support. *Oh God, I don't know if you can do it.* Gravity or not, it wasn't going to be easy to drag the wiring from the bow all the way back to the engine compartment.

"How big are the conduits, Rogers?"

He bent over to study the screen before answering, "Two feet at best. It's going to be a tight fit."

Shaking his head, Cole said, "That's not a tight fit. It won't work. We won't be able to cut through the cable at all. It just won't work."

The room went silent for several seconds as the others absorbed the news. Several broke into tears, hugging those near them.

"*No,* we have to do something," a woman called out.

"I'm telling you, it won't work," someone else said.

"We're just too big. We won't fit," Rogers agreed reluctantly, shaking his head.

"I'd fit," Selene offered, then added, "And Sam."

Chapter 16

The crowd fell silent. She could see most wanted to speak, but none could muster the words. But as soon as Selene mentioned his son's name, Anthony asked, "What was that?"

Selene turned to him. "Where's Sam? Get me Sam. Quick."

"What do you need him for?" his father asked.

Glancing around the room, Selene said, "We have a limited window in which to get the wiring we need for generators, and I can't trust these people to do it properly."

"What does that mean?" Cole asked, absently rubbing his wound.

"It means that you are all experiencing the first stages of thawing. I don't know if it will take an hour or ten, but pretty soon you're going to feel the second stage. Some of you are going to want to set fire to the ship just so you can warm up—but it won't work, because nothing will warm you up and nothing will stop your shaking. That is why I need Sam. He was never frozen and he's small enough to crawl through the conduits."

Someone was sent for the boy. Satisfied, Selene turned back to the terminal, muttering, "None of you are going to make it to the planet."

The room went still again.

Selene looked up, saw their faces, and shook her head. "I don't mean you're going to die," she explained. "I mean you aren't going to make it to the planet before you feel the effects. That's why there is a crew. Four people can't crew this ship."

"Then what do you suggest?" Rogers asked. The look on his face was enough to tell Selene he already knew the answer to his question. He gave a quick nod before adding, "It isn't like we can go back to the station."

Taking a deep breath, Selene said, "Yes, we can. With the engines at full we can circle around the system and come back to the station when it is back on the light side."

"And that makes it easier?" Captain Tyner asked. "I didn't let you go so you could just take us back into danger."

"It isn't dangerous now," Selene said as she turned on the woman. "Think about it. The fires have been put out. All we have to do is navigate around the radiation. At least out here we don't have to—"

"You're just trying to get us back to the station," Captain Tyner countered, frowning.

Selene spun around to stare at her. "Good God, woman, don't you get it? Do you think I would go back there to die? I'm trying to save you. You don't have enough medical personnel and they're going to be feeling the effects soon too, if they haven't already. That means there will be four people still able to keep our heads up in a couple hours. Four people to navigate the ship. And that means only four to land it. Yeah, that's right, *four*. How many seats are on the bridge? Or do you want a repeat performance of your last attempt at flying a ship? I guaran-goddamn-tee that if we leave it up to you, we'll die."

Eyes on Selene, the woman swallowed hard. After several seconds, she nodded and looked away, her eyes bright with tears.

I hate you, Selene thought at her. *I hate you.* At least with her parents, there was no one to blame. Even by accepting responsibility, her Uncle Callum wasn't really to blame. He hadn't made the choice that had killed her mother. Her parents had died heroes. They'd made the choice to save others which in turn had caused their own demise. *But is that any different?* The words almost seemed like her father's. *Different? Yes. No. I don't know.* It was true that Meghan Tyner had made the choice that had sent these people on their crash course. She was responsible for her actions. But Benson had chosen to press the button that had sucked him into space. He'd acted of his own free will. *Why is it so hard?* she screamed at herself. *She made a choice. She chose to take me. She chose to detach the ship.*

Selene sighed and looked away. Meghan Tyner had chosen all of those for her own reasons. She thought she was doing the right thing for Selene. She thought she was protecting her. She thought Selene's grandfather would cause them trouble. Selene snorted as she remembered another thing her father used to say: *"Punish someone not for stupidity; ignorance, yes, but not stupidity. The one they can change, the other they are born with."* Meghan Tyner would be punished one day for her choices. But not for murder.

Sam floated through the hatch; his joyous, "Selene!" pulled her from her thoughts. Grabbing everything in his path to pull himself forward, the boy swam over to embrace her.

"We need your help, Sam," Selene said as she pulled back afterward.

Sam nodded. "Okay."

Finally, someone who could follow an order. Sam acted as if he understood the stakes. He glanced around the room once before returning his attention to her. *You aren't the boy I met on the Orphan,* Selene thought as she studied him. *What did they do to you?* No time for that. Selene turned back to the others. "Okay Rogers, pick your people and send the rest out to us. Sam and I will head for the conduit. Cole, you come with us. Anthony—er, sorry, Captain, can you start on our trajectory?"

As Anthony began to chuckle, Selene flushed and added, "I mean . . . with your leave, Captain?"

"I guess I still have that rank," he said, nodding.

"Thank you," Selene said. "Okay, people, get moving."

Dragging herself to the hatch, Selene made her way down the main hall to the access panel. When several more people arrived she told them, "Sam and I are going to go through the conduit and remove the wire from either end of the hallway. The rest of you will pull it gently through the panels."

"It's so cold. D-d-do you think we'll get it done before . . . ?" The man fell silent.

Looking up at the man, Selene said, "Find one of the doctors and explain that you are experiencing cryogenic thaw syndrome. They won't be aware of the condition, but tell them it's true. They can find it on the ship's computer. Go!"

"Here," another man said, sending a belt filled with tools up to her through the crowd. A second was passed to Sam as someone else fitted a radio to his ear.

"Here's the deal, Sam," Selene said to him. "As soon as Rogers gives you the signal, I want you to start here. Cut the wire straight through and then unbuckle the harnesses. No one else is small enough to get it, so you'll have to do it all. If you have any questions, just ask them through your radio."

You can do it. I have faith in you, Selene wanted to say to him. Instead she smiled at him and gave him a hug. The she pulled away and motioned for the others to follow as she pushed herself toward the far end of the hall.

Reaching the final access panel, Selene flipped the lid off, activated the flashlight strapped on her forehead, and stuck her head into the dark cavity beyond. After a quick inspection she withdrew and said to those with her, "We have to do this quickly. Someone find out how much Rogers needs in each length so we can get them cut and sent down."

No one moved; they all stared at her. *Are you kidding me? Doesn't anyone know how to follow a damned order?* "You." She stabbed a finger at the woman nearest to her. "What's your name?"

The woman was shaking, in the initial throes of the thaw. "S-S-Susan," she stuttered.

"Susan, I want you to find out what Rogers needs. While you're down there, get some radios for everyone. We can't afford to waste time on people running back and forth."

Selene ducked her head and slipped into the utility tunnel. Air and power conduits ran its length as far as she could see, narrowing the space even further. She swallowed hard. *It's so tight.*

She had to keep her arms stretched ahead of her as she pulled herself along. When she wanted to use the radio she was forced to activate it by pressing her arm up against her ear. It was awkward, and it took her five attempts before she heard the chirrup of acknowledgement and said, "Cecile. Which wire do we need?"

"The wire you need is labelled with serial number *0259223.*"

Selene pulled herself along, eyes on the wires, until she found the serial number. When she'd confirmed that she had the correct line, she activated her radio with her arm again. "Cecile. Confirm with Lieutenant Rogers when we can cut through the line, and relay to Sam . . . uh . . . someone get me Sam's call—"

"It's okay, Selene. I can hear you," Sam's voice said in her ear. He sounded full of energy, as if his task offered him new life. *I wish I had your energy,* Selene thought. Her feet were itching, the callus gel worn from the burns. *The only good thing is the lack of gravity.*

Speaking as though she hadn't noticed the interruption, Cecile said, "Lieutenant Rogers has indicated that you can go to work now."

Taking a deep breath, Selene pulled out her saw. "Start at the beginning and move back, Sam," she instructed. "Cut the line first, then move to the clamps. It will float—"

"It's okay, Selene. I know what I'm doing," Sam said with a laugh.

She smiled. *Of course you do.* He'd likely dreamt of this moment a thousand times: helping his father with a real emergency. He was right to call her out, though. She had treated him like a child. *I'm sorry.* Relying on him was the right thing for everyone. His people would learn his worth and he would get the respect he'd yearned for.

Selene pushed the saw back and forth until the plastic lining broke free. The rubber coating gummed up the saw at first, but someone suggested burning it with the butane torch on her belt, and she shifted a wriggled until she had the torch above her head, thinking, *I should have figured that out.*

By the time she pulled the conduit free, Selene was coated in sweat. Chest heaving, she pulled herself to the clamp and began working to set it free.

Selene didn't know how long she worked at the cables. Minute after minute she pried or cut until her fingers bled. Blisters developed on her palms and spots of blood stained her pants where tiny wires from the cut conduit poked and scratched her as she passed. The ship had been rocked so many times with the explosions of misfiring thrusters that Selene had several bumps on her head. She wanted to suggest that they shut the engines down, but she knew better. Even at quarter-speed, they were still moving out of the radiation field.

When she reached one of the other access holes, Cole stuck his head through and cleared his throat loud enough to break her concentration. "It wasn't a coup," he said when she looked at him.

"What?"

"I s-s-said that it wasn't a coup. We didn't s-s-storm the bridge and kill the officers," he said. His hands slipped on the wire he was pulling through the hole.

"Oh," Selene said, and turned back to her work. She knew there was always a reason for things. Some reasons made sense, while others didn't. Her impression of these officers was bad enough. *Please don't tell me. I don't want to find out that you're like him.* Jameson's face flashed in her mind, sending a shiver down Selene's back.

"There was an accident," Cole continued. "We were in hyperspace flight and there was an accident. We—when we woke up, there w-w-were ten of us. We found Rogers, Anthony, and his son unconscious. The rest of the crew had been burned. We . . . we didn't know what to do."

Turning to look at him, Selene began, "But why did you . . . " She stopped. *No, don't tell me.*

"Please," Cole said, "let me finish."

Selene sighed. "Fine, go ahead."

"We tried to wake them up, but Rogers was too far gone. I . . . I think he had a concussion. That's why he didn't recognize anyone. I don't think he even woke up until we were putting him in the pods on the ship here. We thought . . . we thought the best thing was to put him in one of the working pods, but we didn't put him into long sleep. Anthony woke up, though. He told us about the accident. He said he needed help to slow the ship down. That was when Meghan took control. She was good. She had some experience leading people on Earth, so it came to her naturally. Anyway, that's when things went bad. We got the ship under control for the most part, but it was still a little slow. I don't really know what happened between Anthony and Meghan, but they had a—"

"She found out that I was responsible for the accident," Anthony said in her ear. Cole pulled back out of the hole, hitting his head on its edge.

Selene felt tears on her face. *Please, not you.* He'd been the one shining beacon that Selene had looked to ever since she'd been ordered to submit to his command. That order had been the ultimate endorsement.

Anthony heard her quavering sigh. "I know," he said. "I'm sorry." After several seconds, he continued. "When Meghan found out that I was responsible, she threatened to tell the station's crew about it . . . and about Sam."

"I know about Sam," Selene said, hoping the boy couldn't hear the conversation.

"I couldn't think of anything else except to go along with it," Anthony said. "And by the time we got to the station and then with the crash . . . It was too late to tell anyone. I just wanted to take Sam and get away. That's all I could think of—just getting Sam to safety."

Selene pulled on the last piece of wire. "That doesn't really paint a good picture of Meghan," she observed. She still considered the woman a two-headed demon, sent to the station to steal Selene away; a succubus of terrible fame, worse than any dragon could ever be. Not only had she taken Selene, she had caused the death of so many officers. *I will never forget what you did. NEVER!*

"That's not my intention," Cole interjected, pushing his head back through the hole. "She's helping us now, but that doesn't change what she's done. It doesn't change what I've done. I just want you to know that there was a reason. We didn't do this on purpose."

Purpose? What purpose is there in causing so much pain? Selene thought as she stared at him. "How do I know you're telling me the truth now?" she asked, surprising herself.

Hanging his head, Cole said, "I don't know. All we've done is lie to you since you got here. I . . . I'm sorry."

"There is a way to determine whether he is telling the truth," Anthony offered in her ear. "And I think it's the only fair way. I submit that as soon as we return to the station, we offer ourselves up to their justice. The ship's black box has recorded everything."

Cole nodded his acceptance to the suggestion as half a dozen other voices added their agreement over the radio. As their voices faded, Sam asked, "Does that mean we aren't going to the planet, Da?"

"Yes, son, that's what it means."

Selene heard Sam sniffle. *You want to go back as bad as me,* she thought. I *think I get it now.* She wiped away her own tears. Looking up to Cole, she said, "I guess I should apologize too."

Cole squinted at her. "For what?"

"I lied about the station having control over the ship. It was me."

Cole nodded as a smile played on his lips. Then his mouth spread in a rueful grin and his eyes sparkled. "I know. I could hear you talking to Cecile, though at the time I didn't know what it meant. I wouldn't tell Meghan that just yet."

For several seconds, Selene studied Cole. Captain Tyner's weapon of choice—the man who'd physically taken her. At the time, he hadn't known what Selene was or what she was capable of. He'd learned, however, and offered her something her father would have accepted. *"A smile,"* her father had often said, *"is all it takes. Get them to smile, and learn the truth."*

"I'm sorry for biting you, too," Selene said as she pulled herself forward. Cole ducked back out of the way and she pushed out of the utility tunnel.

Cole's smile faded. "Yeah . . . I'm sorry too."

They made their way to the engine rooms, bustling with people at work. Most were busy behind the first line of generators, where welders crackled and threw shadows around the room.

Finding Rogers, Selene asked him, "How is it going?"

Sweat poured down the man's face as he pulled on one of the old power lines connected to a generator. Selene could see dark, smoky lines radiating from the conduit on the floor and on the generator sidewall. He cleared his throat and said, "I almost forgot how young you were, kid." He shook his head. "I don't know. The welders are almost done six and seven back there. Your cable is the last one for this generator here. I'm hoping the circuit board hasn't been cooked because we ran out of replacement boards an hour ago. Pudgy fingers over there knew how to solder so he did what he could, but—"

"How are—"

"We're close," Anthony said as he joined them. "We're ahead of the radiation by about two hours, but the calculations aren't perfect and we can't correct our path. I've already seen an increase in the millirems. I'll let you know when—" The rest of what he said was lost in a cacophony of noise as the generators groaned again.

"I've never been so glad for a lack of gravity," Rogers said as the shuddering stopped. Selene could see he sported as many new gashes on his forehead and arms as she had sustained while pilfering the ship's wiring.

The final wire didn't take long to install. Soon they were all waiting for Rogers and another man who spoke in a thick accent to make their final assessment. The old wires were tied down in the far corner so they wouldn't cause more damage. When they finished, Rogers turned to Anthony and said, "I am ready for your orders, Captain."

"I think it's best if we clear the house a little," he replied. Raising his voice, he said, "Everyone—if you aren't essential, then you shouldn't be here. Get back to the pods and take a nap. We'll wake you when we get to our destination."

There was a collective sigh as most of the passengers moved toward the exit. Most needed to help one another. *They won't even care if they get back before falling asleep,* Selene thought, watching them. She assumed the doctors who hadn't already fallen asleep themselves would sedate them as soon as they arrived, for fear some might become vocal or violent. Most of the pseudo-officers had already departed. They had been the first to wake.

Selene turned to Cole. His hands were balled into fists. "Are you okay to continue," she asked, "or should you all be . . . ?"

A doctor floated by, stopping when he overheard her. "Here," he said, handing Cole a pill. "I've given everyone else one. It will help stave off the effects, but—" He shrugged. "Well, I'm not sure what the effects are going to be. We were never informed of this syndrome before we left Earth."

"That's because they didn't want you to know," Selene said as she watched the man leave. *Who would want to know they would end up burning and freezing at the same time when they woke from the dream everyone promised them would only feel like ten minutes? Not me.*

Selene couldn't remember how long she had been awake, but her body was screaming at her. Her muscles were stiff and her bones ached. She didn't want to think about how bad it would become when she was standing on the floor under gravity again. *I'll likely fall over,* she thought. Her legs wouldn't be able to hold any weight; they already felt like rubber.

As the engine room cleared, Anthony said, "I'm going back to the bridge to talk to Davies. He's strong. He won't screw up."

Nodding, Lieutenant Rogers said, "Yes sir. Let me know when you're ready."

Selene soon discovered that waiting was the worst. The seconds ticked by in silence. It was so quiet that she imagined she could hear the heartbeats of the five people in the room. She kept blinking as her vision blurred.

Lieutenant Rogers nodded to her and smiled before yelling, "Strap yourselves in, people."

Someone handed her a harness strap just as the generators roared to life. She used the strap to pull herself into the seat that had been pulled from the wall, then locked the harness around her waist and across her chest. By the time she finished, gravity tugged her legs against the hard, unforgiving leather of the seat. She was grateful for the straps as they accelerated, so fast that she could feel the pressure in her temples.

Everyone in the room moaned as gravity pulled at them. Selene knew they would have more experience with its force, but the thawing process was taking a serious toll. Blood flowed unabated from Cole's nose, and Victor passed out.

"Th-th-this is getting hard," Selene said, her teeth chattering from the turbulence.

"S-s-soon," Rogers called back through clenched teeth. Tears streaked down his face as he pulled at the straps cutting into his shoulders.

"He's going to push it too far," Cole shouted as he wiped the blood from his lip.

"No," Rogers said. "He knows what he's doing."

Selene nodded. Her grandfather trusted Anthony. That had to count for something. *He's a Met tech. He plots trajectories. It's his job. It's been his job since before I was born.*

One generator lifted to a crescendo as another fell. An ark of blue electrical current shot up the generator, fading as a pole dropped down from the ceiling to absorb the blast.

The pressure mounted as the ship accelerated. Selene felt her ears pop, and everything was quiet. Then, with no notification, the pressure released and the straps pulling against her body relaxed. Opening her mouth several times, Selene tried to adjust the pressure in her ears. "Is . . . is it done?"

There was no answer for almost a minute. Then Rogers jerked his head up and looked around. "Ugh," he said. "That was harsh."

Rolling his head back and forth against his headrest, Cole asked, "Did it work?"

"I . . . I think so," Rogers said as he glanced back to the generators. They had returned to a low thrum. Selene rubbed her nose as an acrid smell wafted around her.

"Davies tells me we've cleared the path of the radiation storm. If there is anything anyone wants to say, I suspect you'd better say it now."

Selene didn't need an explanation. Without the generators running at full capacity, the passenger's screams echoed through the hall. Frowning, she looked at Lieutenant Rogers. "What do we do now?"

Rogers chuckled. "I thought that it was your plan."

Chapter 17

Selene floated alone in a hall, splitting her attention between staring at the hatch and out a porthole into space, all while tapping her fingers against her legs. Though she hadn't found any new clothes, the time she'd spent on the ship had offered her the opportunity to clean the blood-soaked uniform she'd been wearing since she was kidnapped. *Kidnapped,* she thought. *That was so long ago.* Taken as a child, returned as an officer, Selene had no doubt of her abilities. There was a ship filled with passengers to attest to that.

Selene shuddered at the clanging echoes as something shifted on the outside of the hatch. When they quieted, the hatch retracted. *Please be safe. Please be safe, Benson.* But she knew it couldn't be him. He'd been blown into space and though he had been wearing an environmental suit, he would have died of suffocation by now. He hadn't been tethered and the station was orbiting so fast, he would have been torn apart. Even if the man had been able to navigate his way back to the station for some reason, he wouldn't have enjoyed the protection of the shield. He would have succumbed to the radiation.

"Sub-lieutenant Sotana?"

She didn't recognize the voice for the pounding in her ears. Then she looked toward the hatch and her chest heaved as she dragged herself out to embrace the man. She'd spent so long keeping her tears from flowing that as she reached out, everything spilled over. She could barely breathe as she gasped, "I . . . I . . . tried so hard, but—"

"It's okay," her grandfather said. His voice was deeper than she remembered, almost hoarse, but she didn't care. It was just because of her ordeal. *I'm just remembering it wrong.*

Her lower lip trembling, Selene said, "I tried to save Benson and the others, but I couldn't get—"

"It's okay," he said again.

Selene couldn't lift her head high enough to see him through the helmet. She was Sub-lieutenant Selene Sotana, space explorer. She'd broken free of her captors and even went on to lead them to safe harbour. Something as simple as being okay seemed suitable somehow. "It's okay?" she repeated. She smiled as a muffled bark came through the radio on the man's suit. "But, I came back Grandfather."

Bending down, her grandfather said, "I know, Selene. I know. You did well. I am proud of you. You saved us."

"But Grand—Captain, I . . . I brought . . ." Selene swallowed hard and took a deep breath. "I'm sorry you lost part of your crew. I . . . I think I have a solution, though."

"Oh?" he replied as he pulled the helmet off. "And what's that?"

Selene licked her lips and nodded back to the hall behind her. Anthony and all the passengers who'd played at being officers came around the corner.

Selene pushed away from the captain of Orphan Station so she could lock gazes with him. "Sir, they've proven themselves skilled. They can join us."

"Oh?" Her grandfather raised his brow, then looked from her to them.

"They can do it," she said with a nod.

"Selene, they've done some terrible things," he said.

"Captain," Anthony said as he approached. He held his head high and met the captain's gaze. "Sub-lieutenant Sotana doesn't plead for our sake, but for our passengers. We submit ourselves to your judgement."

Selene's grandfather glanced from Selene to Anthony and back again. When he was looking her way, Selene smiled and nodded. "I've learned something from them that I couldn't learn on the station, sir: compassion. They thought they were doing the right thing. I can't fault them for that, even if the consequences for their actions are so terrible."

Her grandfather sighed and shook his head for a moment before saying, "I'll think about it, Selene. In the meantime, I think there's someone who wants to talk with you."

Selene cocked her head when she heard the bark. *That wasn't on the radio!* She looked around, then grinned when she saw Bentley swimming madly through the air toward her. She giggled. "Bentley, you can't do that," she said as she pushed off her grandfather to fly toward the dog. Opening her arms, Selene caught the dog in an embrace as the others began to laugh.

"Hey," Sam said as he approached. "Can I pet him?"

Selene turned back to the boy and smiled. "Sure, kiddo. If you're gonna be on the station with us, then you'll be seeing a lot of him."

She glanced around to see more officers pouring through the hatch. *I'm home,* she thought. Glancing back to the porthole out into space, she thought, *I'm sorry, Uncle.* She sniffed and buried her head in Bentley's neck.